Berkley Prime Crime titles by Jenn McKinlay

Cupcake Bakery Mysteries

SPRINKLE WITH MURDER
BUTTERCREAM BUMP OFF
DEATH BY THE DOZEN
RED VELVET REVENGE
GOING, GOING, GANACHE
SUGAR AND ICED
DARK CHOCOLATE DEMISE
VANILLA BEANED

Library Lover's Mysteries

BOOKS CAN BE DECEIVING
DUE OR DIE
BOOK, LINE, AND SINKER
READ IT AND WEEP
ON BORROWED TIME
A LIKELY STORY

Hat Shop Mysteries

CLOCHE AND DAGGER
DEATH OF A MAD HATTER
AT THE DROP OF A HAT
COPY CAP MURDER

Vanilla Beaned

Jenn McKinlay

BERKLEY PRIME CRIME, NEW YORK

BERKLEY PRIME CRIME

An imprint of Penguin Random House LLC
375 Hudson Street, New York, New York 10014

VANILLA BEANED

A Berkley Prime Crime Book / published by arrangement with the author

ISBN: 978-0-425-25894-1

PUBLISHING HISTORY
Berkley Prime Crime mass-market edition / April 2016

PRINTED IN THE UNITED STATES OF AMERICA

10 9 8 7 6 5 4 3 2 1

Cover illustration by Jeff Fitz-Maurice.
Cover design by Lesley Worrell.
Interior text design by Laura K. Corless.

Penguin
Random
House

For my son, Wyatt Orf. With your sharp wit and kind heart, you are one of my very favorite people. I am so proud of the fine man you are becoming, and I look forward to watching you pursue your own happiness as you go forth in life. Love you forever.

ACKNOWLEDGMENTS

This is for you the readers who have loved the Cupcake Bakery Mysteries and the characters who inhabit them. Writing these books has been an absolute joy because I had such cool people with whom to share them. Thank you, all, from the bottom of my mixing bowl.

One

"Viva Las Vegas!" Tate Harper sang at top volume. Then he did some sort of shimmy shake thing that Melanie Cooper was sure was supposed to look like a suave, swively hipped Elvis but more resembled a person suffering electrocution.

"Viva, viva Las Vegas!" Angie DeLaura slid across the bakery floor, bumping hips with Tate while they sang together.

Mel was behind the counter loading the display case with vanilla cupcakes and ignoring them, well, trying to ignore them. Her two best friends in the whole wide world were making complete jackasses out of themselves so it was pretty hard to remain indifferent.

"What? Now we're offering cupcakes and a show?"

Marty Zelaznik asked. He'd entered from the kitchen and stood beside Mel while he tied on his apron.

Marty was the main counter person for Fairy Tale Cupcakes, the bakery that Mel owned with Tate and Angie. He was a bald, shriveled-up prune of a man, but the older ladies loved to baby him and he had a special charm with the young ones as well. To Mel, he was as integral to the success of the bakery as the flour in her cupcakes.

"They're a little overexcited about our upcoming trip," Mel said.

"So, you're really going?" Marty asked. He kept his voice low as if he didn't want Tate and Angie to hear him, although Mel was sure there was no way they could over the racket they were making.

"Yup," she said.

"You know you don't have to do this if you don't want to," Marty said.

"Yes, I do," she said. She put the last cupcake in the display and closed the back of the case. "We are three equal partners in this venture, and they want to franchise."

She tried to keep her voice neutral but she couldn't help it if the word *franchise* came out sounding more like *black death*.

"So what if they do?" Marty asked. "You're the master chef, the creative genius behind every flavor; I think that gives you extra say."

Mel reached over and squeezed his hand. "It'll be o—"

Whatever she'd been about to say was interrupted by the front door being yanked open with an enthusiasm that did not ring of joy.

"Vegas? As in Las Vegas? Oh, hell, no!"

Tate and Angie stopped singing and their sick dance moves tumbled to a halt.

"Liv!" Marty goggled at the woman on the other side of the shop. "What are you doing here? You know we have an agreement. Neither of us sets foot in the other one's bakery."

"Oh, sugar lips, relax," Olivia Puckett said. She waved a hand at him as if he was being silly.

Marty's bald head turned an embarrassed shade of fire engine red at the endearment and his bushy silver eyebrows rose so high, he almost had a hairline.

He opened his mouth to speak but Mel got there first, mostly so that Angie would not feel behooved to tackle Olivia to the ground and drag her out of their shop by her feet. Olivia Puckett tended to bring out that sort of emotion in Angie, primarily because Olivia owned a rival bakery but also because she was dating Marty, a relationship of which Angie had never approved.

"How can I help you, Puckett?" Mel asked.

Olivia's gray corkscrew curls popped out of the topknot on her head as she strode forward.

"I saw a social media update that somebody is opening a franchise in Vegas, is this true?" Olivia demanded.

She stood across the display case from Mel in her blue chef's coat looking like she wanted some dough to knead, or more accurately some butt to kick. Mel glanced at Marty, and he shook his head. She turned back to Tate and Angie and glared. Tate gave her a sheepish shrug.

"Just promoting the business," he said.

"What if it is true?" Angie asked. "What are you going to do about it?"

She turned and strode toward Olivia, looking like she was getting ready to do some damage. To Olivia's credit, she didn't even flinch, which was saying something since the two of them had tussled before.

Tate deftly slid in between Angie and Olivia and looped his arm around Angie's shoulders, anchoring her to his side. He met Mel's gaze over Angie's head and gave her a bug-eyed look that she interpreted to mean he wanted her to take the discussion elsewhere.

Right, because Olivia was about as easy to move as a three-day-old cupcake at full price. Feeling cranky about the Vegas sitch, she opted to go on the offensive instead.

"Maybe we are franchising. What's it to you?"

Tate's eyes almost popped out of his head while Marty clapped his hands onto his bald dome as if he had just witnessed a car crash and had no idea what to do.

"I'll tell you what's it to me, princess," Olivia snarled. "With a tasty knuckle sandwich."

She began to roll up her sleeves. Mel stepped around the counter. She was feeling just ornery enough to welcome a scuffle. She and Olivia started to circle each other like two boxers squaring off in a ring.

"I can serve up a pretty mean five across the lip when I want to," Mel said. She hoped she was the only one who heard the lack of confidence in her voice. Truth to be told, when upset, she was more of a snacker than a fighter.

"Code Blue," Tate said to Marty.

"What?" Marty squawked.

"Code Blue!" Tate yelled. The veins in his neck began to swell and Mel wondered how much pressure he was exerting to keep Angie in place. "We talked about this; this is a Code Blue situation!"

"I can't remember what Code Blue means!" Marty cried.

"Think," Tate growled.

Marty's face puckered up with the effort. Then he broke into a smile. "Oh, yeah!"

With a smooth move the likes of which was only seen in Fred Astaire movies, he hopped onto the counter, spun around, and slid over the top of it, dropping to his feet right in front of Olivia.

She looked surprised and then went to push him aside, but Marty wasn't having it.

"No, Liv," Marty said. "We need to talk."

Olivia made a face like she'd just tasted something sour.

"You don't want me to pound your boss," she said. She sounded put out about the whole thing and Mel felt behooved to protest.

"Who says you're going to pound me? I could take you," Mel said. She lifted her arm and flexed her muscle. It sagged and she hastily put her arm down.

"This thing between you and me," Marty said. He pointed from him to her and back. "We need to make it official."

Olivia blinked. Her mouth trembled and her eyes got watery with tears. "Oh, Martin, I don't know what to say."

"That's right," he said. He puffed out his chest as if he was quite proud of himself for coming to this place in life. "I think it's time you became my girlfriend."

Olivia's face fell. "What?"

"That's right," he said. "I want to formally make you my main squeeze."

Olivia propped her hands on her hips and glared. "So what, I get a dresser drawer in your bedroom of my very own now? Is that the elevated status you're offering me?"

"I thought you'd be happy," he said. "You're always asking me where this is going. I figured we could make our coupleness official-like."

"Official-like? What does that even mean? We've been dating for over six months. I thought I already was your girlfriend," she said.

"Oh," Marty said. He cast Tate a worried look, who helped him out with a cringe and a shrug.

"Martin Zelaznik, you're about as romantic as a case of beer," Olivia snapped.

"Hey, beer can be very romantic!" Marty argued.

"To a knuckle-dragging Neanderthal," Olivia shouted.

"She has a point," Angie said. "Six months is a long time for a woman to go undefined."

"That's true," Mel said. "You really can't string a girl along like that."

Marty looked outraged. "What? You're on her side now?"

Mel and Angie exchanged a look of understanding with Olivia. Then they nodded.

"Well, if that don't beat all," Marty exploded. He glowered at Olivia. "Fine, if you're looking for more from me, then spell it out. What do you want exactly?"

"Living together," Olivia said. "If we're a couple, then

I want that shriveled-up old face to be the first thing I see in the morning and the last thing I see before I go to bed."

"Does she even listen to herself speak?" Tate asked Angie.

"Shh," Angie hissed.

"But . . . but . . . but . . ." Marty stammered.

"I'm giving you one week to decide," Olivia said. "If you choose not to live together, then we're done, finished, hit the road, Jack, and don't you talk back no more, no more, no more, no more."

Mel glanced at Marty while Olivia sang the rest of her ultimatum. He looked like he'd been slapped upside the head with a rolling pin.

Olivia turned and strode to the door. "Oh, and princess, I hope your Las Vegas franchise blows up in your face but thanks for having my back with him."

Olivia jerked her thumb at Marty, and Mel nodded. She wasn't sure if she and Olivia had just bonded or not. She suspected not since Olivia was still cursing the possible franchise and calling her "princess" in that singularly scathing way she had.

The door shut behind Olivia and they all turned to look at Marty, who slid into one of the bakery booths like he was the melty part of an ice cream cone.

"Live together?" he asked. "As in cohabit twenty-four/seven? No walking around in my underwear, drinking milk right out of the carton, or leaving the john door open? This is a nightmare!"

Tate sat across from him and leaned across the table to pat his arm. "Are you going to be all right?"

"This is all your fault," Marty said. He pointed a bony finger at Tate like he wanted to stick it right in his eye.

"My fault?" Tate asked. "How do you figure?"

"Code Blue," Marty said. "You had to call Code Blue."

"There was going to be a smack-down," Tate said. "We agreed that if that ever happened, you would step up and distract Olivia with relationship stuff."

"Really?" Angie pushed Tate farther into the booth and sat down beside him. "When did you two pumpkin heads come up with that plan?"

"About the time Marty and Olivia started their thing," Tate said. "I knew there would come a day when she would come in here and start something. This was our agreed-upon plan to, er, redirect her ire."

"Well, that sure worked out, now didn't it?" Marty asked. His sarcasm was thick enough to frost cupcakes with. "Now what am I going to do?"

"Looks like you have to make a decision," Mel said.

"Aw, man," Marty whined.

"Look, it could be worse," Angie said. "She could be pressuring you to get married."

Marty gave her a flat stare.

"Or not," Angie added before glancing away.

"One week," Marty moaned. "How am I supposed to figure out the rest of my life in one week?"

"It'll be okay," Tate assured him. "We'll be in Vegas, so you'll have the whole place to yourself, plenty of time to think things through."

"I've got a better idea," Marty said. "How about I go to Vegas and you stay here."

"You know I would absolutely take you up on that if it weren't for the whole franchising thing," Tate said. Mel thought it spoke well of him that he managed to look so earnest. "I mean we're going to be so bored what with meetings with the lawyers and the person wanting to buy in and looking at real estate. Really, it's going to be a total snooze fest. Right, girls?"

"Right," Angie said. She kicked Mel under the table and Mel added, "Ouch . . . right."

One look at Marty's narrowed gaze and Mel knew he didn't believe them, not even a little.

Two

The flight from Phoenix to Las Vegas was a short one. Mel barely had time to get comfy with the in-flight magazine crossword puzzle while the plane leveled out and then they were landing.

The three of them had spent a few memorable weekends in Vegas back in their misspent twenties. It was before Tate and Angie had become a couple and the shenanigans were more about three friends eating all they could at the midnight buffet, particularly the dessert bar, where Mel vaguely remembered pulling up a chair at the chocolate fountain, catching the shows, people watching, and playing video poker all night long.

This time, however, it was all holding hands and giggles from the besotted twosome and Mel felt relegated to the position of third wheel, or more accurately, person in charge of baggage and transportation. She could feel a full-on pout happening, and she did her best to stave it off by renting a badass convertible. Why not? She was young, single, and in Vegas.

When Tate and Angie pried themselves away from the airport slot machine they'd been playing, she led the way to the garage where the cars were kept. The man working the garage took her receipt and said he'd be right back.

"Did you tell them a nonsmoking car?" Angie asked. "Last time we rented a car in Vegas, it reeked of cigars and it took me a week to wash the smell out of my hair."

"I don't think you'll have to worry about that this time," Mel said.

"Oh, man, you went with a minivan, didn't you?" Tate asked. "I don't think my rep can handle being seen in a minivan."

"Your rep?" Mel asked. "Your rep as what, a cupcake baker?"

Tate had the grace to look embarrassed, but he persisted. "You know we have an image to project here. We've got a person who is committing a quarter of a million dollars . . ."

He kept talking but Mel couldn't hear him over the ringing in her ears. Tate was all confident about franchising, but frankly, the whole idea made Mel sick to her stomach. What if this person failed? Was she responsible if they lost everything in a franchise venture with Fairy Tale Cupcakes? Tate assured her that there were measures in place to safeguard against that, but Mel still felt a little hurly.

"Are you listening?" Tate asked. Mel got the feeling it wasn't the first time he'd asked.

"Yes, I am," she said.

Tate grinned. " 'Plastics.' "

Mel blinked at him then she smiled, too, as she realized they had just spoken the dialogue from one of their favorite movies.

"*The Graduate*," Angie identified the movie, glancing between them with a smile.

The three of them had been stumping one another with movie quotes for as long as Mel could remember. It made the tension in her ease. They would be okay. No matter how this mad scheme of Tate's played out, their friendship and the bakery would survive. She had nothing to fear, really, she was sure of it. Mostly.

The rental car attendant pulled up in a silver Mercedes convertible.

"Oh, no you didn't," Tate said. His mouth was hanging open in stunned surprise.

"What?" Mel asked. "You said yourself we have an image to project."

When Tate would have taken the keys, Mel snatched them first. Tate beamed and then opened the driver side door for her while the attendant loaded their bags into the trunk.

"Wait," Angie cried. She put on her oversized sunglasses and fished a white scarf with aqua polka dots out of her purse and tied it around her hair, making her look very much the part of a fifties starlet. She checked her image in the rearview mirror and then said, "Okay, now I'm ready."

Mel pulled out of the garage while her two friends belted out, "*Viva Las Vegas*," and this time she even joined them.

Getting out of the airport was no problem, but the city became more and more congested and then Mel merged onto the Strip and all but parked. The desert sun beat down on their heads while they sat and sat and sat.

"Okay, I made my list of things I want to do," Angie said. "There's a gondola ride at the Venetian, the roller coaster at New York, New York, oh, and we have to visit the Lucky Cat at the Cosmopolitan, and I need to see the eight-hundred-pound replica of the Statue of Liberty at Hershey's Chocolate World."

Mel looked at her in the rearview mirror. "You may want to pare that down. We're here on business. I just don't know if there's going to be time—"

"Oh, and I want to check out the Little White Wedding Chapel," Tate said. He gave Angie an adoring look. "That's where all the famous people elope."

"Like who?" Mel scoffed. "We covered this a few months go. You can't elope, all of your parents will go mental."

"Let's see, we've got Mary Tyler Moore and the first husband, Paul Newman and Joanne Woodward, Michael Jordan, Sarah Michelle Gellar and Freddie Prinze—"

"Buffy? Buffy got married there?" Angie asked. She sat forward in her seat, looking excited.

"No, you are not tying the knot in Vegas. I forbid it," Mel said. She tried to sound as disapproving as her mother. It came out surprisingly easy when she thought of how badly Angie's very Catholic parents and seven older brothers would take the news of her elopement to Tate.

"But it would be so romantic," Angie said. "You could be our witness."

"We could even have Elvis sing to us," Tate said.

"'Hound Dog'?"

"Absolutely."

"Oh. My. God." Mel gripped the steering wheel like she might strangle one or both of them if she didn't keep her hands busy. "No. Hear me now. No."

"You are a complete spoilsport." Angie pouted.

"So sorry, I'm trying to keep your family from putting a hit out on Tate if he elopes with the prodigal daughter."

"They wouldn't," Tate said. "They love me."

"Not that much they don't," Mel said. The traffic began to crawl forward, for which she was vastly relieved. "Now peel your lids and keep an eye open for the Blue Hawaiian Hotel and Casino. I'm not sure where it is, exactly."

They eased forward and Mel tried not to notice that two gray-haired ladies in sensible shoes were making better time on the sidewalk than she was on the road. The streets were crowded with cabs, shuttles, and limousines while the sidewalks were packed ten deep with people walking the Strip, gawking at the sensory overload all around them.

Mel took a moment—she had plenty while not moving—to study the crowd. There were loads of single young men and women, roaming in packs, families of all ages from grandparents to babies in strollers and everything in between, and then there were the groups dressed in matching T-shirts, clearly attending a convention of sorts. She wondered how a cupcake bakery would fit into all of this mayhem. Would these people pause in their gambling and gawking to stuff down a few cupcakes? She had no idea.

"There!" Tate pointed.

Mel felt her eyebrows lift. The Blue Hawaiian was one of the oldest hotel and casino combinations on the Strip, which was why she'd gotten a smokin' good deal on the rooms. Based on the Elvis movie *Blue Hawaii*, one of Mel's favorites, it incorporated everything there was to love about Elvis in Hawaii.

She turned the car into the hotel driveway and they all gawked as they drove under two-hundred-foot-tall tiki torches with real flames bursting out of the top.

"Whoa," Angie said. Neither Tate nor Mel had anything to add.

A valet wearing a Hawaiian shirt, natch, took Mel's car keys while a bellhop in a matching shirt unloaded their bags onto a rolling cart. Mel wondered why they were getting the kid glove treatment and Tate nodded in the direction of their rental's disappearing taillights.

"It's the car," he said.

"Oh, right," she said. "Not exactly a huge pink cupcake truck, is it?"

Tate took care of the tip while Mel checked in. She had decided to do it up and they had a two-bedroom suite in the middle of the forty-five-story hotel. The hotel clerk was a lovely young woman who gave them chilled coconut water in an actual coconut and put leis around their necks. Mel had to admit, the gesture was kitschy and appreciated.

Jenn McKinlay

The lobby was decorated in more of the Hawaii luau motif with tiki torches, potted palms, and a wall-sized screen that ran the movie *Blue Hawaii* in a continuous loop.

Angie stood entranced as Elvis came onto the screen. With his dark hair combed in a perfect pomade-enhanced wave and wearing that heart-stopping Elvis half smile, he really was the perfect male specimen.

Mel stood beside Angie and they leaned into each other, mouthing the words of the movie together.

"All right, ladies," Tate said. "I can feel my manhood shrinking beneath twelve-foot Elvis."

He swooped in between the two of them and hooked their arms with his. He led the way to the elevator with the determination of a man trying to rescue two drowning victims at the same time while also trying to swim upstream. Angie and Mel shook their heads as the Elvis spell was broken.

Tate followed their bellhop into a waiting elevator. The doors stayed open for a few more passengers and Mel shuffled to the back to give them room. When she glanced up, she wondered if she'd hit her head and was seeing triple.

Three Elvises, or would that be Elvi, stared back at her, before they scooted over to the side of the elevator to make room for two more.

Mel leaned close to Angie and asked, "Five Elvises, right?"

"Yup, unless, of course, it's a mass hallucination we're having, and then who knows?"

"It's five," Tate confirmed.

Mel knew she was staring. She knew it was rude. Still, she couldn't help it. The Elvi all wore the traditional white suit with the cape and spangles but they were different in size and shape from tall and gangly to short and potbellied. They also had on the sunglasses, making it impossible to see their eyes. For a moment, Mel wondered if they were bank robbers.

She wasn't the only one staring. Angie was staring so hard, she looked like she'd go cross-eyed, and she reached out to touch the sleeve of the Elvis closest to her.

"Now, now, little lady," the pint-sized Elvis said with a startlingly deep, honey-dipped Southern twang. "Don't touch the merchandise."

Angie cocked an eyebrow at him. "Why? If I break it, do I have to buy it?"

"Ange." Tate's voice was full of warning.

But the little Elvis burst out laughing, and the tension in the elevator broke as the others laughed, too.

"What's with the getups?" Angie asked.

Mel sighed. Someday they really needed to have a talk about the fine line between inquisitive and rude or, in Angie's case, the difference between making friends and enemies.

"We're here for the convention, aren't you?"

"Convention?" Tate asked.

"The annual Elvis impersonators convention," the tall one said. "It's awesome. There's like two thousand Elvises running around here."

"Two thousand?" Mel asked. "All in the white jumpsuit

and sunglasses?" As much as she loved Elvis, this was definitely going to give her nightmares.

"Nah, you got your young Elvises, your old Elvises, it's a mixed bag really, and not everyone auditions to win the title."

"Title?" Angie asked.

"Yeah, the World's Best Elvis Impersonator," the medium-sized one with the spare tire putting an undue strain on his zipper said. "You gotta see some of these guys. I swear last year the winner would have fooled Elvis himself."

"Maybe it really was Elvis," the bellhop said. They all turned to look at him and he shrugged. "The owner of this hotel is an Elvis freak. Most of the memorabilia that you see are really Elvis's personal possessions. He even bought a lock of Elvis's hair for one hundred and fifteen thousand dollars. It's said that Elvis's ghost has been seen roaming the halls of this place."

"Looking for his missing hair, no doubt," Angie said.

"Maybe he enters the body of the contestant of his choice and helps them win."

Mel shivered. Then she felt stupid for doing so. Elvis was not haunting the Blue Hawaiian.

"Young Elvis or old Elvis?" one of the impersonators asked. Mel wasn't positive but the voice was high and sounded like a woman's.

"What's it matter?" the bellhop asked.

"If I'm going to be possessed by Elvis, I want it to be young, hot Elvis," the squeaky voice said. "He can do with me as he will."

"I've got to give her that one," Angie said.

The elevator came to a stop and the Elvises all climbed out on the twenty-seventh floor.

As the elevator doors shut behind them and they began to climb again, Mel looked at the bellhop. "Two thousand Elvises?"

"I heard it was closer to three," he said.

Mel gave Tate the death glare.

"Oh, don't pout," he said. "We'll get you an Elvis outfit so you don't feel left out, maybe something from the *Jailhouse Rock* collection. You'd look good in stripes."

"Not funny."

"Oh, come on," he cajoled. "We're expanding our business with the blessing of hundreds and hundreds of Elvises. What could possibly go wrong?"

Three

"What time are we meeting the woman?" Mel asked.

"The woman's name is Holly Hartzmark," Tate said. "She's a very nice lady, who dreams of owning her own bakery, not that different from someone else I know."

He gave her a pointed stare and Mel rolled her eyes, not where he could see her, however.

"We're meeting Holly, our lawyer Stuart, and the Realtor down in the lobby in an hour," he said.

"Cool, I'm taking a shower," Mel said. She felt grimy from the flight and the drive as if the dusty desert and traffic-clogged streets coated her skin and throat.

"Well, I want to explore," Angie said. She was standing by the window of their room looking out at the city while scanning the hotel's brochure of amenities. "I heard they host a full luau every night. I want to go check it out."

"I'm totally down with that plan," Tate said. He grabbed the spare card key off the table and took Angie by the hand, and the two of them headed out the door without a backward glance.

Mel wondered if this was what their partnership had become now that two of the three were a couple. Would she always be left behind while her two friends went gallivanting?

"Stop it," she said out loud. She shook her head. She was not going to start throwing herself pity parties just because her two besties were engaged and she was single, which seemed to be her status quo.

She knew she could have joined them while they were off seeing the sights, but she had chosen a hot shower instead. She glanced around the suite. It was very modern, very swank, all glass tables and chrome accents, and it was well appointed, offering a view of the Strip that took her breath away. She could even see the water fountain show at the Bellagio Hotel. She tried to find some happiness in this, but it was a struggle.

There was no question that she really wasn't eager to franchise the bakery, but she had agreed to meet the person who was interested so here she was. She knew she had two choices—she could either pout and whine about it, or she could try to enjoy the next few days.

Surely they weren't going to spend all of their time in meetings. She could hit the spa, take in a show, place some bets for Marty, and before she knew it, she'd be headed home. As for the franchise, maybe it wouldn't be so bad.

Tate was right. A woman, like Mel, wanted to own a

cupcake bakery. He said it was her lifelong dream. How could Mel begrudge anyone the happiness she had found running her own cupcake bakery?

She pictured the thirtysomething buyer, Holly Hartzmark, as a happy-go-lucky woman, who would smell faintly of gingersnaps. She would give good hugs, have a contagious laugh, and know how to whip up a cake from scratch out of minimal ingredients. Feeling better than she had in weeks, Mel headed for the showers.

\' \' \' \'

When Mel was wrong, she was, oh, so wrong. As she stood in the lobby of the hotel, waiting for Tate and Angie to appear, Stuart Stinson, the franchise lawyer Tate had hired, arrived with the Realtor and a dark-haired exotic beauty that made Mel feel like hiding behind any one of the potted palm trees until they all went away.

The woman had thick dark brown hair that hung halfway down her back in luscious waves. Her face was sculpted with high jutting cheekbones, a square jaw, and a wide forehead adorned with perfectly arched eyebrows.

Her eyes were an electric blue that Mel could see all the way across the room. Long lashes, a thin nose, and pillow lips completed the knock-'em-to-their-knees beauty that was her face. And that was just her face. The silky turquoise wraparound dress she wore with beige stiletto pumps hugged her every curve while the fabric undulated with each step she took. Seriously, the woman was sex on legs, and Mel had never felt more like a hausfrau in her entire life.

Suddenly her black capri pants and gray sleeveless cotton blouse made Mel feel like Mary Ann to this woman's Ginger, and she desperately wanted to go on a three-hour tour anywhere that would get her out of here and she was not even a boat person.

"Mel," Stuart called out before she could make her getaway.

She gave him a small wave while frantically checking the lobby for any sign of Tate or Angie. They were nowhere to be seen. She tried to tamp down the surge of fury that swamped her. This was Tate's idea. He was the one who'd forced them into this franchise situation that he knew she wanted no part of, and now he was MIA and she was forced to meet the prospective buyer. She blew out a breath through her nose. If he showed up in the next five minutes, she might forgive him, but if he didn't, she was planning to give him a full-on smack-down topped with the silent treatment.

The group approached. Mel tried not to fidget with the buttons on her blouse. She had no idea what to say to a woman who was that stunning, except maybe that it wasn't fair, and instead of hogging all the good looks, Holly should consider passing them around. Yeah, that probably wouldn't go over well because Mel was quite sure a note of bitterness would creep into her voice, keeping the sentiment from being charming.

"Ms. Cooper," Stuart said. "May I introduce your

franchise investor, Holly Hartzmark, and her Realtor, Scott Jensen?"

"How do you do?" Mel said.

"Very well and you?" Holly replied. Even her low voice was sexy.

Holly had a firm, warm handshake and she made direct eye contact, causing Mel to be the one to glance away first. The woman was too beautiful. Mel felt as if gazing upon her too long would render her stupid, as if Holly could put some freaky Greek goddess curse on her or something. It was a relief to turn to the Realtor. Scott gripped her hand a little too tightly and a little too long, and his eye contact ran like that, too.

Mel addressed the group. "I'm so sorry my business partners seem to be running late. I can't imagine what could have held them up."

"It's Vegas," Scott said. He was the quintessential thirty-thousand-dollar millionaire real estate guy with slicked-back hair, veneers on the teeth, Omega on the wrist, skinny-legged trousers, and pointy-toed leather shoes. If there was a cologne that reeked of cold hard cash, he'd be wearing it—heck, he'd probably bathe in it.

"Yeah, well, I'll just give them a quick call," Mel said.

Stuart made an impatient sound. Gray-haired and sour-looking, Stuart was a stickler of an attorney, which was why Tate liked him. Stuart dotted every *i* and crossed every *t*, and he was never, ever late. Mel had a feeling Tate would be groveling to more than just her later.

Mel took her phone out of her purse and stepped away

from the others. What she had to say to Tate wasn't going to be polite. Tate answered on the third ring.

"Where the hell are you?" Mel growled.

Bells and chimes rang in the background, and Mel heard Angie squeal with delight.

"She did it. She hit!"

The sounds of cheering and laughing went on for a few seconds, and Mel felt her temper get hotter and hotter.

"Tate!" she hissed. She could feel the eyes of the group on her, and she walked farther away.

"I can't hear you," he said. "It's too loud. Hang on."

"Tate, you had better get your butts to the lobby right now," she said. "We are all waiting for you in front of the check-in desk. Where are you?"

"Uh," Tate stuttered.

"Do not tell me that you are in a different casino," she said.

"I—"

"Don't."

"But—"

"What do you not understand about *don't*?" she asked.

"I'm sorry, Mel," he said. "Look we'll hop a cab and get back up the Strip in no time."

"Define *no time*," she said.

"Sorry, Mel, I couldn't understand you," he said. "It sounds like you're talking through clenched teeth."

Mel opened her jaw wide to stretch it out before she spoke again so that her words were very clear. "I am going to kill you. I'm going to drag your sorry carcass out into the desert, pour honey all over you, and let the fire ants eat you."

"You're angry," he said.

"Thank you, Captain Obvious," Mel snapped.

"And you have every right to be," he said. "We are so sorry. We just got carried away because . . . Vegas. Listen, go have drinks in the bar and we'll be there within the hour."

Mel shoved her free hand into her short blond hair and pulled. The expression *ripping your hair out* suddenly made perfect sense to her.

"No, I'm not going to entertain your guests," she said. "We are going to press on to the property they are considering for the franchise—you remember, the reason we came here. And we'll see if I think it's appropriate or not, which will determine whether we are franchising or not. *Capiche?*"

"Oh, no, you only use Italian when you're really, really mad," he said. "We are on our way. I swear. We'll meet you at the property."

"Don't bother." Mel ended the call without saying good-bye.

She tugged on the front of her blouse, bolstering her courage. If she was left to handle this, well, wasn't it a pity if she found neither Holly nor the property they were going to look at suitable for a franchise? This might actually work out for the best. She smiled.

She knew without checking her reflection that it was a devious smile, the sort that was usually found on an animated evil queen in a Disney flick. She was okay with that.

"Tate sends his apologies," Mel said as she rejoined the

group. "He and our other partner, Angie DeLaura, were unfortunately detained and won't be able to join us. If it's all right with you, I suggest we go ahead and look at the property."

"Excellent," Stuart said. He led the way to the doors. "It's walkable as it's just around the corner in a small shopping corridor."

Mel followed him, leaving Holly and Scott to bring up the rear. That didn't last as Holly caught up with Mel outside.

"Tate isn't coming?" Holly asked. Her voice matched her looks exactly. It was low and soft and managed to suggest tangled bedsheets. It irritated Mel like the obnoxious bass beat being blasted out of a passing car.

"That's what I said," Mel replied. Holly flinched and Mel cringed. She was not normally a mean person, but this woman looked like she knew as much about baking as Mel did about fixing cars, which was nil.

Just because she had a lot of money didn't mean she was capable of running a bakery. And if she was buying the right to use the Fairy Tale Cupcake brand, Mel was going to make damn sure she knew how to bake a frigging cupcake.

"Tell me, Holly, what's your culinary background?" Mel asked.

She glanced at Holly and saw her bite one of her plump lips. She looked unsure of herself and Mel took a certain satisfaction in that. *Looks aren't everything*, she thought to herself.

"You have studied at a cooking school, correct?" Mel asked.

"I, well, I don't have any formal training," Holly said. She was fidgeting with a ring on her left hand as if she wasn't sure what to do with her hands.

"Oh, huh, I'm going to be honest. I'm not sure how I feel about that. I consider cooking an art and science," Mel said. She knew she sounded snotty but this was business, her business. "A high school home economics class is not really enough preparation to open your own bakery, don't you agree?"

By the blush that darkened Holly's face, Mel knew she had guessed correctly. Holly had no baking experience beyond the minimum. Good grief, she probably wanted to open up a bakery because she thought cupcakes were cute.

Mel pinched the bridge of her nose between her fingers, to ward off an incoming headache, and trudged forward. Well, at least when she said no to the franchise, Tate couldn't fault her. Holly was no more prepared to own and run a bakery than Mel was to be the headlining act at the Blue Hawaiian.

Stuart and Scott paused in front of a small, vacant shop nestled in a narrow alley of shops right off the Strip. There were throngs of people walking up and down the small walkway, and Mel knew Tate would look at the foot traffic as a good sign. Whatever.

She glanced around at the other shops to see what sort of competition they'd be dealing with, but other than a frozen yogurt shop, there were no food places, just clothes and Vegas kitsch. Okay, so that was a point in the "to franchise" column, and now Mel was really glad that Tate had missed checking the place out.

She would be sure to make it sound like it wasn't all that. She glanced at the storefront. It appeared to be under construction. The windows had boards over them, and the front was half painted a deep purple, as if whoever had started the job had run out of paint before they finished. The iron sign holder above the door was empty, as if just waiting for a new owner.

Mel tried to picture her retro fifties atomic Fairy Tale Cupcake sign swinging right overhead. She shook her head. No, it didn't fit in here. She was not buying into the franchise.

"I have the keys," Scott said. He took them out of his pocket. "I'll need to go in and deactivate the alarm. As you can see, it's centrally located on the street. There are no other comparable businesses in the immediate area. And just so you know, I already had a woman looking at this property this morning and she was very, very eager to lease it."

"Well, she's in luck since it's not really what I had in mind," Mel said. She glanced at Holly. "None of this is."

Stuart gave her an odd look and then turned to Scott and motioned for him to unlock the door. "Let's not decide anything until we see inside."

"Right." Scott put the key in the deadbolt.

"You know what, forget it," Holly said. She put her hand on Scott's arm, keeping him from turning the key. "I don't know what I was thinking. I can't do this. I can't do anything. I'm just a stupid showgirl and that's all I'll ever be."

With a sob, she turned and ran down the walkway toward the fountain in the center of the shops.

"Huh," Mel said.

"What do you mean, 'huh'?" Stuart asked. "If you were any colder to her, she would have frostbite."

"I don't know what you mean," she said.

"Sure you do," he said. Stuart gave her a shrewd look. "Tate told me you were balking about franchising and I was prepared for a little resistance, but I didn't think you'd be so mean."

"I am not mean," Mel protested.

"Really? Then why is she crying?" He gestured to Holly where she sat on the edge of the fountain, doubled over and sobbing into her hands.

Mel felt her heart sink into her shoes. She *was* mean. No, even worse, she was a bully, and for no other reasons than she was scared of franchising and Holly was pretty. She was a horrible person.

Four

Mel approached Holly, feeling about as low as a cupcake heading for the floor frosting side down. She hadn't meant to make Holly cry. She just wanted to keep her world in order—was that really so wrong? As she got closer, she tried to see Holly's face. If the woman was a pretty crier, she really didn't think she'd be able to offer her much comfort.

Holly had her face buried in her hands and she was sobbing, not delicate little sniffles but deep-throated wails that sounded like someone was stepping on a duck, repeatedly, so that was promising.

"Listen, I'm sorry," Mel said. "I was being a big jerk and I shouldn't have said what I did. You are probably nervous enough, putting your life savings into a bakery without me making you doubt your abilities."

Holly peeked at her over the tips of her fingers. "You were so mean."

Mel blew out a breath. She would have protested, but Holly and Stuart were right. She had been mean. She glanced over to where Stuart and Scott stood waiting for them. Scott was checking them out and licking his lips. Mel had a feeling he was thinking impure thoughts about them, ew, or maybe he just had a nervous condition.

"I'm sorry," she apologized to Holly again, hoping to get this over with. "It's just that this is more Tate's thing than mine, and when I saw you, well, you really don't look like a baker, and, oh, I have no excuse. I was just an ass. Can you forgive me? Can we begin again?"

"Yes, of course, but where is Tate?" Holly asked. "I dressed like this because of him."

Mel felt her hackles rise, and now she had to rethink being nice to this bimbo. "You do know he's engaged, right? In fact, he's here with his fiancée, Angie DeLaura, who is our other business partner."

"Oh, I know," Holly said. "I didn't mean, oh, we are really struggling to communicate here, aren't we?"

She dropped her hands from her face and reached out to touch Mel's arm. Mel was relieved to see that Holly's makeup had smeared and the tip of her nose was red. She was not quite the blotchy beast that Mel turned into when she cried, but at least she wasn't a pretty crier, either.

"I'm not interested in Tate like that," Holly assured her. "It's just that I find men more manageable when I have all of my weapons strapped on."

"Weapons?" Mel asked. She looked to see if Holly was packing a gun.

Holly gave her a wry look, then she pointed to each body part as she spoke. "Hair extensions, false eyelashes, padded push-up bra, Spanx, butt lifter padded panties—"

"No, sir," Mel protested.

"Yes, ma'am," Holly said and she spun around to show Mel her impressive gravity-defying booty. Then she jiggled it and turned back around and said, "Support hose, platform heels, a half hour spent contouring my face, and about five pounds of makeup. Seriously, if I ditched all of this and passed you on the street, you wouldn't even recognize me."

"I am stunned," Mel said.

"And I am ashamed," Holly said. "It's just that this bakery is so very important to me. I'm a showgirl, you know, and I want to make a different life for myself. I thought all of this would help me negotiate with Tate or at least keep him distracted enough that he wouldn't ask for my credentials, which of course, you did right away."

"That's because all of this intimidated me," Mel said, and she waved her hands at Holly's overall appearance. She gave Holly a sideways glance. "Can I pinch your butt?"

"What?" Holly laughed.

"I just want to see what a butt lifter padded panty feels like."

"Why not? At least you asked first." Holly shrugged.

She spun around and Mel tried to figure out how to pinch her butt in public without looking like a perv. She settled for just jabbing Holly's butt with her pointer finger. Holly didn't even flinch. Mel figured what the heck and she pinched the other woman's behind between her thumb and forefinger. Holly didn't even register the touch.

"Wow," Mel said. "Just wow."

Holly turned back around with a smile. "They come in handy when you have to sit on a hard chair for any length of time."

"I'll bet," Mel said. They grinned at each other. "Well, should we try this again?"

"I'd really like that," Holly said. She fished a tissue out of her purse and used the reflective surface of her smart phone to see her face while she cleaned up her ruined makeup.

"Hi, I'm Melanie Cooper, but everyone calls me Mel."

"Holly Hartzmark, a pleasure."

Mel gestured back to where Scott and Stuart were waiting. Scott had clearly settled in and lit a cigarette while Stuart cast him an annoyed look and moved away from him and his smoke while checking his cell phone.

"So, what made you choose this location?"

"It's close to the Strip, but I think when you see the inside of this place, you'll see the same potential that I do. It's not huge but it's big enough to start. We can always move when we get a following going and demand increases."

Mel forced a smile. Holly's enthusiasm was a bit alarming, but Mel liked it so much better than Holly crying that she nodded and gestured for Holly to lead the way.

When Stuart saw them coming, he turned and shouted

something to Scott. Scott nodded and turned back to the door, unlocking it. Mel and Holly were still several storefronts away when Scott dropped his cigarette. He pulled the door to the shop open and was about to step on the cigarette at the same time, but there was a loud *whoosh* as flames shot up from the ground, covering Scott who screamed. Stuart dropped his phone and ran toward him, yanking off his jacket at the same time, and he began beating the flames off Scott, who had fallen to the ground.

The roar of an explosion sounded and the boards that had covered the windows blew out. Holly shrieked and Mel grabbed her and ducked down to the ground. Covering her head with her arm, Mel couldn't move while bits of board rained down over their heads and clouds of dust and smoke filled the air, making her eyes tear and her lungs burn.

When it stopped, she glanced up to see Stuart on the ground with the front door on top of him. She couldn't see Scott. Smoke and flames shot out of the opening where the boarded windows had been.

Mel waited until there was no more flying debris then she ran toward the storefront, shouting at Holly, "Call 911!"

The other pedestrians in the area had scattered with screams and shouts. Several were on their phones calling in the explosion while others were filming it and taking pictures.

Mel shoved the heavy wooden door off Stuart. He was unconscious with a gash on his forehead. But she didn't see any other signs of injury. She quickly undid his tie and used it to bandage the wound on his forehead.

Holly came running up to her. "The ambulance is on its way. Is he all right?"

Mel checked Stuart's pulse. "I think so, but I don't want to move him in case of an unseen injury."

Holly nodded. "Where's Scott?"

They both glanced back at the doorway. There was a pile of rubble on the ground and a man's hand was just visible.

"There!" Mel cried. Holly ran to Scott while Mel grabbed a woman standing nearby, pulling her down beside her. "I need you to stay with him."

The woman crouched beside Mel, looking scared. "I don't know how . . . what do I do?"

"Just stay with him," she said. "Talk to him. If he wakes up, call me."

Mel hurried to help Holly. They began pulling the debris off Scott and Mel was relieved when more people stepped up to help. The sight that met their eyes beneath the boards and bricks was fit only for a horror film.

Scott was severely burned. The left side of his face was a boiled scarlet red along with his arm and his chest. He was moaning even though his eyes were shut and he seemed to be drifting in and out of consciousness.

Holly knelt down beside him. "It's okay, Scott, we're here and we're going to get you to the hospital."

Scott moved his lips as if to speak but nothing came out except more moaning.

"Shh," Holly crooned. "It's going to be all right."

She glanced up at a man standing beside her. He was

wearing baggy jeans, a sideways baseball cap, and was covered in tattoos and piercings.

"I need you to run to the ice cream shop and get cool, *not* cold, clean towels to put on his burns. Hurry!"

The man nodded and ran. Holly looked at Mel and said, "We have to get his jewelry off. These burns are going to start swelling."

Mel nodded. She reached around his neck and unhooked the thick gold chain while Holly removed his ring from the pinky on his left hand. Mel glanced at his body and felt her gag reflex kick in as the smell of charred skin and hair infiltrated her nose.

"What about his belt?" she asked Holly.

Holly was swallowing convulsively and Mel knew the smell was getting to her, too. She wiped her nose on her arm and nodded. Together they carefully unhooked his belt buckle. Holly lifted his hips, while Mel pulled the belt free.

Scott moaned and the women froze, fearing that they'd hurt him. Then he licked his blistered lips and croaked, "If you wanted my pants off, all you had to do was ask."

Holly choked out a sob-laugh and said, "Shut up. You're going to be fine. Do you hear me?"

The Hispanic man who'd run for the towels returned and Holly gently placed the damp cloths on Scott's burns. Sirens broke through the crowd noise and Mel glanced up.

"You've got him?" she asked. Holly nodded and Mel hurried back over to Stuart and the woman, still kneeling beside him.

She checked his pulse again and the gash on his head. His pulse was steady and the tie around his forehead was saturated in blood but the wound beneath looked to have stopped bleeding and was beginning to congeal. He didn't appear to have been burned.

Mel looked at the woman beside her. "Thanks."

The woman nodded but didn't leave. Mel understood. Once you watch over a person in danger, you become invested in their well-being. She'd been here before.

An ambulance parked at the top of the street and three paramedics came running. They reached Mel first and she pointed to Stuart and said, "Head injury," and then at Scott, "Severe burns."

One man knelt beside Stuart while the other went to tend Scott. The third ran back to the ambulance to get the stretcher. Mel backed up to give the man room to work. While he checked Stuart's vitals, he asked, "What happened?"

"We were here to look at leasing a property," Mel said. "When Scott, the man who is burned, unlocked it and opened the door, there was an explosion and the whole place went up in flames."

More sirens sounded. The smoke had cleared and there didn't seem to be as much fire coming from the storefront. The fire truck pulled in behind the ambulance and the firefighters jumped off the truck and came toward them, hauling on their gear as they ran.

Several men started pushing the crowd back. Holly came to stand beside Mel as Scott was put on the stretcher and taken to the ambulance. Another stretcher appeared and Stuart was placed on it. He was unconscious.

"Are you family?" the paramedic asked. Both Mel and Holly shook their heads.

"Business associates," Mel said. She noticed that she sounded apologetic as if she wished she could offer them more of a relationship than the acquaintanceship she had with both men.

"Where are you taking them?" Holly asked.

"UMC," the paramedic said. "He'll get excellent care there."

His partner arrived and they pushed off with Stuart between them before Mel could ask any more questions.

"University Medical Center," Holly explained. "It's a hospital northwest of the Strip."

"We need to evacuate the area!" One of the firefighters came at them at a run. "There's gas in the building. We need everyone to leave the area."

Mel and Holly exchanged a look and began to back away.

"Gas?" Mel asked. Then she felt dizzy as she realized it had been Scott's cigarette that had probably ignited the gas into a fireball. "Could a cigarette have caused this?"

The fireman looked at her. "Explain."

"The man who was burned was smoking a cigarette. He dropped it to the ground right before he opened the door."

"If the gas was concentrated enough, yes," the fireman said. "That will help us deal with this. Thanks."

"Is the gas coming from a line?" Holly asked. Mel knew Holly was thinking the same thing that she was. As bad as it was that Scott and Stuart had been hurt, and that was horrible, a gas leak meant that this could have happened after they'd opened their shop, killing staff and customers.

The fireman looked harried. "No, in fact, it appears someone left the gas oven in the kitchen on. The whole shop was full of it. Damn lucky it was caught early or it could have blown up the entire street."

"Not so lucky for the two men caught in the explosion," Holly said. The fireman nodded and said, "Sorry."

"I don't understand," Mel said. "Shouldn't the gas to the premises have been shut off if the building was vacant?"

"You'd think," the firefighter said. He escorted them farther away from the area. "Please stay back. We don't want anyone else to get hurt."

"Come on." Holly grabbed Mel's arm and they began to move away from the fire, which had now engulfed the small storefront.

"Mel!"

"Oh my god!"

Five

Mel glanced up and saw Tate and Angie running toward her. They both looked frantic, and at the sight of them, she felt all the terror of the past few minutes bubble up inside her. Tate got to her first and wrapped her in a hug that threatened to crack her ribs. As soon as he released her to study her face, Angie lunged in between them and hugged Mel tight, not releasing her even when Mel patted her back to let her know she was okay and the hug could stop now.

"We heard the explosion," Tate said. "Then there were sirens and people were running and screaming. They blocked off the area and we couldn't get through. I've never been so scared in my entire life. What the hell happened? Oh . . . hi."

"Hi," Holly said back.

Mel unhooked Angie from about her neck and stepped

back. She took Angie by the upper arms and met her terrified gaze.

"I'm okay, Angie," she said. "Honestly, I'm fine."

Angie sucked in a breath, nodded, and then burst into tears. Tate put his arm around her shoulders and pulled her close.

"It's all right," he said. "She's safe. Where are the others?"

"Scott was severely burned," Mel said and she explained about the unfortunate meeting between Scott's cigarette and the gas. "Stuart had a head injury but no burns. They've both been taken to the hospital."

"What about Holly?" Angie asked, glancing around to see if their future franchise owner was anywhere to be found.

"This is Holly," Mel said, and she gestured to the woman beside her. "Holly, these are my partners, Tate, who you've spoken to, and Angie, my fellow baker."

Angie's eyes went wide as she took in the woman beside Mel. Even covered in dirt, with her dark hair mussed and her makeup half cried off, Holly was never going to be confused with Betty Crocker. Mel knew Angie was thinking the same thing Mel had, that there was no way in heck this woman knew her way around a convection oven.

"You're Holly?" Tate asked. He was smart enough to turn his high-pitched note of surprise into a small clearing of his throat. "Sorry, I just . . . you're not . . . cupcakes, huh?"

Mel exchanged a glance with Holly. They both looked back at the blown-out storefront. The firefighters were soaking down the interior, and were now milling around the front, waiting to see if any hot spots flared. The place that just minutes ago had had the potential to be a cute little cupcake shop in a high-traffic area was now a charred gaping maw, looking like it would devour anything that crossed its path.

"That was the plan," Holly said. "But I think it's safe to say that it's gone up in smoke."

Mel patted her shoulder. "I'm so sorry."

Holly shrugged and Mel could tell by the sheen in her bright blue eyes that she was trying very hard not to cry.

"You were really amazing during the chaos," Mel said. "You didn't panic at all but jumped right in and started taking care of Scott. I was very impressed."

"Performing a live show, where anything can go wrong and frequently does, is great training for a crisis," Holly said. "You were quick on your feet, too. I'd say for first responders, we did all right."

"The hospital they took Stuart and Scott to is UMC," Mel said to Tate. "We should check on them. Scott in particular looked . . . rough."

"I'll go," Tate said. "The police will want to talk to you two. Text me about what's happening and I'll do the same."

"I'm staying with Mel," Angie said.

"Of course." Tate planted a kiss in her hair before he took off in the wake of the ambulance.

Two police officers arrived and Mel and Holly were separated and questioned about what happened. Angie moved from group to group, clearly not wanting either woman to feel abandoned.

Mel felt terrible that she didn't have more information for the officer, but the truth was she didn't know anything about Scott Jensen or Stuart Stinson. She hoped Holly knew more about Scott and she referred the officer to Tate for more information on Stuart. She had never felt more useless in her life.

When the officer left her, Mel took a moment to get her head together. Angie was comforting Holly, who was looking at the charred remnants of what was once her dream bakery with the despair that came with watching a dream die. Mel felt terrible for her, she really did, but at the same time there was a tiny sliver of relief.

There would be no franchise now. Fairy Tale Cupcakes would remain hers, all hers, with no quality-control issues and no sharing her recipes or baking secrets. She felt a sigh of relief well up inside her, and she let it out in one long breath.

"That sounds as if it came all the way up from your feet," Angie said. She and Holly joined her where she stood in the shade of a cluster of palm trees.

"I think it did," Mel said. "You know, it's a good thing you didn't lease this place, Holly. If it was something faulty causing the gas to leak from the oven, well, you could have been killed."

Holly shivered. "I really hope Scott and Stuart are okay. I'll just feel terrible if . . . well, you know."

Mel understood. Holly didn't want to say the worst possible scenario, which would be for either of the men to die from their injuries. Mel agreed. She didn't even want to think it. She'd had enough dead bodies to last her a lifetime.

"I have to say that despite this disaster," Mel said, "it was really nice meeting you. Maybe our paths will cross again someday."

Holly looked surprised and then sadly accepting.

"Wait . . . what?" Angie asked.

"Well, since there is no place to put the bakery now, I just assumed . . ." Mel's voice trailed off.

Angie propped her hands on her hips and narrowed her eyes at Mel. "Really? Did you really think we were only looking at one property?"

"Well, I hoped . . ."

"Ah-ha!" Angie pointed at her. "You're still fighting it. You still don't want to franchise."

Maybe it was the near death experience but Mel found herself incapable of denying the truth.

"That's not news," Mel cried. "I've never wanted to franchise, and that was before I knew we were looking to partner up with a person who doesn't even have any baking experience." She paused to look at Holly. "No offense."

"It's okay," Holly said. She sounded resigned.

"No, it isn't," Angie said. "Mel, the three of us have been over and over this. We have to franchise for the good of the business."

"No, you and Tate have muscled me into franchising ever since he quit being a wheeler and dealer and decided to be an entrepreneur with *my* bakery."

"It's *our* bakery," Angie argued, looking like she

wanted to bang her head on the first hard object she could find.

"Listen, I don't want to cause any problems," Holly began but they both interrupted her.

"Hush!" Mel and Angie said together and then Mel softened it by adding, "Please."

Holly nodded. "I'm just going to wait over there."

As soon as she was three feet away, Angie turned on Mel. "What is the matter with you?"

"Oh, I don't know," Mel snapped. "Maybe it's the near death experience I just enjoyed."

"Oh, stop being dramatic, you were nowhere near the explosion."

"I could have been seriously injured," Mel said.

"By what?" Angie asked. "Tripping?"

"A shard of glass—"

"The windows were boarded up."

"A very large splinter, I could have been impaled by a very large splinter."

"What is your issue with Holly?" Angie asked.

"I don't have an issue, I mean, other than her lack of formal training in the culinary arts."

"I don't have formal training; neither does Marty or Tate," Angie said.

"Okay, look at her," Mel said. "Does she look like a baker to you?"

"Sure, if you slap an apron on her and put her in some sensible shoes, why not?"

"She's a showgirl," Mel said. "With no kitchen experience, and you want to sell her a franchise of our bakery. I just think this plan is fraught with disaster."

"Bigger than the one you just lived through?" Angie asked.

"Yes, because if she's a lousy baker and the product is no good, our reputation will be finished," Mel said. "It won't matter how pretty she is. People are very unforgiving about their baked goods."

"So, what's really bothering you is the fact that she's pretty?" Angie asked.

"No, yes, I don't know," Mel said. "Doesn't it bother you?"

"Nah," Angie said with a dismissive wave. "Looks fade. Besides, I think she has a lot of artificial enhancements going on. You always have to wonder what the poor guy thinks when he wakes up and his va-va-voom woman turns into a ho-hum girl."

Even though Mel knew what Angie said was true, and how irritating of Angie to see all of the enhancements right away, she didn't feel like confirming it and proving Angie's point.

"You know, you have to get over this prejudice," Angie said.

"What?" Mel gasped. "I am not prejudiced."

"Yes, you are," Angie said. "Overly pretty women make you uncomfortable and self-conscious. I think it harkens back to your awkward adolescence."

"That is so not true," Mel protested. "I treat everyone exactly the same."

"Okay, then, how did you determine that Holly can't bake?" Angie asked.

"Well, just look at her . . . oh, crap," Mel said. She hung her head. "Oh, man, I *am* prejudiced."

"In your defense, the mean girls in school were usually the pretty ones, so it stands to reason that you are innately suspicious of them," Angie said. "Remember that witch Madison Arthur? She was a blond, blue-eyed stunner with her phony ski jump nose and her inflated ta-ta's. She rode your case for years."

"The one whose boyfriend Dwight nicknamed me 'Melephant' until Tate punched him out?" Mel asked. "Yeah, hard to forget her. I can still see her pointing and laughing at me when my chair broke during band. I should have stuffed my clarinet right down her throat."

"I'd have paid to see that," Angie said. "She used to mock my eyebrows and blame my hairy Italian heritage. She told everyone that I probably had a hairy back. Man, I hated her."

"I hope she's married to a jerk," Mel said. "And she has six kids and the birthing hips to show for it."

Angie laughed. "Time to focus. Holly isn't Madison, and we're grown-ups now. We can let go of all that stuff, yes?"

"Yes," Mel mumbled then twisted her head to the side in a full-on sulk. "It's just not fair. Even if Holly is enhanced, she's still a knockout, and I really think that if she can cook, I'm going to be super irritated."

"No, you're going to be nice and supportive," Angie said. "Come on, you know Tate's right about the longevity of the company. If we want to be able to keep paying everyone, we have to expand."

"I know, I know," Mel said. Her tone was grudging at best and she knew it.

"All right, then, let's tell Holly that we'll keep looking for new locations," Angie said. "Who knows, we may find the perfect spot and the cupcakes will practically sell themselves."

"Fine," Mel said.

Holly looked wary when they approached, and Mel couldn't blame her. Even after the trauma they'd gone through, the woman still looked great, a little smudged perhaps, but still great. She wondered what Angie would say if she knew about the butt lifter padded panties. Knowing Angie, she'd want to pinch Holly's butt, too.

"So, Angie and I talked," Mel said. She couldn't meet Holly's gaze. "And I guess we'll plan on going to look at more properties, say, tomorrow?"

Holly sagged in relief. "You mean it? Oh, thank you so much! You won't regret it. I promise. In fact, I want you to come over to my place tomorrow and I'll prove it to you."

"Prove it?" Angie lifted her eyebrows. "Do I understand from that that you're going to bake for us?"

Holly nodded. "And trust me, I am going to blow your minds."

Six

"How is he?" Mel asked the nurse who came into Stuart Stinson's room while she stood awkwardly by his bed, not knowing what to say or do for a man she had only known briefly.

"Resting comfortably for now. He was awake early this morning and he didn't appear to have any permanent injuries," the nurse said. "They are keeping him a bit longer for observation but he should be free to go soon. Are you family?"

"No," Mel said. Relief that Stuart was going to be fine almost made her buckle at the knees; she hadn't realized how worried she had been. "I'm just a business associate, but I was there yesterday when he and Mr. Jensen were caught in the fire."

The nurse nodded. "Mr. Stinson was lucky he didn't get burned. Mr. Jensen, well, it's been touch and go."

"They wouldn't let me in to see him," Mel said. Her throat felt tight and she drew in a shaky breath. "Can you tell me anything?"

The nurse reached over and squeezed Mel's forearm. "It doesn't look good, I'm afraid. I'm sorry."

"Thank you." Mel nodded.

She turned and saw Tate standing at the nurses' station. He was undoubtedly getting the same report she had gotten. When he turned around, his wavy brown hair looked mussed as if he'd been running his fingers through it. Angie came up beside him and looped her hand through his arm. Tate leaned over and kissed the top of her head. It was a gesture of comfort and affection.

Again, Mel was pierced with a sense of aloneness that was so acute, it actually hurt. Was this how it would always be then, her two friends comforting each other while she stood on the outside looking in?

She shook her head. She was being a selfish brat while Scott Jensen was fighting for his life. She had no right to feel sorry for herself. She was fine, absolutely fine.

"You ready?" Tate asked as Mel approached. She nodded. They all knew the situation; talking about it only made it worse.

✴ ✴ ✴

Mel grumbled all the way to Holly's house, which turned out to be well off the Strip. Even though it gave her an excellent excuse to zip through town in the silver bullet, as she had dubbed the Mercedes, she still felt grumpy. She didn't particularly like change and it sure felt like it was coming hard and fast with no break.

On the one hand, she knew that it was her protectiveness of the bakery that was making her so franchise resistant, but on the other hand, she knew Tate was right that expanding was key to their survival.

She wondered if Holly had shown up yesterday looking a little pudgy with short-cropped hair and no makeup whether she would have felt more kindred with her. The answer would only validate Angie's observation that Mel had a pretty girl bias, but yeah, in Mel's head when they had talked about franchising, she had pictured someone, well, more like her.

Personal maintenance fell by the wayside when you had to be up at the crack of dawn to bake every day. Elaborate hairdos didn't go so well under the old chef toque or hairnet, makeup melted when confronted with a 350-degree oven, and when you spent all day using your hands to mold fondant and had to wash them a million times to keep the germs off the product, manicures seemed pointless. So yeah, Mel had expected someone a little more kitchen goddess and less bedroom siren.

That being said, Holly did seem nice. She had a quick response time in a crisis, and really, how could Mel dislike anyone with a fake hiney? It was so ridiculous, it actually bought Holly some points with Mel.

Tate navigated using the directional app on his phone. When they started rolling toward the McMansions on the west side of Vegas, Mel had to wonder how much being a showgirl paid if Holly could afford one of these places.

"Huh." Angie grunted from the backseat. "I think I may need to look into how much a girl gets for high kicking."

"I don't think she makes enough to live here," Tate said. "Do we have the right address?"

"Let's double-check at the gatehouse," Mel said.

She pulled up to the small brick building with a uniformed guard stationed in the doorway.

"Good morning, how can I help you?" the guard asked. He was middle-aged and a little pudgy, which was unfortunately accentuated by his emerald green uniform. He had a righteous handlebar mustache that was trimmed to perfection, framing his mouth and accentuating his pouty lower lip.

"Hi, we're guests of Holly Hartzmark," Mel said.

"Just for the day?" he asked.

"Yes," she said.

The guard ducked back inside his little house.

" 'Who rang that bell?' " Tate squawked from the passenger seat. " 'Who rang that bell?' "

Angie burst out laughing but Mel refused to react, fearing the guard would hear them.

"Stop it," she hissed at Tate.

"Oh, come on, you were thinking it, too. He's a dead ringer for him." Mel was silent so Tate cajoled, "You know what movie I'm talking about. 'Who rang that bell?' "

"*The Wizard of Oz*, now shut it." Mel identified the movie just to hush him up. "Behave."

The guard popped back out of his house, handed Mel a dated pass to hang on her rearview mirror, and gestured for her to go forward.

"You're all set, ma'am, have a nice day."

"You, too," Mel said. She moved the car forward and a massive wrought iron gate slowly glided open to the right to let them through.

Angie leaned forward and said, "Well, the joke is on them."

"How do you figure?" Tate asked.

"Because I'm pretty sure these exclusionary gates were designed specifically to keep our sort out," Angie said with a snort.

Mel laughed and Tate turned around and planted a kiss on Angie's lips. "That's my girl. Don't ever change."

"All right, you two, no making out while I'm driving, or I'll need a carsick bag," Mel said. "Tate, where do I go now?"

"Head straight for half a mile and then take your first right. Basically, head straight for the big red rocks up ahead. We're looking for number 6844."

"Got it," Mel said.

The massive houses surrounding them were gorgeous; there was everything from fancy Tudor-style homes to starkly modern palaces. It was definitely a mishmash of styles with the only thing they all had in common being their ostentatious show of wealth.

Mel was happy to admire them from afar, but she knew she would hate living in a house where she needed GPS tracking to get from the bedroom to the kitchen. And what if she had children? You could lose a child in one of these colossal casas, quite possibly for days. It reminded her of what her dad always used to say about conspicuous consumption—just because you can doesn't mean you should.

Mel drove down the wide street, slowing to read the numbers in front of the mansions. Each one was again gated, because the uniformed guard at the front station clearly wasn't enough security to keep the riffraff out.

Finally, they stopped in front of a mansion with the matching number. A cobblestone driveway led from the street through another huge wrought iron gate to an enormous mansion beyond. Mel pulled into the drive and stopped in front of the gate. There was a buzzer mounted on a stone pedestal to her left and she pressed the button.

"Oh, you're here!" Holly's voice greeted them. "Come on up to the house."

The spiky gate opened as if by an invisible hand. Perfectly manicured lawns hugged both sides of the drive while a line of tall palm trees led the way to the house.

"Okay, I am definitely working on my high kick," Angie said. "This is unfreakingbelievable."

A three-story gray stone building that was all sharp corners and jutting angles, with walls of sheer glass on the upper stories framed by burnished steel, loomed ahead. Mel parked in front, feeling as if her silly Mercedes wasn't good enough even to be parked in front of such opulence.

As they climbed the stairs to the front door, Mel caught her breath. The doors were two huge steel half circles that met on their inner edge to make one large circle.

"I feel like I'm going into a superhero's lair," Tate said. "At least, I hope it's a superhero's. If it's a villain, I am so out of here."

One of the half circles opened and a young woman wearing baggy shorts and a Hawkeyes football jersey with her dark brown hair in a high ponytail poked her head out.

"Hi, guys," she said.

Mel blinked three or four times. She glanced at Tate and Angie. They looked equally perplexed.

"Holly?" Angie finally asked.

"The undone version," Holly said and she held her arms wide.

"I didn't even recognize you," Tate said. "You look so . . . normal."

Holly laughed. "I'll take that as a compliment, I think. Come on in."

Tate and Angie filed into the house while Mel brought up the rear. She took a second to study Holly. Tate was right. She was unrecognizable and in the best possible way.

Mel grinned at her. "So, all of that . . ." She waved her hands around Holly's face and body before she added, "Really was just makeup and filler."

"And attitude," Holly said. "Don't ever underestimate the attitude component."

"Clearly, that's what I've been lacking all these years," Mel said. She put her palm to her forehead as if she'd suddenly seen the light.

"Truthfully, *filler* is the perfect word," Holly said. "Being a showgirl, you learn how to work with what you've got and make it bigger. This is Vegas, after all."

"Well, it's incredible," Mel said. "You were right. If I passed you on the street, I wouldn't have recognized you as the same woman I met yesterday. I never would have believed it if I hadn't seen the transformation or more accurately the un-transformation myself."

"I like to think of it as the equivalent of taking flour, eggs, sugar, and butter and whipping them into something much more lovely and yummy than they are by themselves," Holly said.

"I like that metaphor," Tate said. "See? She even thinks like a baker."

Mel was spared having to answer when a little girl, who looked to be about five, came tearing into the foyer of the house wearing a chef's hat and an apron, both of which were entirely too big for her.

"Mom, Mom, Mom, the buzzer's going off!" she shrieked.

Seven

The girl was tiny and blond with round silver-framed glasses that made her blue eyes enormous. She was missing a front tooth on the bottom and she had a smear of chocolate batter on one cheek. She was also carrying a spatula like it was a weapon.

"It's okay, Sydney, we're on our way," Holly said. "Thank you."

Sydney gave her mother a stern look and waved her spatula. "But the buzzer!"

Tate held out his hand to the little girl and said, "Lead on, young chef, we can't have anything burnt on your watch, now can we?"

"No, sir!" The little girl grinned at him with a smile as big as the sky. Then she slapped her hand into his and began to run, leaving Tate no choice but to jog to keep up.

"Your daughter is adorable," Angie said before she hurried after them.

"That's one word for it," Holly said. She and Mel fell into step behind the others. She glanced at Mel and said, "Thanks for coming today."

"No problem," Mel said. She glanced at Holly. Somehow knowing that she was a mom changed everything. "Can I ask you something?"

"Sure," Holly said although she sounded wary.

"Why exactly do you want to open a bakery?" Mel didn't want to be the one to break it to her that houses like this were generally out of a baker's salary range, even if they owned the bakery, but it was clear they were going to have to discuss it at some point.

"Well, I love baking," Holly said. "But mostly, it's for Sydney. She'll start school next year, and unless I find something with different hours, I will literally never see her except on Monday afternoon and evening. I want to be a baker, but even more I want to be a mother."

"How does your hus—"

"I'm not married," Holly said.

"Oh, sorry," Mel said. She desperately wanted the details but she knew it was rude to ask, so she said nothing, although it about killed her.

"No, it's fine," Holly said. "We divorced when Sydney was just a baby and it actually saved our relationship. We co-parent better than we ever did the whole husband and wife thing. Billy's a great father and it works quite well, actually."

The hallway to the kitchen was a long one. The floor

was a rich hardwood, and the walls were painted pewter gray. Recessed alcoves with track lighting illuminated the various pieces of art. Mel couldn't even hazard a guess at how much the little gallery of eye-popping paintings was worth. She didn't want to know, fearing it might make her queasy.

If Holly was this well-off, why did she want to buy a franchise? She could easily redistribute some of this largesse and open up ten or twenty bakeries all on her own. She didn't need Mel or Fairy Tale Cupcakes. Mel wanted to ask, but again, it felt rude.

They turned the corner into the kitchen. Mel stopped in her tracks. Tate and Angie were already staring openmouthed at the plethora of cupcakes that littered every surface of the enormous kitchen.

Many of the flavors Mel recognized from her bakery. She saw Blonde Bombshells, Tinkerbells, Death by Chocolates, but also there were cupcakes that were eye catching in their artistry. A dozen vanilla cupcakes sat front and center on the sparkly granite counter. Perched on a fat dollop of vanilla buttercream on each cupcake was a miniature fondant version of the iconic WELCOME TO FABULOUS LAS VEGAS NEVADA sign that has greeted visitors to the city since 1959.

"Oh, my," Angie breathed. "How did you do this?"

"It was easy. I made an edible transfer onto the fondant," Holly said. "Sydney was happy to eat the ones that didn't come out very well, weren't you, cutie pie?"

Sydney giggled. "I got a stomachache."

"She did," Holly confirmed. "I felt terrible. Of course,

it might have been all the chocolate icing that she ate on the sly."

Holly gave her daughter a sideways glance and Sydney giggled again and then said, "I don't know what she's talking about."

This was said with such wide-eyed earnestness that the grown-ups all laughed. The affection between mother and daughter was evident in the way they smiled at each other like they shared secrets. It made Mel miss Joyce, her mother, who was manning the bakery back in Scottsdale.

"Now you have to try them," Sydney said. She pushed her chef's hat back off her head and passed out paper plates and napkins.

"I don't know," Mel teased. "I had a really big breakfast. I don't know if I can manage all these cupcakes."

"Not all of them, silly, just most of them." Sydney gazed at Mel with the inexhaustible stubbornness of the young.

Mel took a plate. She was a little nervous about trying the cupcakes. She realized that she liked Holly and she was anxious on her behalf. She didn't want the pretty confections to prove too dry or too sweet and ruin the amazing first impression that they had made. Then again, they looked so delicious, she was a little afraid that they might actually taste better than hers. The thought horrified her.

Tate had no such qualms. He went right for a vanilla one with the Las Vegas sign. Angie took the almond-flavored Blonde Bombshell. Mel decided to stick with the lighter-flavored lemon and raspberry combo in the Tinkerbell. The three of them glanced at one another and then Tate counted down.

"Three, two, one . . ."

They each took a bite. Mel was pleasantly surprised to find that Holly's cupcake tasted exactly like her own. Tart lemon cake with sweet raspberry icing, it was a one-two punch of cupcakey goodness. Mel nodded at Holly while she chewed, and as soon as she swallowed, she smiled at the other woman.

"This is excellent."

"This one is even better," Angie chimed in. "I think it might even be better than yo—"

"Yum!" Tate interrupted his fiancée with an enthusiasm that didn't fool Mel one bit. He'd tried to cut off Angie before she said that Holly's cupcake was better than Mel's.

"Where'd you get the recipes?" she asked Holly.

"I asked Tate—"

That was as far as she got before Mel whirled on Tate. "You gave away my recipes?"

He had his mouth full of fondant so he was forced to shake his head back and forth.

"He didn't," Holly said. "I swear. He just described them to me and I made them to the best of my ability based on his information."

Mel glanced between the two of them. Tate was pointing at Holly and nodding, clearly backing up her story.

Mel glanced at Angie and asked, "Did you know about this?"

"Nope," she said. Unfortunately, her attention was caught up in scraping every bit of cake and frosting off her paper plate.

"Why don't you just lick it?" Mel snapped.

Angie lowered her plate and frowned. "Why are you not happy? You should be happy. Holly is a fantastic baker. You aren't going to have to worry about quality control at all. This girl has it going on."

"Do you really think so?" Holly asked.

"Yes," Tate mumbled through a mouthful.

"Absolutely," Angie said.

Holly turned to Mel, who still had most of her cupcake on her plate. Mel knew that Holly was looking to her for a final say as if she were the mean guy on *Cupcake Wars* who could make or break her.

She sighed. She had to agree with the others. Holly was obviously more than capable of whipping together an amazing assortment of tasty cupcakes.

"She's right," Mel said. "You are truly gifted in the cupcake arts."

Holly and Sydney squealed and hugged each other. Then they exchanged a complicated handshake that ended when they linked arms and did a very Vegas showgirl high kick. Mel couldn't help chuckling. She'd never had an employee who could high kick before. She tried to picture either Marty or Oz busting out that move, and the image made her laugh out loud.

A cell phone began to ring and everyone checked their pockets. Angie was the winner as it was her phone. She checked the display and then glanced at Tate.

"It's my brother Ray," she said. "I'd better take this. You know how they worry."

"Yes, we do, and we don't want them showing up here to hold us prisoner while we're in Sin City," he said. "Talk him down."

"I'll do my best," Angie promised. She wandered over to the floor-to-ceiling windows that overlooked a zero-edge pool and a view of the desert mountains beyond.

Mel sampled another cupcake. She was torn between the Snickerdoodle cupcake and the Elvis, a banana cake with peanut butter frosting, but finally settled on one of the vanilla ones with the Las Vegas sign on it. Good-tasting fondant was tricky for even the best pastry chefs. As she nibbled the marshmallow-flavored decoration, she had to admit that Holly had done an incredible job. It tasted just as good as anything that had ever come out of Mel's kitchen. She wasn't sure how she felt about that.

"Excellent," Angie said into the phone as she rejoined them. "I'll tell everyone the news. Thanks, big brother."

"Ray called with good news?" Tate asked. He looked dubious.

"He called with excellent news," Angie said. "Ray knows a guy—"

"He always knows a guy," Mel said. "You know how Joe feels about Ray's guys."

Ray DeLaura was the brother that flirted with the boundaries of the law the most, so naturally he was the one who gave Joe DeLaura, a county prosecutor, the most heartburn.

"I know, but this is good," Angie said. "Ray knows a guy who has a storefront right off the Strip that he's looking to lease. It was a sandwich shop, so it already has a full kitchen. Ray said the guy is willing to lease it for a song. Apparently, he owes Ray a favor."

"Yes!" Tate cried. He raised his fist in the air.

"Oh, no," Mel said. She shook her head. "No, no, no."

Holly looked at them, her eyes darting back and forth between their faces. "Sorry, you lost me. With my future swinging in the balance, can you clarify if it's a yes or a no?"

Eight

"No," Mel said at the same time Tate said, "Yes."

"Joe will go nuts," Mel said.

"Why?" Angie protested. "This could be totally legit."

"Since when has Ray ever done anything legit?" Mel asked.

"There's always a first time," Tate said.

Mel looked at Holly. "Angie's brother Ray doesn't have the best track record when it comes to staying within the proper legal margins."

"But speaking of his record at the track," Angie said. "He's so good at picking horses, they have his picture up on the wall at Turf Paradise in Phoenix."

"If he can apply his horse sense to my bakery, I'm good with that," Holly said.

Mel looked at Sydney. Her big blue eyes looked

concerned and Mel didn't know if she understood the conversation as much as she understood the note of caution in Mel's voice. She didn't want to be responsible for the look of worry in the little girl's eyes.

"Well, I suppose it's worth checking out," Mel said. "Who knows, maybe it will be the perfect spot."

Sydney beamed at her, and Mel knew she had done the right thing. So what if Joe popped a gasket at the thought that his brother knew people in Las Vegas? Joe was wrapping up his case against Frank Tucci, the mobster, and if the news media was calling it right, it looked like it was going to go Joe's way and Tucci would be doing time well into his golden years.

It occurred to her that if the place panned out, then the responsible thing to do would be to call Joe and tell him about it so he was fully informed. It would be nice to have an excuse to talk to Joe, even if he was worrying about Ray the entire time. Mel smiled as she bit into a chocolate cupcake. After the horror of yesterday, this day was beginning to look up.

Tate got onto the phone with the law firm Stuart Stinson worked for and they agreed to send another lawyer in his place to meet them at the new site.

Angie had already told Ray that they would meet his guy, so they all did a mad scramble to pack up the cupcakes in every available bit of Tupperware that Holly could find so they would keep while they were gone.

"Did you spend all night baking?" Mel asked as she pushed a lid down tight.

"Pretty much," Holly said. "I was too upset to sleep. I

just kept seeing Scott and Stuart in my head in a bad film loop that wouldn't stop. I called the hospital this morning to find out how they are doing."

"It's not looking good for Scott," Mel said.

"Yeah," Holly said. "I feel awful, just awful."

"I know what you mean," Mel said. "I feel horrible about what happened and then I think that we could have been right there, too, and I feel guilty for feeling relieved that we weren't."

"Survivor's guilt," Holly said, and Mel nodded.

"I wish there was something we could do," Mel said.

"Have they confirmed what caused the explosion?" Holly asked.

Tate joined them and stacked his tub on top of the others.

"I called the fire department this morning," Tate said. "They are putting together a report, but the person I spoke to did confirm that it was caused by gas that had accumulated because the oven was on."

"I don't see how that could have happened," Holly said.

They were all silent, mulling over the randomness of it all. Then Mel frowned. On their way to look at the property, Scott had said that someone had looked at it earlier that day. At the time, Mel had thought it was a typical high-pressure sales tactic, but now she wasn't so sure.

"Where should we store all of these?" Angie asked.

"Right around the corner is a second walk-in refrigerator," Holly said.

"I meant to tell you before, this is a dream kitchen," Mel said. "You have two refrigerators, two professional-grade ovens, three dishwashers, never mind the rest of the house, this room alone is worth whatever it cost to build."

Holly gave her a wry look. "I'm not sure it's worth the price I paid, but that doesn't matter anymore. Let's get going and see this new location."

"Do I get to come, too?" Sydney asked. "Please, please, please."

"All right, all right," Holly agreed with a laugh. "Let me call your dad. He's supposed to pick you up soon, but maybe he'll be okay if I drop you off after we see the bakery."

Holly took her cell phone into the other room, and Sydney watched her go with a look that was so nervously expectant that Mel hoped Sydney's father agreed to the plan for the little girl's sake.

"So, Sydney," Mel said, trying to distract her. "What is your favorite flavor of cupcake?"

"That depends," Sydney said. "On happy days, it's lemon because lemon is the color of happiness."

"Is it now?" Mel asked. It was official. She was thoroughly charmed by this girl. "What about sad days?"

"That's easy. Sad days are chocolate days, because everything is always better with chocolate."

"So true. Okay, what about boring days?"

"Doesn't matter what flavor when you're bored. Just put some sprinkles on it and then—*pow*—no more boring."

Tate, who'd been listening, leaned down so that he was eye level with the young girl. "Sydney, my dear, you are brilliant."

"I know." She looked back at him without pride or guile,

just a complete sense of herself and her place in the world. "My mom taught me most of that so she's pretty smart, too."

"Agreed," Tate said.

"Are you excited for your mom to open a bakery?" Angie asked. She had just put the last of the containers in the walk-in and was washing her hands at one of the two sinks.

"Yes!" Sydney shouted. "I get to pick the flavor of the day, every day."

"Whoa, that's an important job," Tate said.

"That's what Mom said, but she still won't let me leave school to work in the bakery." Sydney frowned. "It's not fair."

"Sydney, we talked about this," Holly said as she came back into the room. "Your job is to go to school."

"Kindergarten is for babies," Sydney protested.

Holly rolled her eyes and Mel had the feeling this was an argument they had had before.

"All set to go?" Mel asked.

"Yes," Holly said. She looked at Sydney. "And you get to come with us but you must be on your best behavior. This isn't our bakery . . . yet."

"I promise," Sydney said.

They took separate cars to the location. Ray's friend the Realtor was to meet them, as well as Peter Kelly, a man from Stuart Stinson's law office, who would take over the franchise paperwork for Stuart while he was in the hospital.

Mel felt guilty for moving ahead with the franchise plan without Stuart and Scott, but Tate, who was the most corporate minded of them all, assured her that it was okay.

"Stuart is a man of business. He would expect nothing less than for us to move forward," he said.

Both Mel and Angie gave him doubtful looks then Angie turned to Mel and asked, "Do you think that's a corporate thing or a guy thing?"

"Guy thing," Mel said. "Definitely."

They were driving out of the neighborhood and Mel waved to the man at the gate as they went. Holly was right behind them in a sporty little sedan with Sydney in her booster seat in the back.

"What do you mean by 'a corporate thing or a guy thing'?" Tate asked.

"That ability to compartmentalize," Angie said. "Is it a guy thing or a business thing? Would a female executive shrug and say 'Let's move forward, it's just business, nothing personal'?"

"Absolutely," Tate said. "In fact, a few of the women I've worked with were even better at separating the personal from the business and managed to make some really tough decisions, ones I don't think I could have made if I were in their shoes. So, it's definitely a corporate thing."

"Interesting," Mel said. "See? This is why I went into baking. The corporate dog-eat-dog world is most def not for me."

"And it was going so well until Tate decided to franchise you, making you corporate by default," Angie teased.

"I know I've been reluctant," Mel admitted.

"Reluctant?" Tate asked. "You had your heels dug in so deep, you left drag marks all the way from Phoenix."

"Whatever. I've come around to the idea, plus I like Holly. She can bake, and I like that we're giving a single mom a real chance to have a normal life that she's in control of," Mel said. "This is going to be great. I can feel it."

"Okay, who are you and what have you done with our friend Mel?" Tate asked, giving her a suspicious look.

Mel and Angie both laughed, and then Mel began to sing, " *'Bright light city gonna set my soul, gonna set my soul on fire.'* "

When it came time for the chorus, Angie and Tate did not hesitate to join in, singing, *"Viva Las Vegas!"*

It wasn't a long drive to the Strip where they were meeting the lawyer and the Realtor. Mel was curious to see what sort of person Ray had them meeting and she couldn't help wondering if Joe would approve. She doubted it.

Knowing Ray, it was going to be a thuggish sort of guy with slicked-back thinning hair, a shiny suit and dress shirt open at the collar, so the sun could shine on his thick gold chain. Mel even figured his name would be something short and blunt like Dave or Nick. For sure, it would be interesting.

Mel found a spot in the narrow parking lot of the small shopping center where the vacant shop was located. Holly pulled in behind her and they all walked over toward the glass front store on the end.

Two men in suits were standing in front of the shop. FOR LEASE signs were hanging in every window. It was a snug space but it was on the end of the row of shops, giving it optimal visibility from the street and extra parking along the side.

Mel checked to see if there was another food joint in the cluster of shops. There was not, which was another plus. Instead, there was a karate school, a hair salon, a photographer's studio, and a pet groomer. All in all it seemed like a low-crime, family-friendly cluster of shops within walking distance to some of the Strip's biggest tourist attractions.

The two men standing in front of the vacant store both wore charcoal gray suits, white dress shirts, and snappy ties. As she got closer, Mel tried to guess which one could be Ray's friend. Surprisingly, thug didn't really come off either of the men, making it harder to hazard a guess.

The man on the right had a head of silver hair. An Omega watch was strapped to his left wrist and he had on cuff links. Mel figured he had to be the lawyer, plus he looked like a no-nonsense sort of guy, which did not match Ray, who was generally full of shenanigans at all times.

She glanced at the other man. He was younger with dark hair, but his suit looked to be just as expensive and so did his tie. He had on a Rolex but no cuff links. She guessed him for the Realtor, especially since his fingernails looked to be buffed into better shape than hers.

Tate led the way, looking casually official in his blue jeans and dress shirt. He held out his hand to the younger, dark-haired man. "Pete Kelly? I'm Tate Harper."

Mel exchanged a surprised glance with Angie.

"I had that figured all wrong," Angie said.

"Me, too," Mel said. "How did Tate know which one was Peter?"

"Must be some secret corporate eyebrow twitch or something," Angie said.

"Or I saw his picture on the website when I looked up the firm to get his phone number," Tate said as he turned around. He gave them an exasperated look that said everyone could hear them.

Mel and Angie exchanged a sheepish glance, and Holly, who had joined them, laughed.

"I had it backward, too," she said.

"I'm Quentin Ross," the silver-haired man said. He had a crisp and precise way of speaking that made Mel suspect he used to have a thick accent of some sort but had studied to lose it.

Tate shook his hand and then Mel and Angie did the same, with Holly and Sydney being introduced next.

"Tell me, Quentin," Angie said. "How exactly do you know my brother Ray?"

Quentin pursed his lips. He looked as if he was trying to think of what Ray might have told Angie. In the end, he shrugged and said, "I can't really say."

Angie's eyebrows went up. Clearly, he had underestimated Ray's little sister.

"You can't say or you won't say?" she asked.

"Won't," Quentin said.

Mel and Tate both stepped forward. Not that Angie would have put the man in a headlock or anything, but they both felt it best to be prepared for any contingency.

"Why not?" Angie rose up on her tiptoes as she tried to stare down the much taller man.

He leaned down so that they were nose to nose. "None of your business. Ask your brother, if you must know."

"Oh, I will," Angie promised.

It was clearly a standoff. Mel wondered if she was the only one who heard the high noon music in her head. All they needed was a tumbleweed to roll by and for Angie and Quentin to start walking in two different directions for a set number of paces. Uh-oh.

Nine

"How about we go inside?" Holly asked. "You know, check out the shop as a possible bakery?"

"Yes, let's do that," Peter agreed. "You have the keys, Mr. Ross?"

When Quentin didn't move, Peter gave him a nudge with his elbow. Without taking his eyes off Angie, Quentin took his keys from his pocket. He gave her one more second of his flat, dead-eyed stare before he turned away.

He unlocked the door and pulled it open. Mel didn't think she was imagining the fact that no one seemed to want to go first. She shook her head. Just because the other bakery blew up did not mean this one was going the same way.

She stepped forward at the same time that Tate did. She gestured for him to let her go first but he shook her off.

Mel went to cut in front of him just to keep him safe; not that she believed he needed a blocker, it was just instinct. Tate grabbed her arm, holding her back.

"Together?" he asked.

Mel realized she could live with that. She nodded and they stepped through the wide doorway together, with Angie wedging herself right in between them as they went. The three of them stepped over the threshold and nothing happened.

A powerful surge of relief ran through her, and Mel realized she'd actually been holding her breath as if there would be another explosion. She wondered if she had a little bit of post trauma still rocking her world. She glanced back at Holly and saw her holding Sydney's hand, looking as relieved as Mel felt.

They exchanged a look of understanding and Mel smiled. She remembered looking for the location of her first bakery. She had been such a mix of nerves and excitement. She knew that Holly was probably feeling all of that and more at the moment.

She turned away to take in the shop. It was small but cute with black-and-white flooring like Mel's own bakery back in Arizona. The walls were a butter yellow color that she didn't love but paint was cheap.

There was no furniture in the shop and she tried to imagine what it would look like with a few tables or booths. They'd have to keep it to a minimum so that people could move around. She glanced through the windows. The sidewalk in front was big enough for a few small café tables. Overall, space-wise it had promise.

Quentin had begun his spiel on the features of the property and Mel turned back to the group to listen to him espouse the pluses of the site as a bakery. There was adequate display space with the big wide counter and a built-in glass case. Behind the counter the work area was tight, but beyond that was a very well laid-out kitchen.

Holly and Sydney ran from each appliance, squealing and chattering. The oven would have to be replaced with a larger professional convection oven, but the steel workspace and the walk-in cooler were practically new.

"What happened to the previous owners?" Mel asked.

"They went belly-up, which was a surprise to no one," Quentin said. He gave them a look of disgust.

"Why?" Angie asked. "What did they do wrong?"

"It pretty much started and ended with their menu," Quentin said. "They were trying to be food innovators and catch a foodie movement like the cronut, you know the croissant donut thing that was a super hit for fifteen minutes on the East Coast."

"I'm afraid to ask, and yet, I find I must know," Tate said. "What was their product?"

"The jelly dough-burger," Quentin said. He grimaced a bit and Mel suspected he was having a bad taste bud flashback.

"I don't get it," Holly said. "What was it made of?"

"A cheeseburger served on a jelly doughnut which was cut in half like a bun," Quentin said.

"That is . . ." Tate seemed stumped for words.

"Disgusting," Mel offered.

"Revolting," Angie said.

"Gross," Sydney chimed in. Her little nose wrinkled as if she smelled something bad.

"I would vomit," Peter said. He looked green at the thought of eating such a concoction and Mel had to agree.

"I don't know," Holly said. "Maybe it wouldn't be totally terrible."

They all turned to look at her and she shrugged. "I just think you shouldn't knock it until you try it."

"Mom, jelly on a burger is nasty," Sydney said.

"Oh, really?" Holly asked. "Is that your professional chef opinion, missy?"

"No, that's my mouth talking," Sydney said. "And it knows what it likes and a burger wrapped in a jelly donut isn't it."

"I admit it's a little out there," Holly said. "But remember there are some weird flavor combinations that don't seem like they could go together but they do."

Sydney looked dubious.

"How about those ginger milk chocolate cupcakes?" Holly asked. "Those were delicious."

"They're cupcakes," Sydney said. She held out her hands for dramatic effect, as if to say anything in a cupcake would be good, although Mel knew from experimenting that this was not necessarily so.

"Okay, how about the bacon-wrapped dates stuffed with pistachios that we made for the holidays? You ate your body weight in those," Holly said.

Sydney rolled her eyes to the ceiling and declared, "I can never talk food with you."

"I know exactly how you feel, kiddo," Angie said. She pointed at Mel and said, "She's the exact same way."

Mel turned to Holly. "Recipe, please?"

"For which?"

"All of the above," Mel said. She paused and then said, "If you have cupcake recipes of your own that you want to sell, we can talk about that, too."

Holly beamed at her.

"So, can I assume you approve of this space?" Quentin asked. He looked eagerly at Holly and then Tate, as if he knew Tate was the driving force behind franchising.

Mel took a moment to picture a Fairy Tale Cupcakes bakery here in this spot in Las Vegas. Instead of the usual crippling doubt and panic, she found cautious excitement in the idea.

She glanced at Tate and Holly, who were both looking at her, and said, "Works for me."

Holly jumped up and down and clapped her hands. Sydney did the same. Tate smiled, looking proud of her, which made Mel feel as if she'd grown exponentially as a person.

"All right," Peter said. "If we're all agreed, we can go back to the office and initiate the paperwork."

Holly took a minute just to look over the place one more time. She glanced out the front window at the view she would have when she opened her shop.

"I really think this will work," she said. "I think we're going to be very successful here."

Mel stood beside her. "I think so, too."

Peter led the way out of the bakery. Tate and Angie followed and then Holly and Sydney. Holly took some pictures of the inside and then took her camera outside to get some more shots of the storefront. Mel and Quentin were the last to leave.

Quentin set the alarm and locked the door while Mel went to stand beside the others. She had almost reached them when the sound of a car engine revving caught her attention. She turned back just in time to see a large four-door sedan hop the sidewalk, roar across the parking lot, heading straight for the bakery.

"Quentin, look out!" she yelled.

Quentin glanced over his shoulder. His eyes went wide and his jaw dropped. He was stunned into immobility and instead of jumping out of the way, he raised up his arms as if he could ward off an entire car.

Before Mel could register the movement, Tate shoved her and Angie aside and dove forward, grabbing Quentin by the sleeve and yanking him out of the way just before the car launched itself right through the windows of the shop in an explosion of glass.

Tate almost made it, but Quentin's right leg was clipped by the car, knocking them both into the side of the building before they crumpled to the ground.

"Tate!" Angie screamed. She ran toward him and Mel was right behind her.

The two men lay on the ground. Holly had her arms shielding Sydney while Peter was already on the phone calling 911.

"My leg, my leg," Quentin moaned.

"I'm okay, I'm fine," Tate said as he rolled over onto his back.

Mel checked him over anyway. He had minor cuts and

scrapes and he was wheezing, but that could have been because Angie had him in a hug that was probably compressing his lungs as she was holding on so tightly.

Mel could see the unnatural angle of Quentin's leg. She grabbed his hand and told him that an ambulance was on its way. He nodded and then he fainted, which Mel figured was probably a blessing.

"What about the driver?" Peter asked. The car had stopped with its nose planted in the glass display case.

Mel looked in through the smashed window. As she watched, the driver's side door was pushed open and a man wearing a motorcycle helmet climbed out of the car. He was limping slightly but managed to haul himself through the broken window and out onto the curb.

"Hey! Are you all right?" Mel cried.

The driver started and glanced up at her. Then he began to back away, moving slowly at first but rapidly picking up speed even though he was still limping.

"Hey! You! Hey!" Peter yelled.

The man, dressed all in black leather, turned and began to limp run across the parking lot. Holly had her cell phone up and was taking pictures of him. Mel thought about giving chase but running really wasn't her gift. She'd be winded by the time they reached the corner and even at his slower pace the driver would outrun her.

"Don't just stand there," she said to Peter. "Go after him."

"What? Are you crazy?" he asked. "He might have a gun or something."

"Where?" Mel asked. "In his helmet?"

The man had disappeared down the street and around the corner. It was a moot point now.

"I do not get paid to chase down crazy drivers," Peter said. He looked defensive about it.

Mel gave him a scrutinizing glance. Under the impeccably cut suit, she noted there was a bit of a paunch and his eyes had tiny lines in the corners. Upon closer inspection, his hair also appeared to be thinning in the front. So, Peter Kelly was not nearly as young as she'd first guessed and she suspected he was in about as good a shape as she was. Fine. She supposed she'd have to give him a pass, but still, it was very disappointing.

Mel saw a flash of red and blue at the same time that she heard the sirens. An ambulance arrived first followed by a police car. They parked right in front of the storefront and the emergency medical technicians went right to Quentin and began checking his vitals.

The police officer approached and Peter stepped up to tell him what had happened. Angie had loosened her grip on Tate and helped him to his feet. He looked steady enough but Mel kept one eye on him just in case as they joined Peter with the police.

Mel saw Holly standing off to the side. Her bright blue eyes were filled with tears and Sydney was sobbing softly into her mother's belly.

Mel didn't think about it. She just reached out and pulled the two women into her arms. They were both shaking and Mel tried to absorb some of their fear while she braced them with her arms.

"It's going to be all right," she said.

"But that man," Holly said. "That's not normal to wear a crash helmet while driving. He must have done it on purpose. But why, why would someone drive through a storefront window? And why when we were looking at it? Does someone want to stop us from opening a bakery? I just don't understand."

Mel had been pushing that thought aside ever since the man had popped out of the car. She didn't want to think that this incident was intentional, because if she did, then she had to assume that yesterday's exploding bakery had been on purpose as well and that was bad, very very bad.

She glanced at Tate and Angie. Angie was staring at her and Mel knew exactly what her lifelong friend was thinking. This was their fault. Somehow, someway, the explosion yesterday and the crash today were because of them. But how? And why?

Ten

"I don't know what's going on," Mel said. "But we'll figure it out. One way or another, we'll find out why these horrible things are happening."

"Sydney!" A man was running across the parking lot toward them.

He was good looking in a rugged sort of way with broad shoulders and stubble on his chin. His honey-colored hair was cut short and he was wearing a dress shirt with the sleeves rolled up, khaki pants, and loafers.

"Daddy!" Sydney cried. "Over here, Daddy!"

The look of thankfulness that passed over the man's face hit Mel right in the gut. He looked like he might faint with relief.

He barreled toward them with his arms wide and Sydney launched herself into his embrace. He swung her up into his arms and held her close, pressing his cheek on the top of her head.

"What happened?" he asked Holly.

"We were looking at the location for the bakery and then this crazy driver showed up out of nowhere and drove right through the front windows," Holly said. "It was terrifying."

"Is everyone all right?" he asked.

"Sydney, sweetheart!" A dark-haired woman joined them. She took Sydney out of her father's arms and hugged her close. "Are you okay, darling? I thought you were getting picked up by your father this morning. What are you doing here?"

"I wanted to see the bakery, Lisa," Sydney said. She patted the woman's back as if to reassure her. "I'm okay. I promise."

The woman let out a little sob but then closed her eyes and seemed to get it together. Mel noted that she and the man stood hovering over the little girl. She looked at the three adults and realized that this was obviously Holly's ex-husband and his new wife. She glanced at the woman's left ring finger to confirm it. Yes, a very nice diamond ring and wedding band sat flush against her knuckle.

"Melanie Cooper, this is Sydney's father, Billy Eastman, and his wife, Lisa," Holly said.

"Nice to meet you," Billy said. He nodded at Mel but she could tell by the vee in between his eyebrows that he was clearly still upset.

Lisa glanced at her and nodded in greeting, but like Billy, she still looked rattled. Her face was deathly pale and she was trembling, although to her credit, she was forcing her lips to curve up in a facsimilie of a smile. Given what could have happened to Sydney, Mel couldn't blame either of them for being upset.

"I'm going to let you all talk," Mel said. "I'll just go check on Quentin."

"Who's Quentin?" Billy asked.

"The Realtor," Holly said. "He got clipped by the car as it went by. I think his leg is broken."

"Damn it, Holly, I don't like this," Billy said. He was clearly winding up and Mel wondered if she should stay but Holly didn't look overly alarmed and Mel would be just a few feet away if Holly needed her.

When she joined the others, they were loading Quentin into the ambulance. Peter was still talking to the police while Angie argued with Tate about whether he needed to be checked over or not.

"I'm fine," he said. "Besides, I'm going to follow Quentin to the hospital, and if I get woozy, I'll be in the right place." He kissed Angie and squeezed Mel's hand. "I want to make sure he's well taken care of until his family arrives."

Angie stood on tiptoe to kiss Tate's cheek.

"You're a good guy," she said. "That's one of the many reasons I love you. Now, be careful, and if you so much as feel a twinge of a headache, I want you to have them check you over, clear?"

"Aw, and here I thought you only loved me for my sweet DVD movie collection," he said.

"That, too," she said. She took out her phone and began swiping the display.

"Call us and let us know what's happening," Mel said. "Since he's Ray's friend, you may want to call him and let him know what happened. You know Ray will freak out if he hears this from Angie."

"I will and I'll check on Scott and Stuart as well," Tate said. "Listen, I want you two to go back to our room and stay there. I'm not sure why all of this is happening, and until we do, I think we all need to be on high alert."

"Agreed," Mel said.

"I have a theory. Want to hear it?" Angie asked as she glanced between them. Then she held up a finger for them to give her a minute.

Tate gave Mel a bewildered look, and she shrugged.

"Listen, I need to know if you've seen your girlfriend or had any contact with her over the past twenty-four hours."

This time Mel gave Tate the bewildered look, and he shrugged. What was Angie up to?

"Yes, it is, too, my business," Angie argued. "Someone has tried to kill us twice in the past twenty-four hours and my money is on your girlfriend."

"Marty," Tate and Mel said together.

"You don't really think it's Olivia, do you?" Mel asked Angie, who held the phone away from her ear while Marty was yelling.

"I always think it's Olivia," Angie said.

Although Mel could hear Marty squawking on the other end of the phone, she was glad she couldn't make out the words. She suspected they were not flattering.

"Quit howling and answer the question," Angie said.

Then she blew out an outraged breath. "You kiss your mama with that mouth?"

Mel snatched the phone out of Angie's hands.

"Hi, Marty, it's Mel," she said.

"Mel, do you have any idea what Angie just said?" he asked. "She actually thinks Olivia is up in Vegas, trying to kill you guys. That's crazy, right? I mean I know you and Olivia had your differences but she's changed since we hooked up. I swear."

Mel hadn't seen much difference over the past few months, but she didn't want to burst Marty's bubble, especially since he was in the middle of having to make a major life decision with Olivia. She didn't think the bakery crew should influence his decision in any way.

"Yes, I know you believe she's changed," Mel said. "But you know how Angie gets, and in her defense, we were almost killed twice."

At this, Angie raised her hands in exasperation. As if she couldn't believe that Mel wasn't going after Marty's girlfriend as strongly as she thought she should.

"When you say you were almost killed, what do you mean exactly?" Marty asked.

Mel told him the events of the past two days. Marty grunted a couple of times but didn't say anything until she finished.

"Well, I think it's obvious who is trying to keep you from opening that bakery," he said. "It's got to be tied to the mob case your ex-boyfriend is prosecuting, especially since they have gone after you before."

"But everyone who went after us has been locked up," Mel said. "There is no way they could be after us here."

"You really think these guys don't have a reach beyond their prison cells?" he asked. "Please, these guys have rubber for arms and they never stop and they never forget. You need to call Joe and tell him what's happening."

A shiver rippled through Mel. "I have to go, Marty. Be careful at the shop just in case this is connected to Joe's case against Frank Tucci. And by careful, I mean super freaky ultra paranoid careful. Got it?"

"Done," Marty said. "And you do the same."

"I will," she said. "Be sure to tell Oz what's happening, but maybe you could not mention it to my mother and just keep a close eye on her. I don't want her to be scared for no reason."

"You got it," Marty said. "And I'll have a talk with Olivia, you know, just to be sure."

"Thanks, Marty."

Mel ended the call and handed the phone back to Angie.

"He's going to talk to her," she said.

"Talk? That's it?" she asked.

"What did you think he was going to do?"

"Take out a restraining order," Angie said. "Handcuff her to something, oh wait, no, I don't want to picture that. Oh, darn, too late."

"Thanks," Tate said. He made a bad face. "Now you've got it in my head, too."

Mel went right to her happy place and pictured a pastry bag loaded with buttercream frosting swirling around the top of a freshly baked cupcake. There. No icky images in her head.

"No, Holly, this is completely unacceptable!" Billy said. His voice was raised not so much in anger as in fear, but still, he was loud and they all turned to see what was happening.

"It was just a coincidence," Holly protested. "You can't be serious. I won't let you deny me visitation based on nothing but a couple of freak accidents."

"Holly, think!" Billy snapped. "Both locations you looked at for a bakery had some seemingly random disaster happen. That is not a coincidence and I won't let you put Sydney in danger."

"But Daddy, I'm okay," Sydney protested. She reached out and grabbed her mother's hand. "Please don't take me away from Mommy."

There was a note of desperation in the little girl's voice that made Mel's heart clutch.

"I'm sorry, Sydney, but it isn't safe," Billy said. He took her out of Lisa's arms and squeezed her tight. "That car . . . look . . . if anything happened to you . . . I . . ."

Holly bowed her head but not before Mel saw a tear streak down her face. She knew Billy was going to win this argument and there was nothing she could do about it.

"You have to deal with this, Holly," Billy said. "For Sydney's sake. I know you thought this crazed fan of yours would just go away, but it is clear that they won't. They've now crossed a line into dangerous and scary. If you won't file an order of protection, I will."

"Against who?" Holly cried. "Don't you think if I knew who was calling and hanging up all the time, messing with my dressing room, and sending me creepy gifts that I'd deal with it, but I don't know who it is."

"Are you two getting this?" Angie asked with wide eyes. Mel and Tate nodded. The three of them were standing in a knot as if having their own conversation when they were really blatantly eavesdropping on Holly and her people.

"Which is why it isn't safe for Sydney to be with you until you do," Billy said.

"No, Mommy, no!" Sydney let out a sob and Billy looked crushed.

"I'm sorry, baby, I'm so sorry," he said. "But it's for your own good, to keep you safe."

Mel realized that every single time someone told her something was for her own good, she hated it. Whether it was Brussels sprouts or a trip to the dentist, it had never felt like it was good for anything. Seeing Sydney's face, she knew the little girl felt the exact same way.

"We'll take really good care of her, Holly, and we'll figure out a way for you to be together safely," Lisa said.

It was the first time she'd entered the conversation and Mel admired how understanding she was in what had to be an awkward situation, given her role as the second wife and stepmother.

Holly glanced from Lisa to the car planted in the shop like it was the aftermath of a Hollywood movie stunt. She stiffened her spine and turned to her ex and her little girl.

She wiped away the tears on her face and forced a smile.

She hugged Sydney tight and whispered something in her ear just before she kissed her cheek. Then she stepped back and patted Billy on the shoulder.

"I know you're just looking out for our girl and you're right," she said. "Until I know what's going on, it isn't safe."

"Noooo!" Sydney protested. She looked anguished. Mel knew it had to be killing Holly to keep smiling and not cry anymore.

"Sweetie, it's just for a few days. We're going to find out why so many strange things are happening and then you and I will be together again," Holly said. She looked at Billy for confirmation and he nodded.

"I'll make sure you get to see her. We'll find a safe place," he said. His face darkened as he added, "And now might be a good time to get out of that gilded cage Byron has you in. I don't trust him. He's weird about you, he always has been."

"I can't talk about this right now, Billy," Holly said. She looked as if she was barely keeping it together.

"Fine," Billy said. "I'll have Sydney call you tonight before bed."

Sydney let out a wail and reached for her mother. Holly hugged her tight one last time. Mel felt her own eyes water up and she glanced at Tate and saw him surreptitiously wipe his cheek.

"Damn allergies," he said. His voice sounded gruff. Angie slid her hand into his and he held it over his heart as if she could make the hurt stop.

But Mel knew nothing was going to stop the hurt, except finding the person who was terrorizing Holly. The only problem was they had no idea who or why.

Eleven

Tate wanted to drop off Mel and Angie at the Blue Hawaiian on his way to the hospital, but Mel insisted on staying with Holly, and Angie did, too. Because Holly had to report to work at the show, they went with her.

It was a tight squeeze in Holly's sports car, but Angie gamely took the backseat as she was the shortest. Aside from their love of Elvis, part of the reason Tate had booked them rooms at the Blue Hawaiian was that it housed the Casablanca Theater, where Holly performed in a showgirl revue every night except for Monday.

They had planned on catching one of her shows while they were staying at the hotel, but now Mel felt like it was imperative that they stay with her and hear every detail about this alleged stalker and find out who this Byro character with the gilded cage was. She hated to admit that she

94

was relieved that Holly had people in her life who might want to harm her, but there was no denying it made her feel better than thinking it was a bad guy who had followed them from Arizona.

They walked through the casino to the accompaniment of shouts, bells, laughter, cheers, the artificial noise of slot machine levers being pulled and change clanging. Most everything was electronic now but the old sounds prevailed.

Holly waved to the pit boss as they walked by the blackjack tables, and a few of the dealers called hello as the three of them passed by on their way to the theater.

The Casablanca was everything that was vintage Vegas in its heyday. The theater had been newly remodeled to showcase its midcentury modern features, and Mel felt as if she were stepping back in time when she walked through the Casablanca's huge revolving doors on the west side of the Blue Hawaiian's casino.

A buxom girl, wearing what looked like a form-fitting bellboy's outfit and the cutest little pillbox hat with two cherries attached at the stem and sporting a big leaf, met them as they stepped out of the doors.

"Cigars, cigarettes, chewing gum," she said.

Mel gaped. Nowadays, she wondered if the girl sold more gum or smokes. Then again this was Vegas.

"What decade is this?" Angie asked.

"More like what century?" Mel asked.

"Hi, Gina," Holly greeted the girl. She fished some money out of her bag and bought a pack of gum. "Do you two want anything?"

"Yes," Mel said. "I want to know where you got the cute hat."

Gina shrugged. "Wardrobe."

Holly smiled. "They are specially made from a hat shop in London called Mim's Whims, very famous among milliners. They make a lot of our hats for the show."

"Really? They order them all the way from London?" Mel asked.

"Well, the Casablanca has been doing this gig for fifty years so they can afford the best," Holly said.

"Time for me to hit the floor and promote the show," Gina said. "See ya, gals."

"That's wild," Angie said, gesturing at Gina with her head. "I feel like I'm on the set of *Mad Men*, the early years."

"Has the Casablanca always had cigarette girls?" Mel asked. "I'd think with smoking losing popularity, there wouldn't be enough demand."

"Vegas isn't called sin city for nothing," Holly said. "All the vices come out to play when people are here. Mostly their job is to work the casino and advertise the show. I started out as a cigarette girl."

"No, sir," Angie said.

Holly laughed. It was the first time since the afternoon's upheaval and Mel was relieved to hear the sound.

"Yes, ma'am," Holly said. "I spent a year trolling the casino, trying to break into the show."

"And you did," Mel said. "That must have taken a lot of perseverance."

"My mother would say bullheadedness," Holly said. "The surest way to get me to do something is to tell me that

I can't. So every time I blew an audition, I became more determined than ever to succeed."

"You've got grit, kid." Angie made a clicking sound with her tongue, closed one eye, and pointed at Holly like she was a gangster.

Again, Holly looked cheered.

"Come on," Holly said. "I'll give you a tour of my home away from home."

Holly never broke her stride. She unhooked the velvet rope that cordoned off the theater entrance and gestured for Mel and Angie to go on through.

A huge framed portrait of comedian Levi Cartwright stood on a pedestal and Angie stopped in her tracks.

"Oh my god, Levi Cartwright is here?" Her head swiveled around as if he'd appear behind a potted palm or faux alabaster pillar.

"He's been our headlining act for a while now," Holly said.

Angie gasped. "Can I meet him?"

"Sure, I'll introduce you," Holly said.

"Is he as funny in person as he is in his act?" Angie asked. "He just cracks me up."

"Well . . ." Holly drew out the one word as if she didn't want to disappoint Angie but she didn't want to lie, either. "You can decide when you meet him."

Angie turned to Mel with a grin so big, Mel couldn't help laughing. She looked as young as Sydney.

A big, burly man with biceps the size of Mel's head and a name tag that read CARLOS smiled at Holly as she led them up the short staircase to the main door.

"Bring me any cupcakes tonight, Holl?" he asked. Mel noticed that his muscles flexed below his short-sleeved polo shirt when he talked.

"Carlos, your sweet tooth is your weakness, you know that, right?"

"Sugar is what gives me my superpowers," he countered. Then he posed in a Mr. Universe stance that made Mel's pupils contract.

The man looked as if he were carved out of granite. She had to curl her fingers into her palms just to keep from poking his muscles to see if they were as rock hard as they looked.

"Tomorrow," she said. "I promise."

"I'll hold you to that," he said.

"These are my friends Mel and Angie," Holly said. "They're going to be hanging out at the show tonight."

Holly didn't ask permission and Mel realized it was a sign of how important Holly was that she could bring guests in without question.

"Welcome, ladies," Carlos said. "If you need anything, don't hesitate to ask."

"I don't know about you, but I am feeling very VIP," Angie said.

Mel smiled. There was a certain cachet to getting to go where no one else was allowed. The theater was a big one with rows upon rows of movie theater–type seating behind fifty or so tables decked out with tablecloths and cushy chairs. The tables were definitely the prime seating.

"We have to get to the green room from backstage,"

Holly said. She led them down a side aisle and up onto the stage, where they cut across the shiny black floor and slipped behind the heavy velvet curtains.

A man with a tool belt was working on a set of lights and he glanced up when they entered.

"Hey, Holly," he said. He was an older man with puffs of white hair sticking out over his ears but nowhere else on his bare head.

"How's tricks, Benjy?" Holly asked and winked at him.

"Fancy is on the warpath," he said. His voice was just above a whisper. "Be careful."

"Thanks for the heads-up," she said. She gestured for Mel and Angie to hurry after her.

"Who's Fancy?" Angie asked.

"Fancy Leroux, she's our stage manager, production manager, you name it," Holly said. "She was one of the original Casablanca girls back in 1959 when the Casablanca first opened."

"Wow, so she's really old," Mel said.

"And really mean," Holly said. "But I still love her."

Mel must have looked as confused as she felt because Holly said, "Fancy was the one who discovered me as a cigarette girl. She took me aside and taught me what I needed to know to pass my audition. After that, she groomed me to take the lead, which I've had since just after Sydney was born."

"Are you sure you want to give all of this up?" Mel asked.

"Yes." Holly didn't even hesitate. She led them to a side door, which she pulled open.

"Um, I don't want to pry," Angie said. "But I couldn't help but hear your ex-husband say you have a stalker."

Holly's chin dropped to her chest. She let the door close as she crossed her arms over her chest and stared at the floor.

"Hey, we're sorry," Mel said. "We didn't mean to get into your business. We just want to know what's going on so we can help you."

"What 'we'?" Angie asked. "I'm the buttinsky. I'm sorry. I shouldn't have said anything. I'm just worried."

"It's a deal breaker, isn't it?" Holly asked.

"What do you mean?" Mel asked.

"My stalker," Holly said. "I didn't want to tell you all because I was afraid you would decide I was too much of a risk to buy a franchise. Clearly, if today's incident was my stalker, I was wrong not to tell you and I am so sorry."

She looked like she was going to cry. Mel reached out and patted her shoulder.

"Hey, it's all right. It's not a deal breaker."

Holly's head snapped up. "How can you say that? You could have been killed twice. If the person destroying the bakeries is my stalker, this is all my fault."

"No!" Angie said. "It is not your fault if someone has a weird fixation on you and is acting out. It's their actions causing the harm, not you. You can't give up on what you want because of someone else."

"Angie's right," Mel said. "We can't let them win."

Holly gave her a tentative smile. "It's just maddening. I don't know who they are or where they are or how they know me. They've never done anything violent before, so I don't know why it's happening now. I'm sorry to have dragged you into this mess."

Mel looked at Angie, and Angie nodded. It was time to come clean.

"It might not be your stalker," Mel said. "You say they've never been violent but have they ever threatened violence?"

"No," Holly said. "Mostly, they send me letters and presents, but lately, they've started calling the theater asking for me, and when the person who answers the phone tries to get their name or number, they hang up. Billy's been worried that the behavior is escalating."

"Still, calling the theater is a far cry from driving a car through a window," Angie said. "That seems like something a real hard-core criminal would do."

Holly tipped her head to study them. One eyebrow rose, and she asked, "Do you have something to tell me?"

Holly Hartzmark was one smart cookie.

"Possibly, the explosion and the car thing were aimed at us," Mel said.

"Really?" Holly's whole face lit up and she clapped her hands. "Oh, wait, I shouldn't look happy about that, should I?"

"It is a bit bad form," Angie said but she was smiling.

Holly forced her features to look duly serious and then said, "It looks like maybe we have more in common than a love of baking cupcakes."

"Quite possibly," Mel said. "The short version is that Angie's brother Joe—"

"Who also happens to be Mel's ex-fiancé," Angie chimed in.

"Is currently prosecuting a mobster, who is known for murdering the loved ones of anyone who opposes him," Mel said.

Holly was quiet for a moment while she absorbed this information.

"I think I'll keep my stalker," she said. "Wow, do you really think it's him doing this to get to you?"

Mel and Angie both shrugged.

"There's also this rival baker," Angie began but Mel interrupted.

"But we have no proof that it's her," Mel said.

"Yet," Angie added.

"I think maybe we all need to stick close together until we know exactly what is going on," Holly said.

"Agreed," Mel said.

"Why don't the three of you stay with me at the house?" Holly asked. "It's got eight bedrooms. We could all stay there and we wouldn't even have to see each other."

"It did feel safe, what with the security guard at the gate and all," Angie said. "I'll text Tate and tell him the plan."

"Great, now follow me," Holly said. She glanced at her phone. "I have to get moving if I'm going to be in costume in time to get back up here."

"Back up?" Mel asked. "Where exactly is your dressing room?"

Holly widened her eyes and opened the side door again. "Welcome to the catacombs, ladies."

They followed Holly down three flights of stairs into a

brightly lit basement that looked as if a flock of sparkly ostriches had come to die. Racks upon racks of glittery, feathered, sequined gowns filled the space while up on shelves above the gowns were huge elaborate feathered headdresses, some as high as four feet tall.

"Wow," Mel said.

"And how," Angie added.

"It is awesome, isn't it?" Holly asked.

A gaggle of girls in high heels and not much else were shimmying into their dresses.

"You'd better hurry, Holly," a pretty blond woman said as her headpiece was adjusted by a costumer. "Fancy is in a mood today."

"She's in a mood every day. Sunny, you'd better get used to that if you're planning to take the lead," Holly said.

"I told you, I don't want the lead if it means you leave," Sunny said.

Holly squeezed her hand. "These are my friends, Angie and Mel. We'll do proper intros and talk later."

"Hi," Sunny said. She gave them a small smile that turned into a grimace as the costumer wrestled her headpiece into place before letting her turn back to the mirror to touch up her make-up.

"That didn't look easy," Angie said. "How much do those things weigh?"

"Some weigh as much as thirty pounds," Holly said. She led them past the main dressing room and opened a door off the main room and entered. "Now imagine trotting up the three flights of stairs we just came down with that on your head and having to do it ten times a show for costume changes."

Mel's hand went instinctively to the back of her neck and she noticed Angie did the same. She was pretty sure she would die if she had to run those stairs even once.

As they stepped into the tiny dressing room, a voice barked, "Where have you been? Do you have any idea what I've been through trying to find you?"

Twelve

But apparently, the person was just warming up as she continued her tirade. "Do you know what time it is? How could you do this to me? It is just so irresponsible! You never used to be like this. Ever since you got that crazy idea to open a cupcake bakery, you have changed and not for the better."

Mel glanced past Holly into the dressing room and saw a tall, stout woman with ten pounds of makeup topped off by a pair of purple eyelashes that had to be about two inches long. *Wild guess*, she thought, *this must be Fancy Leroux.*

"Uh-oh, the warden is looking unhappy," Holly teased. Fancy frowned but Holly was unfazed. She strode into the room and kissed the older woman right on the cheek. "Be nice. These are my friends."

"Friends wait upstairs," Fancy said. She turned her head and sniffed as if she was not the least bit interested in meeting Angie and Mel.

"I asked them to come down here," Holly said.

"And now you ask them to go," Fancy said. She crossed her arms over her considerable bosom and stared at Holly with one drawn-on eyebrow significantly higher than the other. It was a look that clearly stated there was no wiggle room here.

Holly turned back to Mel and Angie. She took them by the arms and walked them to the door.

"I'm sorry, guys," she said.

"That's all right," Angie said. "Truth? She kind of scares me and I don't scare easy."

"She's harmless, really," Holly said. "But I'm going to have Carlos hook you up with a table front and center for the show." She lowered her voice and said, "I think something is up with Fancy, and I'd better deal with it solo."

"Are you sure you're safe down here?" Mel asked. She didn't like to think of Holly making the dark trek up three flights by herself.

"Oh, yeah," Holly said. "There is always someone around down here. Besides, it really is my home away from home."

"If you're sure," Angie said.

"Positive," Holly said. "I'll text Carlos and have him meet you at the bottom of the stairs. After the show you can come backstage and I'll introduce you to everyone. It'll be fun."

"Including Levi?" Angie asked.

Holly laughed. "Most definitely."

They left, and as soon as Holly shut the door behind them, Mel heard Fancy start in again.

"I'm beginning to see why Holly is ready to leave," Angie said. "Do you think 'the warden' is like that every day?"

"I hope not," Mel said. "That would be demoralizing to even the stoutest heart."

"You know without all the hustle and bustle and glittery costumes, this place would scare me," Angie said.

"I know," Mel agreed. They stepped aside to let a man pushing a rack of sparkling red gowns pass. "How far belowground do you think we are?"

"I don't know, two stories, maybe three?" Angie guessed.

Carlos was waiting for them as promised. Mel wondered how he'd gotten down here so fast.

"Elevator?" she asked hopefully.

"There isn't one," he said.

Mel glanced up at the winding stairwell. Coming down had been okay, but up, up was going to suck and she suspected be more than a little embarrassing. She figured she'd be wheezing by the time they got halfway up to the theater. She was right.

"Are you okay?" Carlos asked when they paused on the landing so Mel could catch her breath.

"Yeah, I'm fine." Mel sucked in gulps of air. Her thighs were burning. "Really, I'm good."

"I can carry you if you want."

Mel gave him a death glare. He smiled at her and she

realized the power of her death glare was diminished greatly by her heaving chest and hunched-over posture. She waved him away.

"Have it your way," he said. He turned and jogged up the remaining stairs. *Show-off.*

Angie stayed beside Mel, as a good best friend does, even though she wasn't breathing heavily at all, which was very annoying.

Mel decided to broach the question that had been bothering her since they had met Fancy. Yes, it was a stalling tactic to slow their climb down, making it possible for her to breathe and walk, but also she wanted to know if Angie had gotten the same weird vibe off Fancy that she had.

"Was it just me or did Fancy seem seriously unhappy about Holly leaving to open a bakery?"

"Well, Holly did say that Fancy groomed her for the role of star of the show, so it has to feel like a bit of a betrayal to Fancy for Holly to want to leave," Angie said. "But she's like a hundred years old. It's not like she's suiting up to drive cars through the side of buildings."

"No, but she's been in Vegas a long time," Mel said. "She has to know people."

"And by *people*, you mean, she could find someone to blow up one store and drive a car through another?" Angie asked.

"I'm just putting it out there," Mel said.

"I get that she had the whole dragon lady thing going on," Angie said. "Obviously, she was not thrilled to meet us, but I don't know if I got genuine evil off of her so much as old cranky pants."

"Perhaps," Mel said. "But we should probably keep an eye on her."

"Fair enough," Angie said.

They climbed the rest of the stairs in silence, mostly because Mel had run out of oxygen, but also because it was taking all of her energy to pull herself up the remaining steps using the handrail. Mel was pretty sure she left her dignity down in Holly's dressing room.

As they approached the door where Carlos waited for them, Angie said, "You know you may want to think about—"

"No," Mel gasped.

"You don't even know what I'm going to say."

"You're going to tell me I need to work out, and the answer is no," Mel said. She knew she sounded grumpy while gasping for breath, but she couldn't seem to stop her tirade. "I don't need to diet and I don't need to work out."

"I've been your best friend for more than twenty years—how can you think I would ever say that?" Angie asked.

Mel leaned against the wall while she sucked sweet gulps of oxygen into her lungs and contemplated her oldest pal. Angie had never, not even during her heftiest years, told her she needed to change in any way. Angie was right to be peeved with Mel right now. And judging by the way she was scowling with her arms crossed over her chest, she was very peeved.

"I'm sorry," Mel said. "Clearly, I confused you with my mother, probably from a lack of oxygen to my brain. What were you going to say?"

"That you should consider letting the stud carry you," Angie said with a wink.

"Hey, I resemble that remark," Carlos said. He took the opportunity to flex again.

Mel would have been embarrassed but she didn't have enough strength left to blush. She pushed off the wall and strode into the backstage area, which seemed to have come alive with people in the time they'd been gone. Bodies were buzzing around like bees in a hive while they hurried to set up for the show.

"This way," Carlos said.

He led them down a narrow hallway to a side door that let out into the back of the theater. From there they worked their way to the bistro area in front of the stage. He held out a chair for each of them at a small table front and center.

"If you ladies need me, just give a holler and I'll come running," he said.

"If I were a single gal . . ." Angie said. Her voice trailed off as he left them.

"Yeah, right," Mel said. "Tate has had a lock on you since we were in middle school, so even if you were single, Carlos wouldn't stand a chance."

"Okay, let me change that to if I had never fallen for Tate—"

A phone began to chime, interrupting whatever she had been about to say. They both paused to listen. The ringtone was "It Had to Be You," which was Angie's assigned ringtone for Tate since they felt their love story most resembled the movie *When Harry Met Sally.*

"Speaking of the love of my life," Angie said as she reached into her handbag for her phone.

Mel sat back and relaxed while Angie answered. The tables were beginning to fill up as well as the theater seats behind them. Waitresses were working their way through the area and Mel looked for one to be headed their way. If ever a day deserved a glass of wine, today was it.

"Darn it," Angie said. "I missed his call. Oh, wait, there's a text message."

Mel waited while Angie opened her messages.

"Oh, no," Angie said. Her tone was grim.

Mel glanced at Angie's face, trying to gauge how serious the situation was. A vee was gouged into the space between her eyes as she studied the screen of her smart phone. Not good.

"What is it?" Mel asked. "Is Tate okay?"

"He's fine," she said. "Or I assume he is since he managed to text me, but it's bad news. Scott Jensen died from his injuries an hour ago."

"Oh, no," Mel said. She hadn't known him for more than an hour at most but still, he had died working for them and she couldn't help feeling somehow responsible, or maybe that was just her survivor's guilt kicking in. She dreaded having to tell Holly the news.

"The Las Vegas Police Department has not ruled out homicide as the cause of death," Angie said. She lowered the phone and glanced at Mel. "Shiz just got real."

"And how," Mel said.

Thirteen

Mel's phone started to chime and she glanced at Angie. "That's probably Tate calling me because you didn't answer the text."

"Tell him I'm texting him back now," Angie said.

"Never mind," Mel said when she looked at her phone. "It's Manny."

Angie's eyebrows went up as Mel answered her phone. Mel's Uncle Stan was a longtime detective in their hometown of Scottsdale, Arizona. His partner was Detective Manny Martinez, a man with whom Mel shared a complicated relationship since he had saved her life and was very clear that his intentions toward her were more than that of a buddy. It was further complicated by Mel's attraction to the detective despite being steadfastly head over heels for county prosecutor Joe DeLaura. It made for a complex love life that weirdly left Mel single more than she would have thought possible.

"Hello," Mel answered. She glanced at Angie, who was texting Tate while obviously trying to listen to her conversation.

"Mel, how are you?" Manny asked.

"I'm in Vegas, I'm great," she said. She hoped she sounded more enthusiastic than she felt, because frankly the news that Scott had passed away felt like a cinderblock on her chest.

"You can't even lie over the phone," he said. "Pitiful."

"What makes you think I'm lying?" she asked.

"Tate called Joe, Joe called me," he said.

"Tate called Joe?" she asked, looking at Angie, who tipped her head to the side as if she was uncertain what to make of all this. Mel felt the same.

"Yes, Tate was concerned about the possibility that Frank Tucci's reach extends all the way to Vegas and that you were in the crosshairs."

"We're all a little jumpy because of Tucci," Mel said. She didn't want Joe and Manny to be concerned for her in Vegas, where they were powerless to help. It wouldn't do anyone any good. "But I don't see how a Realtor's tragic and accidental death could be viewed as an attempt on any of our lives."

Angie was blatantly listening and she nodded. Mel knew she was thinking the same thing as Mel. There was no need for their friends and family back in Scottsdale to get worried and upset for no purpose.

"Listen," Manny said. It was his stern cop voice, which

always got Mel's attention, whether she liked it or not. "A random explosion would have been weird, and I could have let it go if a car hadn't been launched into the second location you looked at for your franchise."

"Sounds like Tate really has given you the four-one-one on what's happening. But isn't this out of the Scottsdale PD's jurisdiction?" Mel asked.

"Maybe," he said. "If it's Frank Tucci behind the two incidents, I will consider it extenuating circumstances."

"It might not be," Mel said.

People had filled the tables around them and there was a hum of excitement filling the air.

"What do you know?" Manny demanded. She noticed that Manny's cop voice sounded a lot like her Uncle Stan when he was in pursuit of the truth. She never had been able to lie to Stan when he used that tone of voice, and she couldn't lie to Manny now.

"Not much, just that Holly, the woman looking to buy a franchise with us, has a stalker," Mel said. "She doesn't know who they are or if they mean her any harm, but she receives gifts, notes, and lately the person has started calling the theater and asking for her and then hanging up."

"So creepy but not violent as yet," Manny said.

"That's what Holly thought, but who knows if the person has upped their game for some unknown reason," Mel said. The music grew louder and she couldn't hear as well. She plugged one ear and said, "The show's about to start. I have to go."

Manny's voice was muffled but she heard him say he'd

be in touch, or at least that's what she thought he said. She shouted a good-bye and ended the call.

"What was that about?" Angie called out.

A waitress stopped by their table with a bottle of champagne and a tray of appetizers.

"Compliments of Holly," she said. She deftly popped the cork and poured them each a half glass of the pink bubbly before she left.

Angie leaned back in her chair. "I've got to say our girl has style."

"She does, doesn't she?" Mel sipped her champagne as she recounted her conversation with Manny. "Any more news from Tate?"

"Just that he's on his way," Angie said. She glanced at the door and Mel saw the wistfulness in her expression. It had taken a long time, years in fact, for Angie to land their boy Tate and Mel knew she was still getting used to the idea that he was hers, that they would be married and do the whole happily ever after thing.

Mel was happy for them, really she was, but sometimes, well, she wished she had a loving relationship of her own.

Joe DeLaura had owned her heart since she was twelve years old. It had taken her twenty years to get him to notice her that way, but between her skittishness and his career, they'd been apart more than they'd been together. She was beginning to wonder if there'd ever be a happily ever after in their future.

Maybe someday, if he ever got this trial done, they'd get a shot at the same happiness Tate and Angie had found, but for now, she was flying solo.

She forked a pile of stuffed mushrooms onto her plate. As always, food helped.

"Why did Joe have Manny call you?" Angie asked.

"Manny didn't say, but I think Joe's still playing it cautious," Mel said. "I don't suppose I'll hear from Joe directly until Frank Tucci is locked up for good."

"This trial has been going on forever," Angie said. She loaded her plate with several bacon-wrapped jalapeños. "Did you two ever talk after that night?"

"What night?" Mel asked. She was playing dumb on purpose. She hadn't set eyes on Joe in over two months, after a crazy night where they caught a murderer and then Angie and Tate came careening into the alley behind the bakery, honking and yelling that they were going to elope.

Joe had jumped right into crisis prevention mode. Since she was the youngest child and only daughter of a large Italian Catholic family, it would kill Angie's mother if Angie eloped. Tate let go of the rash plan pretty quickly but Angie was harder to convince. It had taken a full-on intervention with the rest of the brothers to get her to see the light. When Angie had finally abandoned the plan, Joe left and Mel hadn't seen him since.

During this trip, Mel had been keeping a close eye on Tate and Angie just in case the elopement bug hit again. Mel would have no problem putting Angie in a body-locking bear hug if that's what it took to keep her from doing something dumb.

Mel was a bit surprised that the brothers hadn't insisted on coming to Vegas to supervise the trip and make sure there were no matrimonial shenanigans. While most of the family welcomed Tate, there were a few holdouts among the brothers, who were convinced that no one was ever going to be good enough for Angie. Period.

"You know what night I'm talking about," Angie said. She waved a celery stick at Mel. "It looked like you and Joe were in the middle of something heavy when Tate and I arrived, but you've never admitted it."

"And with all the badgering you've done, too," Mel said. She sipped her champagne and gave Angie a pointed look, which was summarily ignored.

"I know. I'd be proud of you if I wasn't so annoyed by your tight-lippedness," Angie said. She studied Mel with a look that was understanding and exasperated at the same time.

"There just isn't much to say," Mel said. "We had a moment, but then it passed and I haven't heard from him since."

"Really?" Angie asked.

"Okay, he sent me flowers, forget-me-nots," Mel said. Her throat knotted up at the memory of getting the pretty little blue flowers. "But that was weeks ago."

"How long are you willing to wait for him?" Angie asked.

"I don't know," Mel said. She shook her head. "And I'm coming to realize that even if he does circle back around, what happens when he takes on another bad guy who threatens his loved ones? Will he dump me again? My self-esteem is shaky at best. I don't really know if I can do this again."

Angie was quiet while she thought over what Mel had

said. Then she nodded. She reached across the table and squeezed Mel's hand.

"Joe is my brother, my favorite brother and if you tell the others that, I'll deny it," she said.

Mel laughed. She would never. But she totally understood. She loved all of the DeLaura brothers as much as her own brother, Charlie, but yeah, Joe was her favorite, too.

"But as much as I love him," Angie said, "I love you, too, and I hate to see you . . ."

She stopped and Mel waited. After a few seconds, she said, "You hate to see me what? Fat? Grumpy? Lonely? You're killing me here."

"I hate to see you sad," Angie said. She looked miserable on Mel's behalf, which actually made Mel feel better. "When Tate and I are, well, I just want the same for you."

Mel squeezed Angie's hand tight and then released it.

"I know you do, and I really appreciate it," she said. She took up her glass and drained it. "Can we not talk about this anymore? We're in Vegas, in VIP seating no less, let's try to be happy."

"You're right," Angie said. She raised her glass and drained it as well. "Viva, Las Vegas! Hey, maybe you'll get lucky with one of the Elvis impersonators at our hotel."

"Yeah, right," Mel said.

"Aw, come on, can't you just see one of them sashay up to you and break into 'Hunka Hunka Burnin' Love'? It'd be all over for you, and you know it."

The image made Mel laugh hard. It felt good. Whatever would she do without her friends?

The lights in the theater dimmed, and she and Angie grew serious as they turned their attention to the stage. The rest of the crowd hushed as well. Mel had never been to a show with showgirls before so she wasn't really clear on what to expect. She figured there would be sparkles, feathers, and high kicks, but she wasn't sure what else was involved in the whole performance.

Music started overhead and the theater went completely dark. Mel watched the curtains on the stage, waiting for them to part, but the music swelled louder and louder with no sign of movement from the stage. She could barely make out Angie in the darkness but noted that she was watching the stage with the same intensity as Mel.

With the boom of a drumbeat, the lights flashed on at designated spots in the theater, and as if they had been conjured out of thin air, dancers dressed all in silver with three-foot headdresses stood amid the crowd.

The audience broke into spontaneous applause as the girls began to shimmy and shake to the music. It was light-hearted and joyful and Mel found Holly standing just a few feet away from them. This was the heavily made-up woman she had met the day before, and it took Mel a second to reconcile the glittering vision before them with the mom in the ponytail just a few hours previous.

Angie nudged Mel, letting her know she had spotted their friend as well. The music swelled and the dancers moved among the crowd, working their way toward the stage. Holly was the first on the stage and began to pump turn, spinning while kicking one leg out then in with her arms in a delicate arc over her head, while the rest of the girls moved forward to join her.

Mel watched with her jaw a bit slack as Holly kept spinning and spinning, the footlights hitting her costume just right and making her look like a bit of silver flame. Mel lost count of her revolutions. When Holly stopped, she slid effortlessly into the chorus line and led the girls in a series of choreographed high kicks that moved down the row of dancers one after another in perfect sync.

The girls broke off as the curtain behind them opened. They moved into smaller groups and continued dancing until Mel was breathing hard just from watching them. Their finale ended on a huge staircase that filled up the back of the stage. The girls parted in the middle and a man in a snappy tuxedo appeared at the top of the steps.

Mel saw Angie bounce on her seat. The man held a mic up to his mouth and he started to sing. It was a silly ballad about Vegas, rolling the dice, pretty showgirls, and what happened in Vegas staying in Vegas. His voice was low and rich and he punctuated his words with a wink here and there. The crowd loved him and went wild as he made his way to the front of the stage.

Levi Cartwright was in the house and he clearly owned the stage. He was tall, lithe, and good looking in a traditional Rat Pack sort of way. A glance at the crowd and Mel could see that the women wanted him and the men wanted to be him. The man released charm like the rest of them exhaled carbon dioxide.

Once the song ended and the raucous applause died

down, he went into a monologue about the silly things people did in Vegas that had people holding their sides as they wiped tears from their eyes. He went on for fifteen minutes and then the girls showed up to dance in new costumes. Again, Mel saw Holly leading the flock of pretty girls in complicated dance patterns around the stage. When Levi came back, Mel saw Holly meet his gaze and give him a small nod.

She realized there had been a look of uncertainty on Levi's face that had lasted no more than a second, but still, it had been the look of someone who was afraid. Mel watched him closely for the rest of the show and noted that he and Holly had the same exchange a couple more times. It was as if Holly was his shield against insecurity. Mel supposed she could have been reading more into it than there was, but she didn't think so.

The show ended in a finale that had everyone on their feet, clapping and cheering. Mel counted five costume changes for Holly and knowing the stairs she had to traverse with the heavy headdresses, she really wasn't surprised that Holly was over it. Maybe a life in the limelight just wasn't all it was cracked up to be.

Carlos collected them from their table at the end of the show. He told them that Holly was down in her dressing room and wanted to know if they wanted to meet her down there. Mel almost passed, knowing she would have to come back up those stairs but she really wanted to see Holly and tell her how wonderful she had been. She heaved a sigh and followed Carlos and Angie.

He led them right to Holly's door. Mel went to knock but the grumpy bulldog, Fancy Leroux, who had been upbraiding Holly before the show, yanked the door open before she could.

"You!" Fancy snapped, pointing a bony finger at Mel. "I want to talk to you."

Fourteen

Startled, Mel jumped. As she gazed at the elderly woman, who was giving her a fierce blast of stink eye from the open door to Holly's dressing room, she wondered if she could take her. Sure she could. Right? How tough could the old bird be?

Her confidence was not boosted when Angie moved in beside her as if to protect her from the octogenarian.

"I think I got this," Mel said.

"She used to be a dancer," Angie argued. "She could probably crack you like a walnut with one well-placed kick."

"Your faith in me is remarkably underwhelming."

Angie shrugged.

"Can I help you?" Mel asked the woman.

"You're the bakers," Fancy said.

"Yes." Mel didn't think lying was going to help at this point.

"You are ruining Holly's life and, more importantly, my show," Fancy said. "Why are you encouraging this madness?"

"I'm going to assume you're talking about Holly opening a bakery," Mel said.

"She bakes a mean cupcake," Carlos said. Fancy glared at him with her black eyes and he took a step back. "Yeah, I'm just going to head back upstairs. Call me if you need me."

It would have felt more sincere if he hadn't been running away when he added that last bit over his shoulder.

"I'm sorry that you don't approve of Holly wanting to open her own business but I really think that's between you and Holly and doesn't have anything to do with us," Mel said.

"You don't understand," Fancy cried. She opened her arms wide in a very melodramatic gesture, forcing both Mel and Angie to take a step back. "Every show has a heart. Holly is ours. If you take her away, the show will lose its heart. It will collapse onto itself like a hollow chest and it will die. You can't let her do this."

Mel had no idea what to say to this. Fancy was clearly agitated and she had a feeling there was nothing that she could say that would reassure the woman that the show would be fine.

"It's not really up to us," Angie said. "It's Holly's choice to make."

"Pah!" Fancy waved an age-spotted hand as if she were swatting a fly. "Ever since she had that kid, her priorities have been screwed up."

Mel bit her lip. She disliked it when women weighed in on the choices other women made in regards to having a family or not. It was such a personal decision. How did any woman feel entitled to judge another's journey?

"Holly is a grown woman and can do whatever she wants," Mel said. "Maybe you need to stop trying to keep her here and work on finding someone to fill her spot."

"There is no one!" Fancy yelled. "No one can do what she does. It takes years of intensive training to be able to manage the shows as effortlessly as she can."

A young woman with bright red hair and freckles across her nose joined them.

"Excuse me, Fancy. Maria in makeup is looking for you," she said.

Fancy swung around and looked the girl over from head to toe. "Look at those hips, you look like you just came in off the field. When are you going to slim down? If you want to have a shot at the lead, lose the weight!"

With that, Fancy stomped away, making the floor reverberate as she went. For a former dancer, she sure knew how to make an impact on the floor.

The redhead blew out a breath and glanced down at her body with a look of such self-loathing, Mel had to resist the urge to take her by the shoulders and shake her.

"You know she's just lashing out at you, right?" Mel asked. "You're as slender as a blade of grass."

"She's right," Angie chimed in. "I watched you out

there tonight. You were spectacular and the crowd loved you. Don't let the mean old fusspot get to you."

"Thanks." The woman tried to smile but it didn't meet her eyes. "But I'm going to throw up everything I've eaten in the past twenty-four hours now."

"You are not." The door to Holly's private bathroom was yanked open and there stood Holly in a blue paisley silk bathrobe and with a towel wrapped around her head. Her makeup was half off, which, combined with her ferocious expression, made her a bit scary looking. "Sit down, all of you."

She crossed the room and sat at her vanity table. She began swabbing her face with make-up remover while studying their reflections in the mirror.

"Sorry I didn't get to the door faster to stop Fancy from being hateful. I was on the phone with Billy," she said. "I wanted to make sure Sydney was all right."

"Is she?" the redhead asked.

"Yes," Holly said. She flashed them a small smile. "She's tucked in safe and sound. Now what was Fancy going on about out there?"

"She blames us for you leaving the show," Mel said. She turned to the redhead and said, "I'm Melanie Cooper and this is Angie DeLaura. We're the owners of the bakery in Arizona that Holly is looking to franchise."

"Oh, hi, I'm sorry. Fancy berated the good manners right out of me. I'm Sunny Evans, I'm in the chorus line."

"That's not all you are," Holly said. "You're my understudy, and the person who will take the lead when I leave."

"Not if Fancy has her way," Sunny said. "She thinks I'm too farm girl."

"No, she doesn't," Holly said. "She's just used to having me here to boss around and she doesn't like the fact that she'll have to break a new girl in. You're the best dancer out there and everyone knows it. You've got natural pizzazz and you kick higher than I ever could."

"I don't have your stage presence and Levi doesn't trust me like he trusts you," Sunny argued.

"He will," Holly said. "These things take time."

"Speaking of, I have to go," Sunny said. "I have a tear on my costume for the opening act that I need Stacey to mend."

"All right," Holly said. "Hey, do not let what Fancy said get to you. If you lose so much as an ounce of weight, I'll bake you a dozen rum raisin cupcakes and make sure you eat every single one."

Sunny laughed and held up her hands in surrender. "See? That's another reason you can't leave the show. You're my best friend. Who will threaten me with baked goods if you leave?"

"I can threaten you just as easily from my bakery," Holly said. The door closed behind Sunny and Holly looked at them and added, "Assuming I can find a place to open one."

"About that," Mel said. "We have some news."

Holly glanced at her face and Mel knew she could tell it was more bad news.

"Don't try to cushion it. I'm tougher than I look. I can take it. What is it?" Holly asked.

"Scott Jensen passed away from his injuries," Mel said. "The Las Vegas PD has not ruled it an accident, meaning they are still considering homicide as a possibility."

"Oh, that poor, poor man," Holly said. "I feel horrible. This shouldn't have happened."

"Tate said the police aren't giving any details but they are investigating whether the leak was intentional," Angie said.

Holly finished wiping the last of her foundation off and slowly lowered the cotton cloth from her face. She looked like she was going to cry.

"This is a nightmare," she said. "Why would someone do this?"

"I don't know," Mel said. "But—"

There was a knock on the door and then it banged open. In strode Levi Cartwright, still in his tuxedo but with his bow tie hanging loose about his neck.

"How did I do, was I funny, I didn't feel like I was funny. I don't think people were really enjoying my shtick. I'm washed up, aren't I?" He was halfway into the room before he noticed Mel and Angie. A pained look crossed his face before he forced a laugh and said, "So, enough about me, what do you think of me?"

Angie laughed but it sounded strained as if she didn't really think he was funny but she didn't want to hurt his feelings. Mel smiled but she felt like she was forcing it. Levi turned to Holly, and she saved him from himself.

"Levi Cartwright!" she said. "You are hilarious and you know it. Don't be fishing for compliments from my guests. They saw the show and loved it, didn't you, girls?"

Mel and Angie both relaxed under Holly's leadership and they immediately heaped the praise on Levi. He seemed to puff up visibly with their words.

"Now I need to get going and you need to go home and get some rest for tomorrow's show," Holly said. She rose and put her arm around Levi's shoulders as she escorted him to the door. "I'll see you tomorrow."

"Wait." Levi stopped her from shutting the door.

He glanced past her at Mel and Angie and then leaned in close to Holly to whisper something. Holly whispered something back and their exchange went on for a bit longer and then Levi left.

When Holly closed the door, she leaned against it and closed her eyes. Mel had the feeling she was either exhausted, seeking inner peace, or trying to process all that had happened in the past twenty minutes.

"I love them all dearly," Holly said. She opened her eyes and pushed off the door. She walked back to her vanity and opened the lid on her moisturizer. "But I am tired of carrying this show, everyone's expectations, worries, and neuroses on my back."

"As if the thirty-pound headdress isn't enough," Angie said. "I can see why you're ready to downshift."

Holly smiled at her in the mirror but then her expression faltered. "Unless someone has their way and stops me."

"We won't let them," Mel said. Then in a singularly rash moment of optimism, she added, "I promise."

Mel and Angie cooled their heels in the green room while Holly changed back into her street clothes. She had a performer's nonchalance about changing in front of them and both Mel and Angie studied the pictures on the wall of Holly with different celebrities when Holly dropped her robe and began to dress.

When they arrived upstairs, they found Tate waiting for them in the theater. He hugged Angie and Mel and gave Holly a grim smile and a nod.

"So, I'm thinking what we need is a junk food–infused movie night to clear our minds. Who's with me?" Tate asked.

The vote was unanimous. They all drove back to Holly's place, figuring she shouldn't be left alone until they knew who they were dealing with and why.

Holly's sports car zipped into her driveway with Mel right behind her. Tate was riding shotgun and he frowned.

"I don't like this," he said.

"What?" Mel asked. "Camping out at Holly's?"

"No, the gate being open," he said. "It feels . . . wrong."

"Probably Holly has a remote in her car. Maybe she hit it as she approached," Angie said from the backseat.

"Catch up to her," Tate said to Mel.

Mel hit the gas and roared up right behind Holly. An enormous black limousine was parked in front of the house and Mel had to slam on her brakes to avoid hitting it.

"Way to make an entrance," Tate said. He hopped out of the car and jogged over to Holly's car. Mel and Angie hurried after him.

"Do you know who the stretch belongs to?" Tate asked Holly as she climbed out of her car.

"Oh, yeah," she said. She looked like she was bracing herself as she turned to face the car. Mel and Angie instinctively moved to flank her with Tate standing a little in front of the three women with his arms crossed over his chest.

The uniformed driver hopped out of the limo and quickly opened the rear passenger door. A well-heeled men's shoe appeared followed by an equally snappy pant leg. The man who stepped out of the back had movie star good looks and an aura of power that charged the air like an electrical storm.

"Holly, you're looking as lovely as always," he said.

"Byron," Holly said. If her tone were any chillier, the man would have had icicles hanging off his nose.

"May I have a word?" He gestured for her to join him in his car but she shook her head.

"Anything you want to say to me, you can say to my business partners," she said.

His immaculately shaped eyebrows drew together in a fierce frown. His tone was equally frosty when he spoke. "You're really going through with this bakery nonsense?"

"Yes," she said. "Here, let me introduce you to my associates so you'll know exactly who it is that you're insulting. Tate Harper, Angie DeLaura, and Melanie Cooper, this is Byron Dorsett. He owns the Casablanca Theater among other things."

Byron strode forward and extended his hand. Tate gave him a dark look before shaking it. Mel knew that look. Tate did not like this man, not at all. Byron did not extend his hand to Mel or Angie, letting Mel know exactly how he felt about women, as second-class citizens not worthy of his acknowledgment. Big mistake. It made her want to knee him in the junk repeatedly.

Angie was emitting a low growl in her throat, and Mel was surprised Byron didn't keel over dead from the death stare she had focused on him.

"Let's not forget that among the many things I own, you are one," Byron said. He loomed over Holly. To her credit, she tipped up her chin and met his malevolent stare straight on.

"Not for long," she said. "Negotiations are under way, and I will be opening my new business in a matter of months."

"A bakery," he scoffed. "You're giving up this"—he paused to gesture at the house and the car—"to wake up and bake tiny little cakes every morning. You're going to be as fat as a suburban housewife in a matter of weeks."

"Maybe." She shrugged. "But at least I'll be happy. I'll own my life for the first time in years. No more grueling hours in rehearsals, no more exhausting photo shoots, no more being paraded around at your corporate parties like a trophy."

"No more fame, no more fortune," Byron countered. "No more seeing your ten-thousand-dollar smile up on the billboards all over the city. Are you really sure you want to give all of that up?"

"Yes!" Holly cried emphatically. "I am done. I am out. I have spent the past five years scraping together every extra nickel so that I could be free. Face it. You don't own me any longer."

Rage, white hot and terrifying, flashed over Byron's

features much like the initial whoosh of the fire that had exploded out of the first bakery they had looked at.

"You're going to fail, and then you'll come crawling back," Byron said. He said it with the supreme confidence of the obnoxiously wealthy. Think it and it happens even if you have to pay someone to make it happen. His smug smirk made Mel want to slap him, and she admired Holly for not doing exactly that.

"I'm not coming back," Holly said. "And I'm not going to fail."

Byron opened his mouth to argue but Tate cut him off. He wrapped an arm around Holly's shoulders and said, "No, you're not. Not with all of Harper Investments behind you."

If he had punched Byron in the face, he couldn't have gotten a better reaction. The man actually staggered back a step. Angie flashed her man a smile full of pride and Mel wanted to give him a high five, but she figured that could wait.

"You're Tate Harper of Harper Investments?" Byron asked. "I thought you left the business."

"Does anyone ever really leave the family business?" Tate asked. He was oozing all of his old corporate cutthroat charm and Mel realized she'd sort of missed seeing this side of him.

"You can't be making that much money in cupcakes," Byron said. He looked uncertain.

Tate grinned like a cat that had just trapped a mouse between two slices of cheese. "You have no idea."

Byron's nostrils flared. The four of them stared at him. He pointed a finger at Holly and snapped, "This isn't over."

"Yes, actually, it is," she said. She pointed her thumb at the house. "I'll be out at the end of the week. Don't come here again until I'm gone or I'll call the police."

With a dismissive wave of his hand, Byron strode to the limo and got into the back, barking orders at the driver as he went.

The driver reversed out of the driveway as if he were outrunning the law. Mel wondered if the threat of calling the police had made Byron that twitchy. As soon as the automatic gate closed behind them, Holly sagged in relief.

"Are you all right?" Mel asked.

"I will be," Holly said. "Remember when I said this house wasn't worth the price I paid, well, I didn't pay for it in cash. It's Byron's house. I've been allowed to live here so long as I did whatever he asked, whenever he asked. I am so done with it, all of it."

Mel was silent, taking in Holly's plight without judgment while feeling equally determined to help her get out from under Byron's thumb.

"Popcorn," Angie said. "I need popcorn and peanut butter cups."

"Nah, that was more of a Frito and Ding Dong episode," Tate said.

Holly broke out in a surprised laugh. "Which one of us is the Ding Dong?"

"Byron," Mel said. "Definitely, Byron."

"Really?" Angie asked. "I was thinking he was more of a Ho Ho."

Tate wrapped her in a hug and kissed her forehead. "You didn't punch him in the nose. I'm so proud of you."

"You should be," Angie said. "It took great restraint on my part."

"Come on," Mel said, following Holly into the house. "Let's go decompress."

Twenty minutes later, they were sprawled in the enormous family room, watching *Viva Las Vegas* while eating buckets of buttered popcorn washed down with lemonade and chocolate ice cream.

Mel had to admit as Elvis and Ann-Margret shook their way across the screen, she was feeling better. But wasn't that the whole point of a movie, to take you out of your own scary miserable life and transport you to another one?

Angie and Tate were both staring at the screen, but Holly was curled up on the end of the couch, her fingers plucking at the edge of the pillow she had in her lap. Mel thought maybe the movie wasn't working for Holly, and it was time to go to the source of all comfort.

She nudged Holly and said, "Come on, let's go snarf some cupcakes. They always make everything better."

A ghost of a smile slid over Holly's face and she pushed up from the couch and followed Mel down the hallway to the kitchen. They went right to the walk-in refrigerator and began to haul out the containers of cupcakes.

"Milk?" Holly asked.

"Always," Mel said.

Holly poured them each a glass and they sat at the large granite counter, pried the lids off the cupcake containers, and reviewed their selections.

"When I first decided to open up Fairy Tale Cupcakes,

I was sure I would fail," Mel said. "I don't think I got a full night's sleep for months."

"Did you have someone driving cars through the front of the shops you looked at leasing?" Holly asked. She lifted a carrot cake cupcake with cream cheese frosting out of the container.

"No, but I did take a huge loan from my best friend, which is the number one taboo of friendship," Mel said. "I was sure I would lose Tate's money and then his friendship in that order."

"But you didn't," Holly said.

"No, and you won't, either," Mel said. She gestured to the containers around them and then selected a cherry cola cupcake. "You have real talent, Holly. You can do this and I'm not just blowing sunshine up your backside, I really mean it. I've eaten a lot of cupcakes in my time, and I'm telling you, there are people out there that I wouldn't let toast a Pop Tart, never mind run a bakery—are you listening to me?"

Mel glanced up from her monologue to see Holly staring past her at the dark window.

"Don't freak out," Holly said. "But I think I just saw someone run past the window. It could be Byron. It could be my stalker. Oh, god, maybe Byron is my stalker, and if he is, do you think he's here to kill me?"

Fifteen

Mel carefully put down her cupcake. Dang it, she'd really wanted to try that one.

"Okay, we need to get you away from the windows," she said. "Let's pretend you're going back for more milk."

She chugged down her glass and handed it to Holly, who took it and went around the island to the refrigerator. Once Holly opened the door, Mel got up and stretched her arms, trying to look casual. As she did so, she snapped the light switch off, making the room dark.

Holly yelped and slammed the fridge door closed. Mel scurried around the counter to join her and together they hunkered down and peered over the edge of the counter at the windows.

The UV-tinted glass made it hard to see, and Mel strained as she looked for any sort of motion out in the pool yard and the desert beyond. The sound of their breathing was the only noise she could hear.

"Maybe I imagined it," Holly said.

"Maybe," Mel said.

"Maybe it was a cat or a coyote," Holly said.

Mel saw a flash outside. It was fast. But it was definitely running on two legs. Her heart pounded in her chest.

"You didn't imagine it. I saw him, too," she said. "Come on, let's get back to Tate and Angie."

They kept the lights off, making their way back by crouching low and running. When they entered the room, Tate and Angie were kissing.

"PDA now?" Mel asked.

Tate and Angie broke apart, looking guilty.

"Sorry," Angie said. "We didn't hear you come in."

"That's because we had to sneak back here because we saw someone creeping around the outside of the house," Mel said. Her voice went higher in pitch with each word, making her sound on the verge of hysterics, which she was.

"What?" Tate bolted up off the couch. He grabbed his phone off the table and began to press the screen.

"It's true," Holly said. "They ran past the window while we were in the kitchen."

"Did you recognize them?" Angie asked. "Do you think it was Byron or one of his goons?"

Holly shook her head. She pointed to Tate. "I saw his face when he realized who you were. He may be mad at me, but he won't do anything to damage his rep in the business community. He's afraid of you and your influence."

Tate nodded as if he'd expected as much. He glanced

down at his phone and frowned. "I'm not getting a signal."

Angie picked up her phone. "I'm not, either."

Mel and Holly checked their phones, too. They had no signal, either.

"Do you have a landline?" Mel asked Holly.

She shook her head. "No, since it's Byron's house I never had the phone connected."

"What could cause this?" Angie asked. She was staring at her phone like she wanted to shake it or smack it.

"A cell phone jammer," Tate said. "Someone doesn't want us to be able to call out."

"Do you think it's . . ." Angie paused.

"What?" Tate asked. He frowned at her. "What are you thinking?"

"Do you think it's the zombie apocalypse?" Angie asked. Her eyes were huge.

"The what?" Holly asked.

"Long story," Mel said. "Suffice to say, Angie has not been a fan of zombie stuff for a while now."

"I think it's my stalker," Holly said. She straightened her back. "Maybe having you all here with me has drawn them out of hiding. You should leave. I can handle myself. I've been waiting for this showdown for a while now."

Mel put her arm around Holly's shoulders and said, "Like we'd leave you. You're one of us now."

"Damn straight," Tate said. "The three of you need to get into the car in the garage and go. Meanwhile I'll go out and circle the house and see if I can flush them out."

"Oh, no, you won't," Angie said. "I'm not letting you

go out there alone. What if there's more than one person?"

"I'll be careful," Tate said. "If you won't leave, then the three of you can stay in here. There are no windows so there's no way for the stalker to know you're here."

"Does he honestly think we're going to follow orders?" Angie looked at Mel.

"You're not going outside," Tate said.

"Neither are you," Mel said. She looked at Holly. "You stay here. The rest of us are going to sweep the house."

"I can't let you—" Holly protested but Angie cut her off.

"We have to," she said. "We can't hide in here when the person responsible for Scott Jensen's death might be right outside and we have no way of calling the police."

That sobered them all.

"Fine, here's how this is going to go," Tate said. "I'll scout the downstairs, check the perimeter, and make sure all windows and doors are locked. You two can check upstairs to see if you can get a visual. Keep the lights off and do not stand directly in front of the windows. Clear?"

"Sure, but then what?" Angie said.

"If we can pinpoint where the person is, I can run to a nearby house and get help," Tate said. "But first we need to know what we're dealing with."

Angie was shaking her head, rejecting the idea, and Tate pulled her forward and pressed his forehead to hers. "Let's argue after we've scouted the sitch."

"We can do that," Mel said when Angie looked like she was going to disagree. She looked at Holly. "Lock yourself in here when we leave."

Holly hugged her middle. "I'm not good with this."

"You have to think about Sydney. You're a mom and she needs you. You have no choice," Angie said. Her voice was final.

They left the room, leaving Holly in the dark. Mel squeezed her hand on the way out.

"If you need us, yell, yell as loud as you can," she said.

Holly nodded. They closed the door behind them and snuck down the hallway back to the main part of the house.

At the staircase that swept up to the second floor, Tate crouched low, dragging both of them down with him.

"Okay, stay away from the windows, hide in the shadows, and scream if you need me," he said.

"Same to you," Angie said. She looked at him with an intensity that made Mel look away.

"As you know from our trips to Belmont Park in San Diego, I can scream like a girl when required," he said.

Angie laughed then she grabbed his face and planted a kiss on his lips that was so fierce, Mel wondered if it was Angie's way of putting a lip-lock protective spell on her man. She hoped it was and she hoped it worked.

"Go!" Tate ordered and the two of them scurried up the staircase, staying low on the cold marble steps.

There were windows perched on the wall high above them, and Mel knew there was no way anyone could see them; still she felt better staying as low to the ground as possible.

"This way," Mel said. She headed to the side of the house that overlooked the backyard. She went right into the master bedroom and noted that the floor-to-ceiling windows and sparse furniture were going to make it difficult to hide from anyone looking in.

"Belly crawl?" Angie asked.

"Yeah," Mel agreed. "Let's split up. You take those windows and I'll take these."

They both dropped to the ground and worked their way across the tile floor until they were perched on the edge of the room, hugging separate walls and looking down.

"On three," Angie said. "One, two, three."

On three, they both popped up just a tiny bit and scouted the yard below.

"See anything?" Mel asked.

"No," Angie said. "Next room?"

"Yes, back up slowly," Mel said.

They scurried back and repeated the process with the next three rooms. When they'd finished their sweep of the grounds from upstairs, they headed back to the staircase except they couldn't find it.

"Where are we?" Angie asked. "Wasn't the staircase here?"

"I have no idea," Mel said. "But then I'm the person who gets lost in the mall."

"We have to get downstairs," Angie said. "Tate and Holly need us."

"We will," Mel said. "There has to be more than one way down."

"Do you think there's a servants' staircase?" Angie asked. "Where would it be?"

Mel thought about all the rooms they'd been in. "We didn't go into the laundry room, maybe it's in there."

They double backed to the laundry room they had just passed. Sure enough, opposite the entrance was another door. Mel opened it and found a staircase.

Angie flicked on the light switch and together they crept down the stairs, trying not to make any noise. The door at the bottom opened into the mudroom off the garage. A bag of golf clubs was propped in the corner and Mel paused to take two putters out, one for her and one for Angie. She really hoped they didn't have to use them.

They came to another unfamiliar hallway. There were no windows so they moved quickly down the corridor. Mel was beginning to wonder if they'd fallen through some wormhole into another dimension when she heard the sound of footsteps up ahead.

"Ta—" Angie called out but Mel clapped a hand over her mouth.

"We don't know who that is," she whispered in Angie's ear.

Angie nodded and she released her. Together they moved silently up the hallway. Mel's nerves felt stretched to the point of breaking. Was it Tate? And if not, who was out there? Who was scouting the house? What did they want?

She peered around the corner at the end of the hallway and saw the back of a rhinestone-studded white jumpsuit with a cape.

She gasped and the Elvis impersonator peered over his shoulder at them.

Mel didn't hesitate. She swung her putter right into the back of Elvis's knees, knocking him to the ground with an "Oomph!"

She lifted her putter again to brain him and Angie stepped up to do the same when another Elvis appeared around the corner.

"Stop! It's us!" he cried. He ripped off his black wig and gold-framed sunglasses. His bald dome shone in the dim light. "It's me, Marty, and that sorry throw rug you're about to beat is Oz."

"Oz!" Mel dropped her putter and crouched beside him. Oscar Ruiz, known as Oz to the bakery crew, was an up and coming young pastry chef who worked in the bakery around his culinary school schedule. Mel had hired him as a student intern the year before and he had never left. "What are you doing here? I almost clobbered you."

"Almost?" Oz groaned, rubbing the back of his knee. "Remind me never to take you on in mini golf."

"We came to see if you were all right," Marty said. He reached down and hauled Oz to his feet. "Shake it off, kid."

"All right?" Angie roared. "You two scared a year off of my life. What were you doing skulking around the house?"

"We weren't skulking," Marty protested. "We called your cell phones, we knocked on the door and rang the bell, but no one answered. Luckily, Manny managed to use his badge and detective speak to convince the security guard to buzz us in and use the key he keeps on file to enter the house."

"Manny?" Mel asked.

"You called?"

She spun and saw Manny Martinez walking down the stairs toward them with a uniformed security guard right behind him.

"What are you doing—"

"Ayeeeh!" The screech cut off Mel's words as Holly came sliding into the foyer and launched herself at Manny, taking him down in a tackle that could have cemented her a position on an NFL defensive line.

"Holly, wait—" Mel began but her voice was cut off by the sounds of shots.

"Get down!" the security guard yelled.

They all hit the floor as one. Glass from the windows above the stairs shattered and fell. Mel covered her head, waiting for the shower of shards to stop.

The silence that followed the sound of breaking glass was filled with the pounding of her heartbeat in her ears.

Mel glanced up and saw that everyone seemed okay. Manny and Holly were still in a tangle of limbs, but he had rolled over to protect her from the glass with his back. Marty and Oz were out of the range of the glass while Angie and Mel were covered. The security guard had his gun out and was already rising to a crouched position, despite the gash in his arm that was oozing blood.

"Stay down," he ordered.

Angie ignored him and was already rising to her feet, shaking the glass from her hair. "Where's Tate? Has anyone seen Tate?"

Sixteen

They all stared at her but no one spoke, giving Angie the answer she needed.

"Tate!" she screamed.

It was a cry so full of anguish that Mel felt her heart stutter in her chest. Her own panic at the thought that her best friend could be injured or worse almost leveled her but she refused to let it. Tate was okay. He had to be.

She wrapped her arms about Angie and held her tight, keeping her from running outside.

"Getting yourself killed won't help him," she said.

Manny uncovered Holly, checking her over as he rose to his feet.

"Are you all right?" he asked.

"I'm fine," Holly said. Her voice was shaky and so were her hands. "I'm sorry. I didn't know you were a friend."

"It's cool," he said. "I think you may have saved my life."

He gestured for everyone to go into the hallway, where they couldn't be seen from outside. He and the security guard whose name badge read DAVE stood at either end of the group, protecting them.

"We'll go outside," Manny said. "You all wait here."

Marty looked like he was going to protest, but Manny shook his head. "No."

He paused beside Angie. "I'll find Tate."

Mel noticed that he didn't say he was sure Tate was all right. Manny knew better. He squeezed Angie's hand before he and Dave slipped out the back door.

As soon as they were gone, Angie moved in the opposite direction. Marty stepped in her way and shook his head. Oz was right behind him doing the same thing.

"Move over, Dynamic Duo," Angie said.

"If you go out there, Manny or the other guy might think you're the shooter and shoot you," Oz said. "You can't go. T-man will be all right."

And that was the difference between an eighteen-year-old chef school student and a veteran police detective. Oz hadn't learned that sometimes the good guys didn't win and that you don't make promises you're not sure you can keep.

"I will give them five minutes and then I'm going to look for him," Angie said. Then she started pacing. The rest of them hugged the wall and let her stride back and forth like a human pendulum, working off her anxiety while she checked her watch every ten steps.

Mel was with her. She didn't think she could take much more waiting, either. On the plus side, there hadn't been any more gunshots so perhaps the shooter had left.

Just as Angie looked like she was going to run from the hallway, they heard a shout coming from the back of the house. Mel recognized Manny's voice and she began to run.

The glass French doors that led to the pool were shut and locked. Angie passed Mel, reached the door first, and unfastened the deadbolt. Manny and Dave had Tate's arms over their shoulders and they were hauling him in. His head was hanging low but his eyes were open.

"Tate, oh my god, are you all right?" Angie asked. "Where did you find him? What were you doing outside?"

"It's okay, I'm okay," Tate said as Manny and Dave lowered him to the couch. Angie started checking him over as if she was looking for bullet holes.

"He has a knot on his head, but he roused pretty easily," Manny said. "He should probably have his injury checked out, however."

"I'll get some ice," Holly said and she hurried to the kitchen.

"Angie, breathe," Tate said. He grabbed her hands and pulled her into his arms. "I'm okay."

Angie burst into tears and buried her face in his chest. "I can't lose you. I just can't."

Her voice was so raw that Mel felt her throat get tight. A quick glance at the men around her and she saw them all looking in different directions as if a magical portal taking them away from the emotional female might open up and they didn't want to miss it.

"Come on, let's give them a minute," Mel said.

She took her two Elvises by the arms and led them from the room, leaving Manny and Dave to follow. Holly handed off a bag of frozen peas to Angie and then followed them out of the room.

Once back in the kitchen, Holly drew the blinds over the large windows, preventing anyone from seeing into the room from outside. Then she tended Dave's cut and told Manny and Oz to help themselves to anything in the kitchen. They did not need to be told twice.

"Mel, can I talk to you a minute?" Manny asked.

"Sure," she said.

They left the kitchen and went down the hall to a small study off the main floor. Manny went in first to switch on the light and check it out and Mel followed.

Once they were in the room, he shut the door. Mel blew out a breath. The study had two wing chairs and a fireplace; a small desk sat in the corner in front of a wall of books. It was a cozy room, made even cozier by the amount of space the detective seemed to take up.

"Where did you find him?" Mel asked. She sat in one chair and Manny took the other.

"He was on the side of the house," Manny said. "Face-down in the shrubbery."

"He wasn't supposed to go outside."

"We're lucky he did. It could be that the shooter saw him and got spooked."

"But he could have been killed."

"I don't think that was the plan. Judging by the scene, Tate got hit on the head by a flowerpot that was shot off of the balcony with the precision of a sharpshooter."

"What are you saying?" Mel asked. She sat forward and propped her head in her hands. Suddenly, she was so tired.

"I think this was a scare tactic," Manny said. "Or at least, that's what it feels like."

"You know, when I spoke to you earlier this evening, you didn't mention you were coming for a visit," she said.

"The beauty of flying from Phoenix to Vegas is you're up and down in an hour," he said. "I found Marty and Oz at the hotel, working their Elvis magic, and then we stopped at the Casablanca to find out where Holly Hartzmark lived."

"And they told you? Isn't that a violation of privacy?"

"I think introducing myself as Detective Martinez helped. It doesn't always, but today it did. Well, that and a fifty spot."

Mel reached across the space between their chairs and took his hand in hers. "I'm really glad you're here."

They stared at each other and Mel felt as if there was a mountain of words between them that would never be said. She and Manny had been through a lot. If it weren't for the fact that she was in love with Joe, well, there was no way of knowing what might have been.

"Joe sends his regards," Manny said. It was almost as if he was reading her mind. Uncanny.

"Joe?"

"I called him after you and I spoke. We're both concerned that what is happening stems from his case."

"Wait a minute." Mel let go of his hand. "Are you telling me that Joe *sent* you to babysit me?"

"No, it wasn't like that."

"Oh, please, that's what it's always like," Mel said. "Joe can't ever be there for me, so he sends you, his trusty detective buddy."

Manny leaned back in his chair and crossed his arms over his chest. He was grinning.

"What?" she asked.

"The thought of Joe and I being buddies. That's funny. But you are giving me hope," he said.

"What do you mean?" she asked.

"If you're getting tired of Joe or more specifically the lack of Joe, maybe there's hope for me," he said with a careless shrug.

"Or maybe I'll just join a convent," she said.

Manny looked alarmed.

"And you can tell Joe I said that, too." She rose from her seat and strode across the room. "I'm going to check on Tate."

"Mel," Manny called after her before she slipped through the door.

"What?" she asked over her shoulder.

"Stay away from the windows."

Mel slammed the door so hard, it rattled.

"Why do I get the feeling you wish that was someone's head?" Marty asked.

Mel glanced up and saw Oz and Marty, or rather, the Elvis wannabes approaching.

"Or something even more delicate," Oz added.

Mel glared at them. "Why are you here? Why are you dressed like Elvis?"

Marty and Oz exchanged sheepish expressions. It appeared they were trying to outlast each other in confession mode. Mel was lacking patience.

"Out. With. It."

The Elvises jumped in fright.

"We were trying to blend," Marty said. "The biggest Elvis impersonator conference in the world is going on in our hotel and we figured as long as we're here . . ."

"Oh, no. You're not competing, are you?" Mel asked.

"No!" Marty protested. Then he gave her a sidelong look. "Unless you think I should."

Mel smacked her forehead with her palm.

"We're here because we were worried about you," Oz said. "I baked enough to hold the shop for a few days and filled all of our special orders. We got your mom and her friend Ginny to watch the bakery, which they were happy to do when they heard about the explosion."

"You told my mother?" Mel asked.

"Yeah," Marty said. "And she called Joe."

"Who then called Manny," Mel said. She sighed as she leaned against the wall. "It's all coming into focus now."

"On the upside—" Oz began.

"There's an upside?" Mel asked.

"None of the brothers know about the car collision, except

for Joe," Oz said. "You could have Dom, Ray, Sal, Tony, Paulie, and Al following you around as well."

Mel just stared at him. Suddenly she was tired all the way down to her toenails.

"I'll just hug that pillow of comfort to my chest when I fall asleep tonight," she said. "Come on, I think we need to get out of here."

Mel joined Holly and the security guard in the kitchen. He was taking a report and she was plying him with cupcakes. A small smile tipped the corner of Mel's mouth. Holly was using a maneuver she had employed on many an occasion herself. She had to respect that.

"I think we need to get out of here," Mel said. "I'm going to talk to Tate but I want all of us to stay together in a place with higher security." She glanced at Dave. "No offense."

"None taken," he said. "The police are on their way, and once they've taken statements, I'd bug out, too, if I were you. Whoever shot out those windows was not messing around."

Mel glanced at Holly and saw her shiver.

"We'll figure it out. I promise," she said, hoping she wasn't telling a big, fat lie.

* * *

"How many bedrooms are in the penthouse?" Mel asked.

"Six," Tate said. He handed over his black Amex card, and Mel felt like it was the old days when Tate was rolling in money and bankrolled some seriously luxurious digs for them.

"But there are seven of us," she said.

"Angie and I are bunkies."

"Oh, yeah, duh."

"Unless you were hoping to shack up with Manny," he said. He wiggled his eyebrows at her.

"Stop," she said.

Tate turned so they were facing each other. His nostrils were flared and his lips were compressed. This was the expression he always wore when he had to say something he was pretty sure his listener did not want to hear.

"Manny's here," he said. "Joe isn't."

Mel looked at him. She didn't know what to say.

"I'm just observing a pattern," Tate said. "I know how Joe feels about you, but I also know that he will always choose his career first. So I'm looking out for my best friend. I want you to be happy. You deserve that."

"Thanks but Manny and I are just friends. Period. Maybe you need to lie down and let Angie tend that concussion of yours," Mel said.

"I am feeling a little woozy," he said.

Mel took the room keys from the desk clerk and thanked her. She was feeling a little woozy herself from what Tate had just said and she knew she was in no place to process her emotions right now.

She glanced over her shoulder at their bedraggled group. After an hour and a half of answering the police officer's questions, it was now the wee hours of the morning and no one was looking their best. If it hadn't been for

Manny cutting through the red tape, they'd probably still be at the house recounting the events of the evening.

Marty and Oz were nodding off in their chairs while Angie was again watching the big screen Elvis do his thing. Manny and Holly looked to be avoiding each other's gaze, and Mel figured it had to be embarrassment on both their sides, given that their first meeting had entailed her sacking him like he was a QB who had yet to deliver the ball.

"Rise and shine, troops," Tate said as he nudged Oz with his foot. "We're moving up to the penthouse."

At this, Marty sat up like he'd been electrocuted. "Now this trip is looking up."

Tate turned to Manny. "Do you mind getting these guys settled? We need to stop by our old room and grab our stuff."

"No, not at all," Manny said.

Again, Mel noted that he didn't look at Holly. If they were all going to be staying together, this was just going to get increasingly awkward. She hooked her arm through Holly's and dragged her in front of Manny.

"In all of the chaos, I don't think we got to make proper introductions. Detective Manny Martinez, this is Holly Hartzmark," she said. "I know your first meeting was—"

"Like watching a twister blow up a barn," Marty interrupted. He looked from Manny to Holly and then back at Mel and added, "I like her. She's feisty."

Holly hung her head. "I am so embarrassed. I had no idea you were a friend and not just a friend, but a cop. You could totally bust me for assaulting an officer."

Mel could see her cheeks flame red hot behind her curtain of dark hair. Poor thing, she really was mortified.

"Since I hadn't identified myself as an officer, I think you're good," Manny said with a small smile. "Besides, how can I bust anyone who can execute a tackle like that?"

Holly peeked at him from behind her hair and Manny turned up the wattage in his smile to full grin. Mel didn't think it was possible, but Holly blushed an even deeper shade of red. Interesting.

"Come on, I'll show you up to the suite," Manny said.

He started to walk and Holly fell into step beside him. They were halfway to the elevators when Holly said something that made Manny throw back his head and laugh. Neither of them looked back at Mel, not even for a glance of reassurance.

"Do not tell me you've lost the slavish devotion of the detective," Angie said.

"I think I might have," Mel said. "He actually belly laughed at something she said. He never does that."

"Uh-oh, do I hear upset in your voice?" Tate asked. He gestured for them to follow the others.

"Don't be ridiculous," Mel said. "It's just that I've known him for over a year and I've never seen him laugh like that with anyone ex . . ." She stopped talking, aware that what she had been going to say would make her sound like she cared way more than she did.

"Except you," Angie and Tate said together.

This was the downside to lifelong friends. They could complete your sentences for you with a precision that was usually found only in overpriced European watches.

"Which is totally fine," Mel said. "Overdue, in fact. I've made it clear that I am emotionally unavailable and that we're just friends. It's time Manny found someone who can return his feelings."

"Keep talking yourself into it, kiddo, you'll get there. But we all know you care more than you've ever admitted, even to yourself," Tate said.

Mel punched him on the shoulder, not lightly, before stepping into the elevator that would take them up to their floor.

"Ouch!" he said. "Isn't there an expression about not harming the messenger?"

"Which is null and void when the messenger is being an insensitive boob," Angie said. "She is clearly working through some stuff and you didn't need to point it out to her."

"What?" Tate protested. "I was merely stating the obvious. We both know Mel has feelings for Manny as well as Joe. It's only natural that if either of them moved on, she would feel sad."

"Sad?" Angie asked. "She's not sad. She's relieved. Manny's nice and all but her heart has always belonged to Joe."

"Well, maybe if Joe put her ahead of his career once in a while, she wouldn't be sad all the time," Tate said.

"Are you criticizing my brother?" Angie asked. Her tone was full of warning. Tate did not heed.

"Yeah, I am," he said. "How long is she supposed to wait for him?"

"Until he's done putting away the mobsters who tried

to kill us all," Angie snapped. She tossed her hair and looked like she was going to start pawing the ground. "Or did you forget?"

"I didn't forget," Tate said. "I just want her to be happy."

"I do, too!"

"I'm standing right here," Mel said. She reached around Angie to hit the elevator button. "And for the record, I'm not sad about Manny being interested in someone else, just surprised. I didn't really see a Vegas showgirl as Manny's type."

"Ah, but she's also a cupcake baker," Angie said. "And we all know that's his type and how."

Mel sighed and Angie stepped forward and hugged her. "I'm sorry. Tate's right. I just want you and Joe to work out so much, because I love you both and I think you bring out the best in each other."

"When he's around," Mel said.

All three of them were silent. Tate opened his arms and they both stepped forward for a group hug.

"Better?" he asked.

"A little," Mel said.

"Seriously, all my bias for you and Joe as a couple aside, are you okay with Manny and Holly?" Angie asked.

"Um, they just met," Mel said. "I don't see them as running off to the altar exactly, but yeah, I'm fine with it, really."

Of course, if she had heard from Joe at all during the past few weeks, she would have that to cling to and she probably would be fine, but she hadn't. Up to now, she had refused to make a fuss. He was busy wrapping up his mobster case and she fully supported him.

She glanced at Tate and Angie, who had obviously already made up. They stood holding hands and looking at her with the unintentional pity couples often direct at the single. She tried not to resent it. She knew they loved her and just wanted her to be happy. That was all she wanted as well, but as the weeks rolled on, she wondered if she and Joe would ever find their way back to each other.

Seventeen

It was noon before Mel opened her eyes and faced the day. She wasn't sure what had lured her from her sleep. The bed was harder than she was used to and the room was colder, the surroundings were plush but unfamiliar, and her pillow was hard. She thought it was likely a combination of all these things that made her wake up, feeling stiff and tired.

She glanced around her. Done tastefully sleek and modern, the room was all burnished copper, glass, and black leather. Slowly, it all came back to her. Oh, yeah, Vegas.

Then like a rabbit smelling a carrot, her nose twitched. Bacon. If someone had ordered bacon, then there had to be coffee to go with it. She jumped out of bed, shoved her blond bangs out of her eyes, drew on her thick hotel robe, and strode out of her room to find the others.

The penthouse had a kitchen and Holly was in the center of it with a man who, judging by his uniform, was a hotel chef. Mel had stayed with Tate before in a high-end hotel where a full domestic staff came with the price of the stay. It always amazed her that Tate stayed so down-to-earth given how lavish his life had been.

Holly and the chef were laughing and chatting, and he was teaching her some fancy knife maneuvers while Marty, Oz, and Manny looked on in amusement. There was no sign of Tate or Angie.

"Hey, look who decided to join the party," Marty said.

He patted the seat next to him and Mel slid onto it while Manny poured her a cup of coffee just the way she liked it.

"Thanks," she said. Their fingers brushed when she took the mug from him, but he seemed unaware as his eyes went right back to Holly, where she was chopping up a pile of vegetables under the supervision of the hotel's chef.

"They're making omelets," Marty said. "Hmm-mm."

"You don't like vegetables," Mel said. "Are you actually going to eat one of those?"

"I already did," he said. "I'm waiting for my second."

"Forget the eggs. Mel, you have to taste Holly's pancakes," Oz said through a mouthful. Syrup dripped down his chin and he wiped it with his cloth napkin. "They're light and fluffy with just a hint of lemon. Seriously, I have to have the recipe for these."

Mel glanced at Holly. With a big white apron tied over her long john shirt and flannel pajama bottoms, she looked like a little girl helping out in the kitchen. Her long dark hair had been shoved up into a ponytail on top of her head and her upturned nose made her look all of twelve.

When she saw Mel, she smiled and her happiness shone in her bright blue eyes, making Mel blink. "Melanie Cooper, this is Mario Consuelo," Holly said and pointed at the chef. "He's amazing."

"Hi, Mario," Mel said. "Nice to meet you. So, what's your specialty breakfast dish?"

"Well, since I'm cooking for another cordon bleu chef, I feel I must make my small Normandy-style brioche with apples and an apricot glaze," he said. He was wearing his chef's toque and his whites were impeccable. He looked very serious until he smiled and the deep dimples in his cheeks gave him a dab of mischief.

"You had me at brioche," Mel said.

Mario delivered the small loaf of bread with a thin, crisp apple slice on top to Mel with a side of whipped butter. It looked delicious. Mel tucked into it with her fork and the sweet bread melted in her mouth. Now this was how every morning should start.

"Did you use a touch of Calvados?" she asked.

Mario looked impressed. "Just a few drops of apple brandy but you tasted it. Well done."

"It's exquisite," Mel said.

Mario kissed the tips of his fingers and then touched his forehead in a gesture of gratitude before he turned back to the stove to finish Marty's second omelet.

Holly came around the table with her own breakfast and Manny hopped up to let her have his seat. She looked flustered by the gesture and Mel wondered how a Vegas showgirl could be so undone by basic gentlemanly courtesy. Then again, maybe Holly hadn't gotten to experience much of that in her years as a working girl.

A busboy began to clean up after them and Marty and Oz moved themselves to the lounge chairs out beside their private lap pool on their rooftop balcony. Mel knew this little excursion to the penthouse was costing Tate a small fortune, and she also knew that he thought any expense to keep them all safe was well worth it.

The thing Mel couldn't let go of was what or who exactly they were being protected from? Was the shooter after Holly or one of them? And if so, was it Angie, Mel, or possibly even Tate? Or was there something else entirely going on, and if so, what?

"Can I get the door for you?" Mel asked Mario as the busboy wheeled his loaded cart toward the suite's front door.

"No need," Mario said. "I am taking the back way."

"There's a back way?" she asked.

"Come on, I'll show you," he said. He opened the front door and let the busboy out, and then he went back into the penthouse to a small door at the end of the hallway. It opened into a utility type of closet where extra pillows, linens, and bathrobes were stored. At the back there was a tiny door that looked like an elevator door.

"See, I have my own escape hatch," Mario said.

"What the what?" Mel asked.

Mario tapped in the number to their suite and the door slid open. It was a tiny elevator.

"I'll be darned," Mel said.

"Well, we can't keep the rich and pampered waiting, especially at ten thousand dollars per night," Mario said. "It's only big enough for one, but it gets the staff where they're needed pretty quick."

"That is so cool," Mel said. Although as she registered the cost of the penthouse, everything went gray and she started to see spots.

"I'm glad you think so," he said. "It lets out by the main kitchen. Come visit me sometime and we can cook something together."

He wiggled his eyebrows at her and Mel laughed as the door slid shut and he disappeared from view. Mel shook her head. The other half really did live completely different lives.

She reentered the kitchen to find only Manny and Holly. Mel didn't think she was imagining the tension between the two of them.

"Holly, do you mind if I ask you a few questions?" Manny asked.

Holly glanced up from her empty plate and blushed. "No, not at all."

Mel frowned. The blushing thing was out of control. Was Holly doing it on purpose? Could a person do that on purpose? She glanced at Manny. He looked positively beguiled.

"Great, how about we go to the other balcony so as not to disturb Marty and Oz?" he asked.

Mel looked at him and he shrugged and said, "What? It's police business."

"Sure it is," she said. This time it was Manny who blushed as he escorted Holly outside.

There was still no sign of Tate or Angie. Maybe Tate was sleeping in because of the knot on his head and Angie didn't want to leave him unattended. She was certain Angie would holler if she needed help.

Through the French doors, she saw Marty and Oz looking pretty comfy napping in their pool loungers. The last of the busboys wheeled out of the suite, taking his rolling cart of food with him. As Mel sat at the granite counter sipping her coffee, she felt like an outsider looking in and the familiar feeling of loneliness crept in, stealing the warmth from her and making her shiver.

Her pocket buzzed and she pulled her phone out of her robe. She had been expecting her mother to call. Joyce was a worrier of the first order and since Marty and Oz had told her about the explosion, she was bound to be upset.

Mel looked at the front of her phone and her heart did a little skip jump sort of thing as Joe's name appeared. She hadn't spoken to him in weeks. She missed him and she was mad at him. She loved him and sometimes she really hated him, well, not him so much as his career, or as Tate had so painfully observed, she hated how his career always came first.

"Hi, Joe, what's new with you?" she asked. She tried to sound indifferent, but she was afraid it just came out snotty.

"Morning, cupcake," he said. "How are you?"

His low voice rolled over the familiar endearment laced with concern and caring. It made her breath catch and her head spin. She had to clear her throat before she could speak.

"At the moment, I'm surprised," she said.

"Really?" he asked. "I was going to call you last night after I spoke to Manny, but he suggested I wait. He said you were a little prickly."

"Prickly?"

"I believe he said something about you joining the holy sisterhood," Joe said. He sounded amused, which irritated Mel beyond reason.

"I think I'd make a fine nun," Mel said. "What's it to you anyway? You've sent your minion to babysit me. You should have a clear conscience."

She glanced out the window and saw Holly and Manny standing by the railing of the balcony while they talked. Even from inside the suite, she could feel the sizzle of chemistry between them. She tried to read their lips. Were they talking about the explosion, the car crash, the shooting? Or had they moved into more personal waters?

She couldn't tell and despite what she'd said to her friends, she wasn't really sure how she felt about it. She had begun to like Holly despite not loving the idea of her owning an offshoot of the bakery. But now she was moving in on Mel's personal life and it felt straight-up invasive.

"Mel? Are you listening to me?" Joe asked.

"What? Huh?" Mel turned away from Manny and Holly. She stomped back to her room, away from the sight of them.

"I was cataloging all of the reasons why you might be mad at me," he said.

"Oh, yeah, whatever," Mel said. "Look, I need to go figure out what the plan is, so I don't really have time for this."

"Okaaaaay," Joe said. He sounded hurt and a little irritated. "This conversation has gone from awkward to openly hostile."

"I'm not hostile," Mel said. "I'm just . . ." Her voice trailed off. She couldn't think of what she was other than pitifully lonely and, yeah, a little whiney.

"I sense we need to talk," Joe said. "Really talk. As in you and me, face-to-face. I know this case has—"

"You know what, Joe?" Mel interrupted. "We really don't need to talk. I'm done."

"What?" he asked. She could tell she had his full attention now.

"You heard me," she said. "I'm done."

"Done with . . ."

"I'm officially done with waiting for you, for your cases to be resolved, for the bad guys to all be put away, for all of it. I can't always be the second most important thing in your life. I want to be first. I want to be number one, and I can't keep putting my life on hold, waiting for an elevated status that clearly isn't coming. I'm done, Joe."

"Mel, I know the past few days have been scary and you're probably pretty shaken up—"

"That's not it," she said. "Well, not all of it."

They were both silent. Mel didn't know what more to say and it was clear that Joe didn't, either.

"Listen, I have to go," she said. "I'll call you when we get back to town, but I really don't think there's anything left for us to talk about."

She didn't wait for him to say anything. She didn't want to hear it. To make sure there was no extension of the conversation, she ended the call and turned the volume off on her phone and went to take a shower, where she had a good long cry.

It took holding her breath while she dunked her face in a sink full of cold water to make her nose and eyes stop looking so red, but Mel was confident that when she joined the others, she looked perfectly normal.

She should have known better. As soon as she stepped into the main room, where Angie was sitting with Tate, Angie rose from her seat, crossed the room, and hugged her.

"What's wrong?" she asked. "You've been crying, haven't you? Is it a little post-traumatic stress?"

"No, just allergies," Mel said. She hugged her friend back and then released her.

Angie looked like she was about to argue, but Tate spoke first.

"Yeah, I heard the pollen count was abnormally high."

Angie looked at him like he was thick, but he shook his head. Angie heaved a sigh and gave Mel a look that clearly stated that they would be talking later.

There was a knock on the penthouse door, and Manny appeared in the doorway. He gestured for everyone to stay put while he went to answer it. He arrived back in the room moments later with Billy Eastman and Sydney. She was clutching a large stuffed panda and looking wide eyed at the enormous room.

"Mommy?" she called.

Holly must have had a mother's bionic hearing because

she came running down the hall in a bathrobe with a towel twisted around her hair. She opened her arms and Sydney launched herself into them.

"Oh, baby," she said. "I'm so glad you're here."

Billy glowered as he took in the reunion. "I'm only here because your attorney threatened me with a lawsuit if I break the custody agreement."

"My what?" Holly asked as she glanced over Sydney's head.

"How can you do this?" he demanded. "How can you put our daughter in danger like this? I thought you were a better mother than that."

Eighteen

Holly looked shaken and Tate stood, moving to stand right in front of Billy. "Don't. Holly didn't even know about this. It was my attorney who arranged it." He gestured with his thumb at Manny. "We have our own police detective staying with us. Sydney couldn't be any safer."

Billy glared at Manny, who met his rude stare with one of his own.

"Detective?" Billy scoffed. "From where?"

"Scottsdale, Arizona," Manny said.

"Please," Billy said. "What do you do, spend your days searching for rich ladies' lost dogs? This is Vegas."

"Manny is a homicide detective with an impeccable record," Mel said. She strode forward, staring at Billy Eastman as if he were a wad of gum on her shoe. "Plus, he saved me from burning to death in a fire. You ever save any lives?"

Billy was silent.

"Yeah, I didn't think so," Mel said.

Billy ran a hand over his face. He looked genuinely contrite, and Mel could tell by the fine lines around his eyes and his overall pallor that he was feeling pretty stressed.

"Is everything okay?" Holly asked. "Is Lisa—"

"She's fine," Billy said. "Or at least, I assume she's fine. She won't let me go to the doctor with her; in fact, she won't let me do anything with her. I think she's avoiding me. Is that normal when a woman is expecting? I don't remember you being like that."

"Every woman is different," Holly said. "Maybe she just needs some rest. She's, what, five months along? I remember feeling so tired then."

Billy nodded and looked relieved and then he turned to Manny and said, "I'm sorry I was a jerk. I know you'll take care of our girl."

"With my life," Manny said.

Billy nodded. He turned and scooped up Sydney and gave her a smacking kiss on the cheek that made her giggle. "Be good and I'll be back later, okay?"

"Okay, Daddy." Sydney hugged him back.

Mel could tell that Billy wanted to talk to Holly some more so she turned and smiled at Sydney. "Do you want to go see our pool? Maybe you could go for a swim later?"

"Can I?" Sydney asked her mother.

"Sure," Holly said. "I'll just work out your pickup time with your dad."

Mel took Sydney's hand and the two of them went out to the pool area, where Marty and Oz were lounging like two lizards in the sun.

Mel watched as Holly and Billy worked out Sydney's schedule under the watchful eyes of Manny and Tate. In a way, she couldn't blame Billy for being worried about his daughter, but at the same time, he had no right to keep her from Holly, especially when the only time Holly got to see her daughter was for a few hours in the afternoon. Mel could only imagine how hard it must be.

"What's your panda's name?" Mel asked Sydney.

"Rupert," Sydney said. "He's my baby."

"Well, he sure is a handsome fella," Mel said. She glanced at the bear with his multiple bald spots, missing eye, and torn ear.

"Isn't he?" Sydney asked. She hugged her bear tight. "Do you have a baby?"

Mel glanced over at Oz and Marty, who had moved to the pool and were now bobbing around the narrow space like two turtles on a log.

"No, I have a cat named Captain Jack."

"That's a funny name," Sydney said.

"He's a funny cat. Actually, he has a black patch over his eye that makes him look like a pirate, so the name seems to fit," she said.

"You should have a baby, too," Sydney said. "My stepmother Lisa is going to have one. It's going to come out of the pouch in her belly any day now."

"Pouch?" Mel asked. She bit her cheek and tried not to laugh.

"Uh-huh," Sydney said. "You just strap on your pouch while the baby cooks and then *ding* when the baby is ready, you take it out of its pouch."

Somehow Sydney had gotten the idea that humans birthed like marsupials—would that it were that easy.

"Well, I'm not really ready to have my pouch filled with a baby yet," Mel said.

Sydney nodded. "Lisa says not everyone should be parents. That it takes a special person to be a mom, a person who will do anything for her child."

Mel glanced at the window and saw Billy Eastman leaving while Holly hugged her middle tight and glanced at Sydney. She smiled so that Holly would know Sydney was okay. It was clear that Holly loved her daughter very much, especially as she was abandoning her career and starting over just so she could spend time with her.

"I think she's right," Mel said. "Good thing your mom is that special sort of person, huh?"

"Yes!" Sydney agreed and then added, "And I am, too."

Mel smiled. Sydney was a great kid and so was her mom. They had to find out who was wreaking so much havoc in their lives and stop it.

"Hey, sweetie." Holly stuck her head out the door. "Your dad says you can stay for a few hours so long as Detective Martinez watches over you and he has agreed."

Sydney bounced up from her seat and clapped her hands. She hugged her mother and then went around her into the suite, where she hugged Manny. He looked surprised and then amused. Then he asked Sydney something and she jumped up and down again.

He stuck his head back out the door and said, "We have a game of Go Fish starting up, any takers?"

"I'm in," Holly said.

Manny looked pleased and Mel realized that there was definitely a thing between these two.

"I have to pass," Mel said. "I have some work stuff I have to do."

Manny didn't press it, but turned to Holly instead and said, "Your daughter has managed to wrap me around her finger in about five minutes."

"Really?" Holly asked. "How'd she do that?"

"She looked at me with those big, beautiful blue eyes, the ones just like her mother's, and declared I was her hero," he said. "She is a natural-born charmer."

Holly laughed. "That she is."

Sydney tugged Manny back inside and the two of them made for the dining table in the room off the kitchen. Manny took the cards that Sydney handed him and he began to shuffle.

"Mel, can I ask you something?"

Mel turned to see Holly looking at her with a worried expression.

"Sure, what is it?"

"Are you . . . that is . . . Vegas sure is a long way for a guy to travel to keep an eye on a friend," she said.

Mel had a feeling Holly was talking around the point. She wondered if she should wait for her to get there on her own or help her along.

"I suppose it depends on the friend," Mel said. "Marty and Oz are friends and employees so they're a bit different."

"I was thinking about Manny," Holly said. "He came all the way up here just to make sure you're all right. That's pretty special."

"Manny is a special kind of guy," Mel said.

"Oh," Holly said. She looked momentarily sad and then rallied with a smile. "Well, I'm glad you have such a great boy—"

"Friend," Mel said. "He's just a friend."

"Really, 'cause I could swear . . ." Holly stopped. She looked embarrassed.

"He's a special friend," Mel said. "We met a few years ago when my mother went on a date and her beau ended up dead."

"Oh my god, how awful," Holly said.

"We didn't get on at first," Mel said. "Then this crazy woman tried to kill me and a whole bunch of other people by burning down a building. Manny pulled me out of the fire. He saved my life."

"Wow," Holly said. "And you're really just friends?"

Mel thought about it and knew it was true. Despite enjoying the mild flirtation between Manny and her, they would always just be friends.

"Yeah," Mel said. "Just friends."

"Oh, I get it. He's married, isn't he?" Holly asked. "Or gay, is he gay?"

"No and no," Mel said. "As far as I know, he is one hundred percent available."

"Okay, cool," Holly said. She turned and went toward the house then she spun back around and asked, "And you don't mind if I . . ."

"Not at all," Mel said. "Have at it."

Holly hurried inside, shutting the door behind her.

"How do you get one hundred percent available off a guy who has been pining for you for over a year?" Marty asked. He floated by her on his spongy pool noodle.

"He has not been pining," Mel said.

"Please, he calls himself your number two," Oz corrected her. His dark hair hung over his eyes, shielding his expression and giving Mel no clue as to whether he was teasing her or not. "If that's not pining, I don't know what it is."

"It's pitiful, that's what," Marty said. "A man can't be making a fool of himself like that over a woman."

"This from a man who wore an Elvis wig and jumpsuit to see if he could score with the ladies," Mel said. She reached into the pool and splashed the two of them. While Marty was spluttering, she asked, "Does Olivia know about you dressing up? Should I text her a picture?"

"No!" Marty said. "Let's just keep this excursion on the down low."

"Speaking of your girlfriend, have you made a decision about her ultimatum yet?" Mel asked.

"Don't pressure me," Marty said. "I'm working on it."

"Tick tock," Oz said. Marty gave him a death glare.

Mel and Oz exchanged a smile.

"Besides we have bigger problems than my love life right now," Marty said.

"I'm beginning to think this excursion is going to be just that, one big problem," Mel said. "I don't see how we can move forward with the franchise until we know who is trying so hard to stop it."

"My money is on the ex-husband," Marty said. "I don't like him."

"You don't like anyone," Oz said.

The two of them climbed out of the pool and toweled off. Mel took an available seat beside the pool with them. She glanced back at the suite and watched Sydney and her mom playing Go Fish with Manny. The three of them were grinning at each other and Mel felt a pang in her chest at the thought that this was what Manny was looking for, it was what he deserved, and it was what she could never give him. Not while she was still all twisted up after Joe. She was happy for Manny; really she was. Well, she would be if she weren't so busy feeling sorry for herself.

Mel shook it off. She tipped her face up to the sun and tried to tell herself that everything was going to be okay. She supposed she should call Joe back and apologize. She knew he was trying one of the biggest cases of his career. Frank Tucci needed to be put away and Joe was the man to do it. She was proud of him, so proud, but she missed having a boyfriend and she really resented being alone all the time.

Okay, clearly she wasn't ready to call him back just yet. It didn't matter. He would be so busy wrapping up the case, he wouldn't notice that she was giving him the cold shoulder, or if he did, he'd be able to compartmentalize it until the case was done.

"I think it's a crazed fan," Oz said. He had his head tipped back as he reclined in his lounge chair, soaking up the rays. His long thick hair, which usually hung in a fringe over his face, was dripping wet from his time in the pool and he'd shoved it to the side. Mel realized Oz was a pretty handsome young man when he chose to show his face.

"You mean a stalker?" Marty asked.

"Exactly. I heard Holly telling Manny about him this morning," Oz said. "I think he's the one behind the gas leak, car crash, and shooting."

"Why?" Mel was curious to see how Oz had puzzled this out.

"Assuming the stalker is a fan who likes Holly's show, then they have to be freaking out that she's going to quit and open a bakery," he said.

"Yeah, no more ogling her in her sparkly gee-gaw outfits," Marty said. "Makes sense."

"Only to a man," Mel said with a frown. "We really need to know who is so obsessed with her. You know, it could be someone in the show."

"Like who?"

"Levi Cartwright," Mel said. "He is totally dependent upon Holly for his positive feedback."

"Then why would he hire someone to shoot her?" Oz asked. "He won't really get the love he wants from her if she's dead."

"Unless he's so angry that she's leaving him that he shoots her in a rage," Mel said.

"Whoever shot at the house was a pro," Marty said. "They weren't shooting to kill."

"How do you know?" Mel asked.

"The shots came through the second-floor window when we were all clearly visible through the glass on the first floor," Marty said. "No one is that bad of a shot."

"Maybe," she said. "But here's what I don't get: The first two incidents happened while we were scouting bakery locations. Destroying the shops made certain that Holly would be unable to move ahead with her bakery. So, it seemed the motivation was to stop the bakery. But shooting at Holly's house is a totally different modus operandi."

"What do you think it means?" Oz asked.

"I think whatever is happening is aimed at Holly, and I think it's moved from trying to stop her from opening the bakery to trying to stop her permanently," Mel said. "It could be this stalker she has, maybe they're freaking out so much that she's leaving the show that they'd rather see her dead."

"That's seriously twisted," Oz said.

"I can't think of any other explanation," Mel said. "Can you?"

Both Oz and Marty looked thoughtful and then they shook their heads. They had no answers and Mel didn't have any, either. Either the shooting at the house was about something else entirely or the person after Holly had gone from stopping her dream of opening a bakery to out and out trying to kill her.

Mel fell asleep poolside. She blamed the apple brioche but she knew it was really just her body's reaction to all the stress. There was no greater cure for anxiety than a bowl full of frosting or a nap. Given the extra weight she was now carrying, she was glad the nap had won that round.

Mel staggered out of her chair. Marty and Oz were gone, presumably to another Elvis impersonator event. When she glanced at the suite, Holly was back in the kitchen while Sydney sat at the counter coloring with crayons.

Mel opened the door and stepped inside. The heady smell of vanilla hit her senses and she thought she might just get to try her other stress buster.

"Whatcha doing?" she asked.

"Baking," Holly said. "It's my stress reliever. Mario was super cool about sending up some ingredients so I could play in the kitchen."

"Mind if I join you?" Mel asked as she scrubbed her hands at the sink.

"I don't know," Holly said. She gave Mel a considering look. "Do you have any experience?"

Nineteen

"No, but I am an excellent taste tester," Mel retorted.

"Well, I suppose everyone has to start somewhere," Holly said.

They set to work, finishing up the vanilla cupcakes. They tried a variety of frosting techniques and Mel was pleased to see that Holly had a wide knowledge base when it came to style and technique. She also had a good eye for presentation.

"Where did you acquire your baking skills if you never attended culinary school?" Mel asked.

"I learned by doing," Holly said. "My grandmother, Mammie Cay, owned a bakery in Shellsburg, Iowa, population nine hundred and seventy-three."

"You worked for her?"

"Sort of. My dad ran out when I was a baby, so my mom

and I went to live with Mammie Cay. Mom worked in the bakery, and when I was old enough, I helped out after school and on weekends," Holly said.

"Sounds nice."

"I hated it."

Mel gave her a confused look as she watched Holly squeeze her pastry bag and make a perfect swirl of thick, delicious vanilla buttercream on the cupcake.

"I wanted to be a movie star," Holly said. "That's why I took off at seventeen. I bought a bus ticket to get me as far away from Iowa as possible. I made it as far as Vegas before I ran out of money. I figured it was close enough to Hollywood, and I figured I'd save my money and then I'd get to Los Angeles."

"Never got there, huh?"

"No," she said. "I got hired as a cigarette girl, then a dancer, I met Billy, who was dealing blackjack in the Blue Hawaiian, fell in love, got pregnant, got married, yes, in that order. Then Billy lost his job and I had to work more shows and longer hours to make up the income.

"I was never home and Billy was playing Mr. Mom. We were so unhappy, we separated. Then he went back to school and met Lisa."

"Sounds like it was rough," Mel said.

"It was, but I got Sydney out of it, and after a while when the glitz and glamour started to wear thin, I realized I missed the bakery," Holly said. "I longed for the comforting smell of breads, cookies, pies, and cake, mostly cake, and then I realized that was what I wanted to do with the rest of my life."

"Did you ever consider going back to Shellsburg?"

"No, my mom sold the bakery after Mammie Cay died and retired to Florida. It wouldn't have been the same," Holly said. "Besides, I can't take Sydney away from Billy. No matter what he and I went through, he's always been a great dad."

"How does he feel about you opening the bakery?"

"He hasn't said much, but I can tell he's relieved. With a new baby on the way, it'll be easier for them if I'm available to have Sydney at night. I don't think I slept a full night for the entire first year after Sydney arrived."

"Sydney did mention Lisa's condition," Mel said. "Is she excited to be a big sister?"

"She is," Holly said. "And maybe it's just wishful thinking on my part, but I think she's excited to get to spend more time with me. We've never really had that before. Lisa and Billy have been the ones to tuck her in most nights, they get to do family dinner and bath times, all of it."

"That has to be hard," Mel said. "How about Lisa's family? Does Sydney get to spend time with them?"

"No, her only grandparents are my mom and Billy's parents. I don't know the details but I know Lisa only has one brother that she's in touch with and he's been in and out of jail for a variety of misdeeds."

"When the baby comes, I'm sure she'll be happy to have you available to take care of Sydney," Mel said.

"That's assuming we actually manage to open a bakery." Holly sighed. She went from looking happy and excited to sad and anxious so fast that Mel got whiplash.

"We will," Mel said with far more confidence than she

felt. "I don't know what is going on or why all of these crazy things keep happening, but I am not giving up on opening this franchise and neither should you."

"Did you hear that, Angie?" Tate asked as he entered the room. "Mel has crossed over." Then he lowered his voice and added, " 'Impressive. Most impressive. Obi-Wan has taught you well. You have controlled your fear.' "

"*Empire Strikes Back*," Angie and Holly identified the movie quote at the same time and then exchanged a high five.

"See?" Tate asked. "She really is our people."

Manny popped into the kitchen, and Sydney handed over the seven pictures she had drawn for him. Manny took the time to appreciate each one, pointing out what he especially liked in each picture, even the portrait of him that made him look a bit like Sasquatch.

Sydney slid her hand into Manny's hand as if it were the most natural thing in the world, and he grinned down at her like a man completely beguiled by his little princess. He picked her up and swung her in the air to sit on the counter and Sydney squealed with delight.

"I don't want to go, Mommy," Sydney said. "I want to stay here with you and Manny."

"Oh, sweetheart, I would love that, but I have to work tonight," Holly said. "Besides, your dad will be here any minute to pick you up."

Sydney opened her mouth, looking about to protest, but Manny hunkered down and met her gaze.

"It's only fair," he said. "I need to practice my Go Fish skills so you don't thump me again tomorrow."

"She beat you?" Mel asked.

"Three games in a row," he said. "I'm pretty sure she's a hustler." He looked at Sydney and asked, "You are, aren't you?"

Sydney giggled. "No, you're just really bad at cards."

The rest of the grown-ups laughed at Manny's feigned chagrin. A knock at the door interrupted the moment and Manny excused himself to go answer it.

"That'll be your dad, say good-bye to our friends and we'll go meet him," Holly said. She lifted Sydney down from the counter.

"Good-bye," Sydney said. She grabbed Rupert, her panda bear, hugged each of them in turn, and followed her mom to the door.

"Cute kid," Angie said. She turned to look at Tate. "I think I want a couple of those."

"I don't know," he said. He shook his head, looking doubtful. "I think it takes a lot of practice to make one."

Angie giggled and Mel rolled her eyes.

"Back to the subject at hand," Mel said. "I've been doing some thinking."

"While napping in your lounger?" Angie asked.

Mel gave her a squinty eye. "Yeah, as if you two were doing anything more constructive while I was sleeping."

Tate and Angie exchanged a hot glance and Mel blew out a breath before turning to Tate. "I take it your melon is just fine?"

"Hard like a brick," he said. He knocked on his temple to prove it.

"I don't think what's happening is directed at us," Mel said.

Both Tate and Angie grew abruptly serious, and Angie asked, "What makes you say that?"

"If it were Tucci, we'd be dead," Mel said.

"I had the same thought," Tate said. "His people don't miss, not three times."

"So, if Holly is the target, we need to stick with her at all times, correct?" Mel asked.

"Have you talked to Manny?" Tate asked.

"Not yet," Mel said. "But I'm betting he's come to the same conclusion. I don't know how much the Las Vegas PD can help us, given that we have no idea who is doing this. We could try to convince Holly to go into hiding for a while."

"No," Holly said. She and Manny joined them in the kitchen. "Hiding is only a temporary solution. I need to find out who is doing this."

Mel noticed Manny giving Holly an admiring glance. She tried not to let it bug her.

"You three and Marty and Oz need to head back to Scottsdale," Manny said. "It's too dangerous for you to be here. If this person has gone over the edge, there's no telling what they'll do to anyone who gets in their way."

Tate reached up and rubbed the sore spot on his head. "Oh, I have a pretty good idea."

"I'm not leaving," Mel said. "The more of us to watch over you, the more likely we are to catch the person."

"No!" Holly argued. "If anything happened to any of you, I couldn't live with myself. Really, you have to go back where it's safe. Once this is over, we can try the franchise thing again."

Mel knew that running back to Scottsdale wasn't an option. Much like Holly felt about them, she knew she couldn't live with herself if anything happened to Holly.

"You know that's not going to happen, right?" she asked Manny. "Even if the Las Vegas PD help, how much can they do when we don't know who is behind this? You need us."

Manny ran a hand through his hair. He looked at Holly and said, "She's right."

"But—"

"No buts," Angie cut in. "This franchise thing, it's a 'one for all and all for one' sort of deal."

She put her hand out in front of Holly and Tate put his hand on top of hers. After some hesitation, Holly put her hand on top of theirs, followed by Manny and then Mel. The pact was made. There was no going back now.

"I do *not* see how this makes us blend," Mel said. "Everyone is going to be staring at us."

"No, they won't," Tate said. "If you're going to hang out backstage, then you need to look like one of the girls. Otherwise, you really will stick out."

"Close your eyes, I need to put your eye shadow on," Margie the makeup girl said while snapping her gum.

Mel was a little afraid of her so she did as she was told.

"This is so fun," Angie said. "You have to take pictures before you go. No one will ever believe this, me and Mel posing as backup showgirls."

"I will," Tate said. He was tricked out in a slick suit and looked every inch the wealthy mogul he used to be. Mel knew that if he had his way, they were all going to be disgustingly wealthy from franchising the bakery. Not for the first time, she wondered why she resisted his business smarts. Oh, yeah, it was her obsessive controlling nature.

Mel's eyelids itched and she reached up to rub them, but Margie smacked her hand away. "Don't touch, you'll smear."

"How much makeup remover is needed to take all of this off?" Mel asked.

"A lot," Margie said helpfully.

"And people do this voluntarily?" Mel asked.

"All the time," Margie said.

"Can I open my eyes now?" she asked.

"Yes, but don't touch your face."

Mel opened her eyes. The face staring back at her from the mirror was unrecognizable. She turned to look at Angie, who was in the chair beside her.

"Whoa."

"I know, right?" Angie asked.

They both looked like they'd been hit by a glitter bomb. Mel's eyelids wore a thick coating of silver with heavy eyeliner making her eyes huge to the point where she looked like an anime character. The eyes were balanced by her lips in a hot pink, and the blush on her cheeks was just as dazzling.

"And now for the finishing touch," Margie said. She held up a sparkly costume. "If you really want to blend, you need to be dressed."

"But isn't this someone else's outfit?" Mel asked.

"It's a backup," Margie said. "Just like your friend's outfit. If ever one of the girls suffers a wardrobe malfunction, we keep a few spares on hand."

Mel looked doubtfully at the sheer spangled number. "Do you have a shoehorn to help me into that thing?"

Margie grinned. "It stretches."

"And then it rips," Mel added.

Margie laughed and then she frowned. "It better not. Wardrobe will kill me."

"It won't rip," Holly said. She was sitting in front of her own mirror, finishing up her makeup. Gone was the fresh-faced cupcake baker from earlier. Now she was all eye-poppingly gorgeous with a side of va-va-va-voom. "Remember Belinda?"

"Oh, yeah, she was a big-boned girl," Margie said. "Real light on her feet, though."

"If the outfit didn't rip on her, it won't rip on you," Holly said. "Angie, you're on the petite side for a dancer, so if anyone comes around, make sure you're sitting down."

"That's the nice way of saying I'm too short," Angie said. "Isn't it?"

Holly cringed. "Did it work?"

"No." Angie frowned. "What's the minimum height requirement for a dancer?"

"The shortest is five foot eight," Margie said.

"So, you're all giantesses?" Angie asked.

"It's a leg thing," Margie said.

Angie didn't look comforted by this, and Tate patted her knee and said, "I think you have amazing legs."

"Well, it's a good thing we're not actually participating in the show," Angie said. "I wouldn't want my stubby legs to give us away."

"Your stubby legs, my complete lack of ability, yeah, it's a good thing we're benched," Mel said. She met Angie's gaze and they both grinned.

There was a knock on the door, and a voice called, "Five minutes to curtain, Holly."

Mel knew that voice. It was Fancy and she sounded very cross.

"I have to go inspect the others," Margie said. She grabbed her toolbox full of makeup and headed for the door. "Now remember, if you get busted, I know nothing." Then she glanced at Holly, her longtime friend, and said, "Be safe."

"I promise," Holly said.

"I'd better go," Tate said. "I have Marty and Oz holding a table in the front. We'll be sweeping the theater, making sure there is nothing strange going on. Manny is stationed backstage. He won't let anyone back there who doesn't belong, and he'll be keeping an eye on the ones who do."

"Thank you," Holly said. "I don't know what I'd do without all of you."

"No problem," Tate said. He turned to Angie. "You be careful. Keep your phone with you at all times. Remember you're here to snoop in Levi's dressing room and Fancy's office and the girls' big dressing room if you can manage it, but you are not to put yourselves in jeopardy. Am I clear?"

"Crystal," Angie said.

"Roger that," Mel said.

Tate planted a kiss on Angie and squeezed Mel's hand before he left to go upstairs.

When the door shut behind him, Angie sighed. "I'm going to marry him."

"When we get back to Arizona," Mel said. "Not here. Your parents would skin you alive and you know it."

"But eloping is so romantic," Angie protested. "We could go home as Mr. and Mrs. Tate Harper."

"It won't be romantic when your brothers string Tate up like a piñata and smack the candy out of him," Mel said. "And you know they will."

"How many brothers do you have?" Holly asked.

"Seven," Angie said. "Seven nosy, meddlesome, annoying, buttinsky older brothers, who I love like crazy. How's that for too much sibling?"

Holly smiled at her. "It sounds nice actually."

"Wait 'til you meet them," Angie said.

There was another knock on the door and a shout. "Two minutes!"

Holly jumped up from her seat and adjusted her feathered headpiece and sparkly outfit. "I'm off."

"Break a leg," Mel called as Holly hustled out of the room. She turned back to Angie. "It seems wrong to say that to a dancer."

Angie nodded. " 'Bust a move' would seem more appropriate. So, where do we want to start?"

"Levi won't leave his dressing room until he's about to go on, and Holly said that Fancy is backstage for the entire show every show, except for intermission when she comes back down with the girls," Mel said.

"Fancy's office it is," Angie said.

By mutual agreement, they waited a few minutes before peeking out. The hustle and bustle that had been happening before the curtain came up was over now, and the dressing area was almost eerie in its quiet.

Mel led the way out the door and into the main room. Fancy's office was situated by the stairs, no doubt enabling her to keep an eye on all the dancers as they came and went.

Mel tried the door. She hesitated for just a moment, hoping that Carlos had done what Holly had asked and unlocked it before he headed upstairs. The knob turned and Mel pushed the door open.

Angie gasped. The sight that met their eyes was incredible. It was a decent-sized office and it was covered from floor to ceiling and wall to wall with pictures of Fancy. Some were solo shots of her showgirl days, but most were Fancy in the later years with everyone from Sid Caesar to Katy Perry.

"Look, there's Fancy and Elvis," Angie said.

"And here's Fancy and POTUS," Mel said. "Looks like she gets around."

"Can you imagine meeting all these people?" Angie asked. "What a legacy."

"Yeah, it kind of makes you wonder if her sense of power is out of whack," Mel agreed.

She moved to the far wall, where there were pictures of Fancy with all the headliners and the troops of dancers. Mel saw Holly right away. With a burst of pink feathers coming out of her head, Holly looked like an exotic bird. The two women wore matching grins, and Mel had a feeling this must have been taken when Holly became the lead in the show.

"They sure look happy," Angie said. "I can't really picture Fancy trying to hurt Holly."

"If she feels betrayed because Holly's leaving, who knows what she might do," Mel said. "It makes sense that she would stop us from finding a bakery just to keep Holly in the show."

"Come on, you've seen Fancy," Angie said. "She may be fit for her age, but I don't see her driving a car through the front of a bakery."

"No, but she looks like she's pretty well connected," Mel said. "It can't have been too hard for her to find someone to do it for her."

"All right," Angie said. "Let's find the proof."

Together they searched the office; while Angie checked every drawer, every file, and every shelf, Mel took a look at Fancy's computer. It was turned on and she had left her e-mail open. Hurrah! It seemed to Mel if she was hiring people to explode bakeries, there'd be some sort of trail.

Angie finished the room and checked the time on her phone. "Find anything?"

"No," Mel said. "It's almost time for Levi to go on. We can't lose our opportunity to check his dressing room."

"I'll go on ahead," Angie said. "Meet me there when you're done here."

"Okay, but be careful," Mel said.

Angie slipped out of the office and Mel felt her nerves ratchet up. She shouldn't be in here doing this, but how else were they going to find out who had it in for Holly's bakery? She knew Tate would be unhappy that they had split up, but what choice did they have?

Fancy was one of those people who never deleted an e-mail. As she scrolled through, Mel looked at the in-box and there were over ten thousand e-mails. She had to suppress the urge to bang her head on the desk.

"I am never going to slog through this, never," she muttered. She glanced at the time in the corner of the screen. Nerves made her jog her foot up and down. Suddenly, she was overly aware of her makeup and it felt greasy on her skin.

She decided to stick to the days when there had been incidents. That narrowed it down by a few thousand. She read the subject lines, hoping the words *crash*, *bomb*, *shooting*, or the like would give her a clue. There was nothing.

She glanced at the clock again. Time was running out. Fancy and the others would be down here for the intermission at any moment. Damn it.

She pushed back from the desk, planning to slip out of the room when she saw the words *contingency plan* in a subject line. It was a reply in Fancy's e-mail from a person with the handle *stuntryder*.

Mel's eyes bugged. This had to be the driver. This was her proof. She had to see the e-mail. She glanced at the clock again. She was out of time. She could hear the chatter and laughter of the girls as they passed by the office.

What to do? What to do? Impulsively she forwarded the e-mail to her own e-mail account. Then she opened the sent mail folder and deleted what she had forwarded. That should do it.

"What the hell are you doing in my office?"

Twenty

"Yikes!" Mel jumped. "You scared me."

"I'm going to do a lot more than that if you don't tell me what you're doing in my office, which was locked, right now."

Fancy crossed her arms over her chest. She looked pretty confident that she could kick Mel's behind, which was disturbing because Mel was pretty sure she could, too.

"You know, the door was open," Mel said. "And when I was walking by, I saw this person come running out of here and I thought that was weird, so I just popped in here to make sure everything was okay."

She stood as she spoke. She glanced from side to side as if reassuring herself that all was well. Then she looked at Fancy and said, "You're welcome."

"You're new, aren't you?" Fancy asked.

"Very," Mel said.

"I don't remember hir—"

"Fancy, come quick! Tisha twisted her ankle," one of the dancers cried as she stuck her head around the door frame.

"What? How?" Fancy forgot all about Mel and moved toward the door.

"Coming down the stairs. She's at her dressing table, but it doesn't look good," the dancer said. "It's already swelling."

Fancy turned around and glared at Mel. "Okay, new girl, get suited up for the opening number after intermission. You're taking Tisha's place."

"What?" Mel gaped. "No, I—"

"Go see Denise in wardrobe," Fancy said. When Mel didn't move fast enough, she barked, "Now!"

Mel hurried out of the office. This was not possible. She couldn't do this. She couldn't even fake it. If she tried to high kick, she'd likely throw her back out.

She passed Levi's dressing room on her way to wardrobe. Angie was just slipping out.

"Find anything?" Mel asked.

"No." Angie shook her head. "Unless you count the world's largest collection of indigestion medication. Poor Levi must be the most nervous person in show business."

"Yeah, I sort of got that off of him," Mel said. "Doesn't matter because I found a name in Fancy's e-mail and I think it might be who we're looking for."

"What did the e-mail say?"

"I don't know. I didn't get a chance to read it because

Fancy caught me in there," Mel said. "But the handle was *stuntryder.*"

"No way. We have to tell Manny," Angie said.

"Yeah, I would but I can't," Mel said. "One of the dancers twisted her ankle and I'm supposed to step in for her. I'm supposed to be in wardrobe right now."

"Well, what are you doing here?" Angie asked. "Go!"

"What? No, I thought we'd sneak out the back," Mel said.

"In this?" Angie pointed to their sparkly outfits. "Really?"

"Well, no, I figured we'd change first," Mel said.

"We have five pounds of makeup on," Angie said. "We'll be seen as showgirls or hookers; either way I don't see us getting out of here unnoticed."

"I can't do this," Mel said. "I've never been onstage in my life."

"Just do what the others do," Angie said. "You'll be fine."

"You had dance lessons as a kid, you go," Mel said.

"No can do, too short," Angie said. This time she didn't look bitter so much as relieved.

"This is a nightmare," Mel said.

"Come on, let's get you to wardrobe before Fancy has a cow and our real identities are discovered," Angie said.

Mel let Angie drag her out of Levi's dressing room and down the hall toward the main room shared by the rest of the girls. It looked like a typhoon of shimmer and feathers as the dancers peeled off one outfit and slid into another.

Angie maneuvered her way through the room without breaking her stride but Mel was feeling very self-conscious. She was going to have to change in front of these women. Suddenly every ounce of extra weight she was carrying seemed like a sack of flour. She turned to bolt out of the room but a hand clamped on her wrist, holding her in place.

"Where are you going?" Fancy asked.

"Bathroom?"

"No time," Fancy said. "Denise is waiting for you. Let's go."

Mel felt the walls closing in. Now might be her only chance, so she asked, "Who's *stuntryder*?"

"What?" Fancy asked.

"You heard me." Mel tried to look fierce.

"It's a poodle that rides a tricycle," Fancy said. "They're auditioning for the show. Why? Do you know them?"

Nuts! Mel bit her knuckle. She seriously doubted Fancy could have made that up on the spot.

"Fancy! Fancy, wait!" A dancer came running up to them. She was holding her enormous purple headdress on with one hand while she ran. "Sunny just went to check on Holly and she can't find her anywhere. She says she's missing."

Fancy dropped Mel's arm. "What?"

"Missing! Holly is missing!"

"She should be in her dressing room—why wouldn't she be there?"

"I don't know." The dancer shrugged.

"But she's never missed a curtain, not ever." Fancy looked around her as if expecting Holly to appear out of thin air.

Mel glanced at Angie. Judging by the round-eyed gaze Angie sent her, her panic was confirmed. Mel had tucked her phone into the padded front of her outfit. She pulled it out now, planning to call Manny and see if Holly was with him. Maybe she had already gone back upstage.

They were three stories belowground in concrete. Mel couldn't get a signal on her phone. She looked at Angie, who was doing the same thing.

"Nothing," Angie said. "I'm going upstairs to find Tate."

"Right behind you," Mel said.

"You can't," Fancy cried. "The show!"

"Is screwed if we don't find Holly," Mel said. "If I were you, I'd get her understudy up to speed then worry about your backup dancers."

She didn't wait for an answer but hurried from the dressing room, following Angie as she plowed through bodies to get to the door. They passed Holly's dressing room. Sunny was in there, looking confused, while one of the costume people helped her into Holly's headpiece.

"This just doesn't feel right," Sunny was saying. "I need to go look for Holly."

"We'll do it," Mel said. "When was the last time you saw her?"

"She was right behind me on the stairs when we came down," Sunny said. "I went to the dressing area and then doubled back to go upstairs with her but she wasn't in here and she should have already been dressed and ready to go."

"Anyone check the bathroom?" Angie asked.

"Twice," the costume person said.

"Okay, let's go," Angie said.

They dashed through the changing area to the stairs. Mel felt like cursing all the way up, but she couldn't afford the breath. The stairs were well lit and there was no sign of anything amiss, no explosion of feathers or rhinestones to indicate a struggle. They got to the top of the steps and Mel was doubled over and wheezing.

"You all right?" Angie panted.

Mel nodded and waved her hand for Angie to continue. Angie pushed through the metal door and they stepped into the darkness. They could hear the crowd laughing as Levi paced the stage, shooting out his rapid-fire jokes like they were a barrage of bullets.

Mel blinked, trying to get her eyes to adjust. She knew Manny had planned to stay backstage to keep an eye on everything so she assumed he would be near the door to downstairs.

"Manny!" she whispered. "Are you here?"

There was no answer.

"I'm going to slip out into the audience to find Tate," Angie said. "Come with me."

"No, I need to find Manny," Mel said. She glanced at her phone. Now she had a signal. "I'll call you if I get in a jam."

Angie's face was barely visible in the dark but Mel knew her best friend well enough to see the crinkle of unhappiness in her forehead. She didn't like this plan. Mel didn't, either, but Manny really was their best shot for finding Holly since he was probably the last one to see her before she went downstairs.

"All right, but if I don't hear from you in ten minutes, I'm coming back here with all of the boys."

Mel nodded. She squeezed Angie's arm before turning and walking into the deep darkness of backstage. Like any backstage, there was a shabbiness that came with overuse. The props that looked so glittery from the audience were distressed when seen up close.

Mel stepped over a coil of rope, walked around a stand of lights, and moved even deeper into the backstage. She couldn't hear what Levi was saying but she could hear the laughs from the crowd. She knew she still had some time. She just hoped that Holly did, too.

"Manny!" she hissed.

A man wearing a headset hushed her and Mel jumped. She looked closely at him. Did he look like a stalker in disguise or the real deal? He spoke into the mouthpiece attached to the headset and she assumed he was real or a very good actor.

Where was Manny? He was supposed to be here, guarding the backstage from anyone suspicious like, say, a cupcake baker who couldn't dance for beans but was decked out in showgirl attire. If Mel had made it this far, then who else might have and where the hell was Manny?

Her stomach began to churn. She inched forward in the darkness hidden behind the backdrop from the crowd. The noise from up front, even the laughter, was muffled. Surely, Manny wouldn't have stayed this far back. How could he see anything from back here?

Mel turned to go back toward the front of the stage. She held her hands out in front of her to help guide her in the darkness. It was strange to walk around when she could barely see the dim outlines of sets and equipment around her. It was like walking through nothingness and she felt as if she might step off an unseen ledge into a vast emptiness.

Instead she kicked something soft. She thought it might be a costume or a prop. She reached down to see if she could move it. Her fingertips brushed something warm. She held her hand still and it took her a moment to register that it was skin. She bit off a scream before it could escape her lips. Her heart hammered hard and she knew without even looking more closely that the arm she was touching was Manny's. On the upside, his skin was warm and not cold so that had to be good.

"Manny," she called as she crouched and ran her hands down his chest. It was then that she felt the ropes looped around his middle, binding him to a stone pillar. Oh, no. Someone had done this to him. Someone bad.

He didn't respond and she noticed his head was hanging forward. He was unconscious. Mel tried to rouse him to no avail. She patted his cheeks and then ran her hand over his head. There was a knot the size of a golf ball on the back of his head that she was sure was going to give him a powerful headache when he woke up.

Mel began to fumble with the ropes, but she couldn't get them loose. Whoever tied him had been efficient. She needed help. She took out her phone and sent a text to Angie letting her know where she was and that she needed help ASAP.

Mel continued to work the knots with little success, but

in less than a minute, two Elvis wannabes, Tate, and Angie arrived.

"What happened?" Tate demanded.

"I don't know," Mel said. "I found him like this. He got clocked on the head and tied up but I haven't been able to rouse him to find out if he saw Holly or not."

What Mel didn't add was that she had no doubt that wherever Holly was, she was in grave danger.

Twenty-one

Angie's nimble fingers untied the last of the rope and Manny sagged forward. Mel caught him, staggered under his weight, and then Oz and Tate were lifting him off her. Together they draped his arms over their shoulders and they began to drag-carry him across the dark stage.

"He needs to have his head examined," Mel said.

"Not the first time someone has said that, I'll wager," Marty said.

"Focus, people," Tate said. He was breathing heavily as he and Oz maneuvered Manny through the dark. "We have a man down and Holly is missing."

"Take Manny out front," Mel said. "Carlos can call an ambulance. The rest of us should look for Holly."

"No!" Tate argued. "Whoever did this will not hesitate to hurt any of you. We stay together."

"We can't cover the same amount of ground if we stay together," Mel argued. "If we don't find Holly quickly, it could be dire."

They were near the side door to the stage and Mel could see Tate's face illuminated in the glow of the stage lights. He was straining under Manny's weight but he also looked like he was wrestling with himself over the situation.

"We'll be careful," Angie said. "We'll leave our phones open with a live call so we can hear whatever is happening if anyone finds anything."

"Mel." The voice was slurred but Mel recognized Manny's low growl immediately.

"Manny, are you all right? What happened? Where's Holly?"

His head was weaving and he looked like he was trying to raise his face up but his muscles were having none of it.

"Saw her leave the stage and went to follow, but I . . ." His voice trailed off as he fuzzed out.

"Manny, speak, what happened?" Mel demanded. She moved so she was standing right in front of him. She cupped his face so that he could see her eyes.

"Got jumped," he said. He gave her a wan smile and his eyes rolled back into his head right before he went limp.

"Get him out front for ambulance pickup right away," Mel said. "If he saw Holly go down the stairs, then she must have gotten snatched on the stairs or below. Let's go check it out."

"Use your phones," Tate ordered. His gaze pierced Angie and he added, "Be careful. Marty, go with the girls. I'll be down as soon as I can."

Neither Mel nor Angie felt the need to let him know that their phones didn't work downstairs. They bolted for the door to the stairs just as Tate and Oz disappeared into the theater, hauling Manny as they went.

They wound down one set of stairs before Marty started puffing. "How many levels are down here?"

"Three," Mel said. She paused on the landing to catch her breath but also to be sure that they hadn't missed anything. She did a quick scan of the wall to make sure there were no secret openings or hidden passages.

"What knucklehead thought having the dressing room three floors below was a good idea?" Marty said.

"Try doing it with a thirty-pound headdress," Mel said. "I can't believe Holly has lasted as long as she has with this show."

"She must be very fit," Angie said. "Which may be the only thing that saves her now."

With that grim pronouncement, the three of them picked up the pace and wound their way down the remaining stairs.

"Where do we start?" Angie asked. "Her dressing room and the bathroom have been checked."

"Let's look for a back exit," Mel said. "Maybe there is another way out of here and whoever snatched her took that route. We have to ask Fancy."

"She isn't going to tell us jack," Angie said.

"No, but I'm betting she sings like a bird for Elvis," Mel said.

They both turned to look at Marty. His Elvis wig was askew, he had sweat stains in the armpits of his white jumpsuit, and his aviator glasses with the gold rims hung off the end of his nose as if the earpieces couldn't latch on to his head quite right.

"What? Fancy who? What are you two cooking up?"

"You know that suave magic you use on the ladies at the bakery?" Mel asked. "Yeah, we're going to need a little bit of that right now."

"Whoa, whoa, whoa, that's like my superpower," he said. "You can't just expect me to flip it on for any old gal that comes along. It could have catastrophic consequences."

"Fancy has worked here since she was a showgirl fifty-plus years ago. If anyone knows the layout, it's her," Mel said. "Now get in there and find out what she knows."

Angie opened the door to Fancy's office, saw Fancy pacing back and forth with her desk phone at her ear, and Mel gave Marty a solid shove into the room. Angie shut the door and they pressed their ears up against the gaps in the door frame hoping to hear what was said.

As the girls hurried past them to finish the show, it was impossible to hear what was being said over the clack of shoes, the rustle of feathers, and the whisper of voices. Mel caught snippets of the conversation, and it sounded as if the theories regarding Holly's disappearance ranged from she ran away in a romantic elopement, she was abducted by a crazed stalker, and Mel's favorite, she was snatched by an alien who was disguised as a human.

Of the three, Mel gave the last one the biggest props for creativity, but she also hoped it was the least likely since she barely knew how to deal with human beings, never mind aliens from outer space.

"He's taking an awful long time in there," Angie whispered.

"Maybe his charm is working," Mel said.

"Or maybe he forgot why he is in there?" Angie countered.

A crash sounded from the office. Mel and Angie looked at each other in alarm.

"What do we do?" Angie asked.

"I don't know, maybe one of them just tripped?" Mel said. Her voice went up on the end, as if she were asking a question instead of offering a hypothesis.

"Tripped over what?" Angie asked. "The wall?"

"I don't know."

There was a grunt and the sound of fabric shredding. Mel strained to hear more and she was pretty sure she picked up the sound of a whimper.

"We have to go in," she said.

"Are you sure?" Angie asked. "We could just walk away and pretend we were never here."

There was another crash.

"I'm going in," Mel said.

"All right, all right," Angie said.

Mel shoved the door open. She opened her mouth to talk but the sight before her rendered her too stupid to speak.

"Oh, jeez," Angie said and clapped a hand over her eyes. "Marty, zip up your jumpsuit and let's go. You can swap spit later."

Mel didn't think that was going to be as easy as Angie thought since Marty was pinned to the top of Fancy's desk while she stretched out on top of him, holding him in place while she planted a lip-lock on him that looked like she was trying to suck all the oxygen out of his lungs.

"Marty!" Mel called. She tried to look away, but really, what was the point? She could never unsee this.

Marty ripped his lips from Fancy's. He was breathing heavy, adding credence to the whole stealing breath theory Mel had going.

He'd lost his glasses and his gaze met Mel's when he rasped, "There is another exit. At the back of the main dressing room, there's a door that leads up to the parking garage."

"Oh, no!" Angie cried. "If they took her through it, they could be long gone."

"We have to go!" Mel said to Marty.

"Go! I'll call the police," he said and waved them away while bracing his forearm against Fancy to keep her at bay.

Mel felt a pang of guilt for leaving him but he was reaching for the phone on Fancy's desk, and she knew now that he'd broken out of her lip-lock, he'd be able to fight her off.

Angie and Mel broke into a run, charging through the dressing room to the back wall. The room was lined with shelves that housed the elaborate headdresses with racks below holding the matching costumes. If the door was on the back wall, it had to be behind the costumes.

Angie dove into a section of red spangles while Mel cut through the black feathers. They pushed through the outfits until they found the wall. It was dark behind the clothes and Mel had to feel along the concrete for a door.

"Found it!" Angie cried.

Mel hurried to her side. It was a standard door and Mel hoped against hope that it wasn't locked. Angie grabbed the knob and turned. With a squeak and a squeal, the door opened into another stairwell.

It smelled dank and dirty. Mel felt along the wall for a light switch. The concrete was rough and cold against her fingers.

"I don't like this," Angie said. She took her phone out of the front of her outfit and turned on the flashlight app. She shone it on the wall where Mel stood, and sure enough, there was the light switch just beyond Mel's fingertips. She flipped it on and the entire stairwell lit up.

They took a second to get their bearings. It was just like the other stairwell. Stairs wound up from the floor in a squared spiral of cold concrete.

Mel blew out a breath. She really, really hated stairs. Not for the first time, she promised herself that when she got home, she would eat less of her product and work out more—more, of course, meaning at all.

The clang of a metal door slamming shut echoed from above, breaking the silence and making both Mel and Angie jump. They glanced at each other with the same realization. Someone had just exited the building and it wasn't Elvis.

Twenty-two

"I'm going to run up to the top," Angie said. "Maybe I can catch them."

"Yell if there's trouble," Mel said. "I'm right behind you."

Mel knew she couldn't keep up with Angie, and she didn't want to hold her back if she could catch up to Holly's kidnapper. It was a long shot, but they had to try.

Angie gave her a quick squeeze and took off running. Mel followed, trying to keep up but falling behind Angie's rabbit sprint up the stairs.

Mel was only on the second level when she heard the door above bang open. She moved more quickly but a cramp doubled her over and she paused to suck in a big breath before racing after her friend.

A sparkle at the foot of the stairs caught her eyes. It

could have been from Angie's costume, except Angie was in red and this was definitely blue. Mel's outfit was silver so it wasn't hers, but it wasn't Holly's either since she had been in black. Mel frowned. Maybe some of the girls used these stairs to get to their cars in the garage after the show. Maybe it was just coincidence except just to the right was a crawl space with a metal grate over it.

She leaned closer to examine it. The screws weren't flush with the grate as if someone hadn't put them in all the way, someone who might have been in a hurry. Sadly, her phone didn't have an app for a Phillips screwdriver, so she was forced to make do with her thumbnail. A couple of twists and she had the already loose screw free. She quickly unfastened the next one.

"I lost them," Angie said as she came down the stairs toward Mel. She was winded and her face was bright red and sweaty.

"It's okay," Mel said. "Give me a hand?"

"What are you doing?"

"Following a hunch," Mel said.

Angie frowned at her but set to work on a screw using her thumbnail while Mel finished the last one. They used their fingers to grasp the grate and together they hoisted it off the wall. It was dark in the opening and Angie reached for her phone.

Mel couldn't wait. She reached into the black space, praying there were no spiders or rats inside. Her fingers brushed something feathery just as Angie's light snapped on behind her. It was the same black feathers as Holly's costume. Mel twitched the fabric aside and revealed a foot.

"Oh my god! It's her!" Angie cried. She dropped her phone and together they reached inside to haul Holly out.

Her feathered costume made it hard to grab her and Mel was worried that if she was injured, they could be causing more harm.

"Wait," she said. "I'm going to climb in and see if she's okay. If we yank her out while she's injured, we could hurt her."

"Okay," Angie said. Mel noted her hands were shaking when she picked her phone up and flipped on the flashlight app. "Take this with you so you can see."

Mel aimed the light into the darkness. She pushed aside Holly's legs and crawled into the small space. There was barely any room to maneuver.

She reached Holly's wrist and felt for a pulse. It took her a frantic second to find it, but when she did, it was strong. She then checked the rise and fall of her chest. The feathers rippled on each exhale.

"She's alive," Mel called.

"Thank god," Angie said.

"I'm going to try and rouse her," Mel said. She leaned back over Holly, trying to get up to her face. She felt like she was practically lying on top of her and she worried that if her arm gave out, she was going to crush her. "Holly, wake up! Come on, Holly, I need you to open your eyes."

A grunt sounded from Holly's lips and Mel was encouraged.

"You can do it, think about Sydney," Mel said. "Sydney needs her mom."

Holly lifted one arm as if to push away the sound that was interrupting her unconscious state.

"Yeah, I'm not going away," Mel said. "But I might fall on you, so you really want to wake up."

She said the last two words extra loud and Holly responded by grunting and swearing.

"What the—" Holly's voice trailed off as her eyes opened. Then she screamed.

Mel had no time to move as Holly began to thrash and fight. Mel took a knee to her rib cage, and with an *oomph*, she went down, making Holly panic and fight even harder.

"Holly! Stop! Holly, it's us!" Angie shouted as she grabbed Holly's legs so Mel could get out without taking a foot to the face.

Mel wriggled out of the crawl space and together she and Angie helped Holly climb out. She was blinking against the light and her lower lip wobbled as if she was about to cry.

Mel didn't hesitate. She hugged Holly close, giving her warmth and comfort. Angie did the same, and the three of them sat huddled for several long minutes.

"You're okay now," Mel said. "You're safe."

A sob was Holly's only response and then another and another. Angie and Mel gazed at each other over Holly's head. Angie jerked her head in the direction of the stairs and Mel knew that she was saying that they needed to get out of here since they had no idea who had done this, where he was, or if he was coming back.

"Holly, we need to get out of here," Mel said. "It isn't safe."

Holly's blue eyes were wide and full of tears. Mel felt bad about making her move before she had it together but it was too dangerous to sit here. Holly caught on immediately. She nodded and Mel and Angie helped her to her feet. Together the three of them made their way downstairs.

Before they reached the bottom of the steps, the door banged open and Mel saw Marty run in with Carlos on his heels. When Holly saw them, she paled and began to shake.

She raised her arm and pointed. "You! You did this to me."

Mel and Angie looked at Carlos and Marty. Carlos? Was he involved?

Before Mel could register what was happening, Holly launched herself down the steps right at Marty. She had her fingernails extended like a wildcat. Marty saw her coming, let out a yelp, and ducked behind Carlos.

Carlos caught Holly around the middle and said, "Holly, stop, this guy is like a hundred years old. I don't think he's your man."

Holly was trying to pull out of Carlos's hold but the man was built solid like a mighty oak. She'd have had better luck if she'd been wielding an axe.

"But it was him!" Holly insisted. "It was Elvis."

"Someone dressed like Elvis grabbed you," Mel stated for clarity even though she knew the answer was yes.

"Crap!" Angie said. "There are like what, three thousand Elvises running around Vegas right now?"

"Come on, we need to talk to the police," Carlos said.

He looked at Mel. "They're already talking to your friend with the head injury."

"Manny," Mel said. "He was supposed to go to the hospital."

"He refused," Carlos said. "He was determined to find Holly first. He's making a righteous stink up there."

"Manny was hurt?" Holly asked. "Take me to him."

Carlos led the way upstairs—Mel really, really, really hated stairs now—to the theater's front office. Inside, Manny was talking to a Las Vegas detective. He was holding an ice pack on his head and the worry lines on his forehead were deeper than usual. When Holly stepped into the room, he dropped his ice bag and half rose from his seat.

"Holly, you're all right," he said. He opened his arms and she stepped into them as naturally as if they'd known each other for months instead of hours. "I've been frantic. I sent Tate and Oz out to look for you."

"I'll call them," Angie said and she backed out of the room.

The detective rose. He glanced at Holly. "I'm Detective Barnes with the Las Vegas PD. You look a bit banged up, miss. Can I ask what happened?"

Holly nodded and explained that she was the last to leave the stage area after the first half of the show as she was the one who introduced Levi Cartwright for his part of the show. As soon as Levi took the stage, she headed down the stairs. She glanced at Manny.

"I was surprised you weren't there, but then I thought maybe you had found something out," she said.

"No, I was tied up, literally," Manny said. His tone was wry and Holly gave him a weak smile as she continued.

"I started down the stairs. Even though it's intermission, this is my biggest costume change so I try to give myself plenty of time. I entered my dressing room and then this Elvis person showed up . . ."

"Excuse me?" The detective gave Marty the hairy eyeball and Marty immediately held his hands up in the universal gesture for surrender.

"It wasn't me," Marty said. "I was in the audience all evening."

"He was," Manny said. "I can vouch for him."

Barnes turned back to Holly and asked, "Then what happened?"

"I told him he was in the wrong place and then *wham!* He clocked me in the back of the head and everything went black."

"The same thing happened to me," Manny said. "But when I woke up, I was tied up."

"I was shoved into an air duct," Holly said. "Luckily, Mel and Angie found me before the person who grabbed me came back."

Detective Barnes frowned. "I'll want to see that area."

"Of course," Holly said with a shiver.

Barnes looked at Mel. "What made you look there?"

Mel explained that they had figured that there had to be another exit since no one had seen Holly at all. She mentioned that Fancy had told them about the alternate exit. She did not explain how she found it and noted that Marty looked vastly relieved.

"She's lucky you're so sharp," Detective Barnes said.

"Thanks," Mel said.

The detective was silver haired, with a kind face and a nice manner. She was glad he was the one who would be working with Holly on this. The poor girl was rattled enough as it was.

He turned back to Holly and asked, "Did you notice anything different about the person who did this to you?"

She sighed. "I thought the Elvis outfit made him different but apparently not."

"I'm not following," Barnes said.

"There's an Elvis impersonator convention going on," Marty said. "There are thousands of us."

"Oh," Barnes drew out the word as if it helped him absorb how complicated the problem was. "I don't suppose there was anything distinct about this Elvis?"

Holly shook her head. "It was like he was in uniform." She gestured at Marty. "Same black wig, sunglasses, and sparkly white jumpsuit."

Again Barnes looked at Marty, who put his hands on his chest in a gesture of outraged hurt.

"Marty was the one who helped us find Holly," Mel said. "We couldn't have found her without him."

Barnes frowned. "Perhaps that's because he knew where he'd stuffed her body."

"No!" Mel protested. "Trust me, he sacrificed himself to get the information."

"Really?" Barnes asked. He crossed his arms over his chest and glared at Marty. "Explain."

"Aw, man." Marty's face was so red, he looked like he

was being roasted alive. He scuffed the toe of his white boot on the floor. "If you must know, I romanced the location of the back entrance out of Fancy Leroux."

"When you say 'romanced' . . ." Barnes asked.

Marty glared and Barnes had the smarts not to press it.

Manny choked back a laugh and then winced as his head clearly hurt.

"It's true," Mel said. "We sent him into her office to get the intel out of Fancy and then we heard, well, she had him, oh, boy. Please believe me when I say he went above and beyond the call of duty."

Barnes looked like he was trying not to laugh, too. "All right, I'm going to talk to Ms. Leroux. Please wait here as I'm sure I'll have more questions."

The door shut behind him and Holly looked at Marty. "I think I owe you an apology and a thank-you."

She stepped forward and kissed his cheek. If anything, Marty looked even more embarrassed, especially as the door opened and Oz walked in with Tate and Angie behind him.

"Hoo, dang, Marty was right!" Oz exclaimed. "These Elvis duds really are chick magnet material."

Twenty-three

Detective Barnes was gone for a long time. While Angie took him and Tate back to the place where Holly had been held, Mel and Manny kept Holly company in the front office.

Oz and Marty decided to infiltrate the ranks of the other Elvi to see if anyone mentioned abducting a showgirl that evening. It was a long shot, but they both felt that lingering around Holly in their outfits was going to make her have abduction flashbacks.

While they waited, the door to the office became a revolving door of theater people. The word about what had happened to Holly had trickled out and they all came to see how their star was faring.

The first was Sunny. She was still in her costume and makeup, and when she saw Holly, she hugged her in the closest thing Mel had seen to a choke hold outside of a wrestling ring.

"Holly, are you all right? We were so worried. Then Fancy made me take your place and I was sure I wasn't ready," Sunny gushed. "But she said the show needed me and Levi needed me and that I had no choice. I was so scared, my knees were knocking, actually knocking, but then I got up there and I did it."

"That's wonderful, Sunny." Holly patted her friend's back as if looking for the quick-release button. "Okay, can't breathe."

"Sorry, I'm so sorry." Sunny let her go. "I'm just so excited and so scared for you. Honestly, I'm a mess!"

"Don't be. I'm fine. Now, didn't I tell you that you could do it?" Holly said. "You just needed a chance."

Sunny's eyes moved over Holly's face. Then she looked sad. "Oh, no, you didn't."

"Didn't what?" Holly asked.

"You didn't rig all of this so I'd have to step up," Sunny said.

"Really?" Holly asked. "You want to know if I knocked out a detective and tied him up and then stuffed myself into an air duct to see if I could get you to take my place for the second half of the show."

"Well, when you say it like that, it sounds . . ."

"Crazy?" Holly asked.

"Well, yeah," Sunny said.

"No, I didn't set this up," Holly said. Her voice cracked and she cleared her throat. "Manny and I were attacked and we don't know by who. You didn't see anything strange backstage, like an Elvis roaming around, did you?"

Sunny's forehead crinkled in thought. "Not before intermission, and afterward, I was so freaked out . . . I'm sorry."

"It's okay, but if you think of anything, let me know, okay?" Holly said.

"I will tell you right away," Sunny said.

"Knock knock," Levi said before he entered the office. His face was sweaty from his time on the stage, but he also looked flushed with exhilaration. "Holly, did you see? Sunny took your place and it was . . . she did . . . it was okay."

"Are you kidding?" Sunny interrupted. "It was better than okay. You had the audience in the palm of your hand the whole time. I've never heard people laugh so much."

Levi puffed up with the praise, and Mel forced herself not to roll her eyes. It was official. Levi Cartwright was the biggest, most narcissistic jackass who ever drew breath.

"I'm really glad the show went so well," Holly said.

"So, what happened to you?" Levi asked. "Did you get sick? Is Sydney okay?"

All right, he did ask about her daughter. Mel thawed a little bit toward him.

"Actually, I was attacked," Holly said.

"What?" Fancy Leroux pushed into the room with Detective Barnes right behind her. "What are you talking about? The detective said you were abducted, but I thought he was just being dramatic. I thought you were ditching."

Mel saw Barnes run a hand down his face as if he was trying to rein in his patience. When he removed his hand, he nodded at Holly, letting her know it was okay to tell the others what had happened. Mel suspected he wanted to watch their reactions to the story.

He stood by the door with his arms crossed over his chest while Holly brought everyone up to speed. There were gasps and cries of disbelief, but when Holly was done, the biggest surprise was that Fancy, Levi, and Sunny all moved forward as one and enveloped her in a huge hug.

"You poor, poor thing," Fancy said.

"Just let me get my hands on whoever did this to you," Levi said. "I know how to throw a pretty decent haymaker. I'll lay them out."

"Much as I appreciate that," Barnes said, "what would really help is if anyone saw anyone backstage who didn't belong. Anyone wandering around, looking lost or anything like that?"

They all shook their heads.

"We could check the security cameras for the theater," Fancy said. "They don't cover the backstage area since we do costume changes back there but they would show if anyone came backstage who shouldn't have been there."

"Do you think either of you would be able to identify your assailant?" Barnes asked.

"I would," Holly said. "My Elvis wannabe lost his glasses for a moment right before he knocked me out, and I saw he had crazy eyes. I'll bet I could pick him out in a sea of Elvises."

Manny put his hand on the back of his neck. He looked

chagrined when he said, "I wish I could. He clipped me from behind. I never even saw him coming."

Mel knew that admission cost him. Holly seemed to sense it, too, and she squeezed his arm in reassurance.

"Elvis?" Fancy asked. "An Elvis did this to you?"

"Don't worry," Mel said. She knew exactly what Fancy was thinking. "Your Elvis wasn't the one. He doesn't have crazy eyes."

Fancy looked at Mel from under her eyelashes in a coquettish look that might have been ridiculous if she weren't so earnest. "Are you sure about that?"

"Quite," Mel said. She didn't think she imagined that Fancy looked a little disappointed by that.

Two crime scene officers arrived and Detective Barnes dismissed everyone while he and his people went back to the stairwell to see if they could bring up any fingerprints or other evidence.

He cautioned them to be careful and to be in touch if they had any cause for concern. He pulled Manny aside and the two of them had a whispered conversation that Mel was dying to eavesdrop on, but she didn't. She figured she'd muscle the information out of him later.

Angie had stayed downstairs to change after showing Barnes the stairwell and then she and Tate headed over to the all-you-can-eat buffet. For once in her life, Mel wasn't hungry, not in the least.

As soon as Holly and Mel had changed into their street clothes, Manny hustled them back to their suite at the top of the Blue Hawaiian. He was in full protective cop mode so Mel let him do his scanning-the-lobby thing while looking considerably forbidding without badgering him with questions.

When they got into their elevator, he flashed his badge at a group of tourists and refused to let them get on. One guy with his Hawaiian shirt unbuttoned to his navel and sporting a carpet of chest hair not seen since the heyday of shag looked like he was going to balk, but Manny quirked an eyebrow at him and he stepped back, feigning interest in his reflection in a nearby mirror.

"Thanks," Holly said. "I think that guy's cologne would have knocked me out for the second time tonight."

Manny gave her a look of such intensity that Mel suddenly felt like an intruder into whatever was happening between the two of them. She glanced away and then back. She couldn't resist the impulse to see what unfolded.

"You are an incredibly brave woman," Manny said to Holly. "A lesser gal would have been reduced to hysterics by what happened to you."

Holly stared back at him as if her world had shrunk to encompass just the two of them. She whispered, "Thank you." As if the tension between them was just too much, she added, "I'd feel better about the praise if I hadn't been taken out by a crazy Elvis. I mean if I had to get abducted, why couldn't it have been a young, hot Elvis, instead of a short, kangaroo-bellied Elvis?"

"Tell me about it," Manny said. He rubbed the spot on the back of his head where he'd been clobbered.

"Kangaroo-bellied?" Mel asked with a laugh.

"Yeah," Holly said. "That's what Sydney calls Lisa's belly. She seems to think people procreate like marsupials and I haven't had the heart to enlighten her as to the real deal as yet."

Mel grinned. "I don't blame you. I don't think that's an easy chat for any parent. So, you think your Elvis had a beer gut?"

"He certainly seemed to fill out his jumpsuit," Holly said.

"That might help narrow it down," Manny said.

The elevator opened up to their floor and Manny checked the area before allowing them to step out. When he signaled for them to follow, Holly looked at Mel and gave her a wry smile.

"I feel like I have my own security detail," she said.

"I think you do, actually." Holly gave her a questioning look and Mel said, "He definitely likes you."

Holly beamed at her and Mel blinked. She didn't know how a relationship between a cop in Scottsdale and a cup-cake baker in Vegas would work out, but she was pleased to see the feelings between them were mutual.

Once inside, Manny had them wait by the door while he checked the entire apartment. Probably she was over-tired and overwrought, but Mel held her breath as she strained to hear any sound coming from the suite. As the seconds ticked by, her tension level mounted to the point where she felt as if her nerve endings were frayed beyond mending.

"All clear," Manny called as he reentered the room. "Stand down."

"More like fall down," Mel said as she collapsed into a chair.

"I'm going to take a shower," Holly said. "I feel grubby from the outside in from being trapped in that air duct with five pounds of greasepaint on. I don't want anyone confusing my actual profession for, well, something less savory."

"Go for it," Mel said.

With a small wave, Holly left them. Manny watched her go and Mel watched Manny.

"So, what do you think of her?" Mel asked.

"No, just no," he said.

"What do you mean no?" she asked.

"I am not talking about this with you," he said.

"Why not?" Mel asked. "I thought we were friends."

"I know you did, but what you had going on in your head and what I had going on in mine were two very different things."

"I know, I never meant to lead you on in any way, if I wasn't already . . ."

"Taken, yeah, I know," he said. "You've always been honest about how you feel, and I appreciate that even though it wasn't what I wanted."

"But now there's someone else that you want," Mel said.

She wiggled her eyebrows at him and he glowered at her, but it lacked heat. He shook his head as if trying to shake her off. Mel thought he should know better than that by now.

"Still not discussing this with you," he said.

"Aw, come on, I could offer you relationship advice as your friend."

Manny snorted. "Listen, friend, I don't know that you're the best person to impart any dating wisdom. I've seen you and Joe together, apart, together, oh sorry, I've lost track. What is your status lately?"

"Apart," Mel said. She almost added that it looked to be permanent, but then she realized she couldn't toy with Manny like that. If he had feelings for Holly and she returned them, then Mel didn't want to do anything that might mess it up so she added, "Or was it together? Even I can't remember."

Manny must have sensed from her expression that there was more going on than she was saying. He stepped close to her chair and gave her a big hug.

"It's going to be okay," he said. "If ever any two people were meant for each other, it's you two."

Mel felt her throat get tight. She nodded against his shoulder. Then she pulled back and said, "So, you want me to ask Holly about you and see how she feels? I could pass her a note and have her check yes or no and tell you at fifth period?"

He stepped back and dropped his head to his chest as if he was embarrassed. "No."

"Are you sure? Really, I could put in a good word for you," she offered. "I promise I won't oversell you."

"No, really, thanks." He glanced around the room and his eyes lingered on the large screen television. Then he tipped his head as if considering something. "I need to make a call."

"Okay," Mel said. Manny took his cell phone and left the room.

She leaned her head back and closed her eyes. Now that she had stopped moving, her adrenaline spike had ebbed and she felt more tired than she could ever remember being. Her body twitched and she knew she was about to doze. She thought she should fight it, but the idea of a fifteen-minute power nap was too tempting to ignore.

"Mel, wake up," a voice roused her.

She opened one eye but it was an effort. Manny was crouched beside her.

"I'm going downstairs to talk to the security personnel about making the tapes viewable in our room," he said. "I think it will be easier for Holly to view them up here than to drag her down to the office."

"Good idea," Mel said. She still had just one eye open.

"A security guard will be posted out front to watch the suite. Do not let anyone in except our people. No one else."

Mel just looked at him. "I got this."

"Really? Because you look like roadkill."

"Thanks," Mel said. "I'm feeling a little flat, now that you so gallantly mentioned it."

"Sorry," he said. He cupped her cheek with one hand. "You know you always look beautiful to me."

They stared at each other for a second with the same awareness that always snapped between them. Though she never intended to do anything about it, it gave Mel a little lift to note it was still there.

"Ahem," Holly cleared her throat as she came into the room.

Twenty-four

Mel started and Manny snapped up to his feet.

"Okay, then, I'm just going to do that thing," he said. He jerked his thumb at the door and backpedaled out of there so fast, Mel was surprised he didn't leave skid marks. He was halfway out the door before he turned back. "Remember what I said."

"On it," Mel said.

The door shut and she turned to look at Holly. In a fluffy bathrobe with her dark brown hair in a ponytail on top of her head and her face free of the layers of makeup, she looked much younger than she was, younger and more vulnerable and emotionally fragile. Mel felt like a heel.

"That"—Mel waved her hand in the air before she continued—"wasn't what it sounded like."

"Huh, interesting," Holly said. She looked grumpy. "'Cause it looked like you lied to me."

Mel gasped. "That was blunt."

"Sorry, but I'm feeling a little abused right now. It's been a rough night."

"I get that," Mel said. "But let's remember who found you behind the grate and act accordingly, shall we?"

Holly put her hands over her face and sighed. "You told me that there wasn't anything between you and Manny."

"There isn't."

"Please," Holly said. "I know a guy who is pining when I see one. This is Vegas. The city is rife with dudes who are trying to forget."

"Manny and I are just friends. That's all we've ever been, and that's all we'll ever be."

"He doesn't look at you like you're a friend," Holly said. It sounded as if the words cost her. As if she'd been trying to deny the truth but was now forced to accept the stark reality of what she had seen when she'd walked into the room.

"Manny and I have a connection," Mel said. "But I'm in love with someone else and have been since I was twelve years old. It's not going away and it's never going to change even if he and I don't end up together, which is sadly what I'm afraid is going to happen."

Holly sighed and gave her a sympathetic look. Then she sat down beside Mel and put her arm around her. "I'm sorry. That blows."

The unexpected compassion made Mel's eyes tear up.

She hadn't really allowed herself to dwell on the situation with Joe since their phone call. Abductions and crazy Elvises had a way of distracting a girl from these things. Holly's sympathy felt sincere and it made Mel realize how much she was hurting over Joe and the end of whatever it was that they'd had.

"Listen," Mel said. She cleared her throat. "If I wasn't in love with Joe DeLaura—"

"DeLaura?"

"Angie's older brother—long story—I would absolutely arm-wrestle you for Manny Martinez. But . . ."

"But you *are* in love with Joe," Holly said.

"Yeah," Mel said. "And Manny knows it and has always known it. I can't ever be with Manny because he would always think he was my second choice and he deserves to be someone's first choice."

"So what's wrong with this Joe guy? Why hasn't he put a ring on it yet?" Holly asked. "Clearly, you're a catch and I'm not just saying that because you're a hot cupcake baker. You really are the whole package."

"He tried. He asked and I said yes, but . . ."

"Uh-oh, that sounds like a *Baby Got Back*–sized butt," Holly said.

"It is. I freaked out."

"Oh," Holly said. "So you're the weak link."

"I was but then I proposed to him," Mel said.

Holly leaned back and studied Mel's face. "Wait. Do we need wine and cupcakes for the rest of this story?"

Mel laughed. She really, really liked Holly and not just because she was offering to drink and eat with her but because she seemed to understand that things with Joe were complicated and she wasn't being judgy about it.

"That might help," Mel said.

Holly went and grabbed an already open bottle and two glasses. While she poured, she asked, "So, you asked him and . . ."

"He said no," Mel said.

"What?" Holly handed Mel her glass and took a sip of her own. "Why? Did he explain?"

She ducked back into the kitchen and returned with a plate full of cupcakes.

"No," Mel said. "He just said no and he left."

"I would have gutted him like a fish."

"He's a county attorney, a prosecutor."

"A really nasty paper cut then," Holly said. "Or two."

"Manny was the one who explained it to me," Mel said. "Joe is trying Frank Tucci in Phoenix. He has been working this case for months."

"Tucci? I know that name," Holly said. "He's connected, like, big-time connected even here in Vegas."

"He also has a reputation for murdering anyone the prosecution team cares about to ensure he gets off."

"So, Joe said no because he didn't want you in the line of fire," Holly said. She put her hand over her heart. "That is so romantic."

"You'd think," Mel said.

"You don't?" Holly asked.

"I did, but I was so mad at him for not explaining it to me," Mel said. "If Manny hadn't told me what was going on, I would have just thought Joe didn't love me anymore."

"Harsh," Holly said.

"The thing is, his career will always come first, always," Mel said. "He's making the world a better, safer place. I admire him for it, but how can I compete with that?"

"I've got some pasties you could borrow, blue sparklies with tassels," Holly said. "I could probably even teach you how to spin them in different directions."

Mel laughed, which sidelined the tears that had been about to fall, which she suspected was Holly's plan.

"Look, none of my romantic drama matters," Mel said. "I just want you to know that Manny is more into you than any other woman I've ever seen him encounter, even me."

Holly's face went pink and Mel was pleased to see that the thought of the detective liking her brought the showgirl to blushes.

"He seems to care very much about you," Holly said.

"Well, we've been through a lot," Mel said. "All I can tell you is that he's a great guy."

"I could use a great guy," Holly said.

"Then give him a chance," Mel said.

Holly nodded and Mel felt relieved that she hadn't gunned down anything between Manny and his new love interest before it had a chance to achieve liftoff. As far as she could tell, they both deserved something good in their life.

"Out of curiosity, how do you envision your life being after you open up the bakery?" Mel asked. She needed a change of subject as she didn't want to have any more relationship heart-to-hearts. The night had been draining enough as it was.

"I'll become a morning person," Holly said with a smile. "I'll see sunrises again."

"That's the truth," Mel said. "Do you think it will be a tough adjustment?"

"Not if I keep in mind that I get to see my daughter after school, in the evening, at night, and on weekends," Holly said. "I am so ready to have a normal schedule, maybe I'll even be room mother at her school."

"You'd be fabulous," Mel said.

"And the best part is that I get to be my own boss—succeed or fail, however this turns out, it's on me," Holly said. "I am so ready for that."

"What about your current custody arrangement with Billy?" Mel asked. "Is he going to be okay with you having Sydney more often?"

"He said it was great timing as it will help them get used to the new baby," Holly said. "Lisa will be able to focus on the baby and get some rest. The timing really is perfect for everyone."

"Does Lisa feel the same?" Mel finished off her wine in one swallow. It had the instant mellowing effect she'd been hoping for. She was pretty sure when she went to bed, she'd be able to sleep for a week, except for that whole someone murdering Scott, stalking Holly, and terrorizing their bakery locations thing.

"Yes . . . er . . . maybe." Holly looked thoughtful. "You know she hasn't really said. I just assumed she did because of the new baby, but now that I think about it, I don't know how she really feels. I don't think she ever said one way or the other."

Holly's phone vibrated on the counter where she'd left it. She rose from her seat to check it. "Excuse me."

She checked the screen and her eyebrows rose. "It's Lisa."

Mel and Holly exchanged a look as if they'd been caught talking about someone. Mel made a motion with her hand for Holly to go ahead and answer it.

"Hi, Lisa, what's up?" Holly's voice had a forced upbeat note and Mel gathered she had no intention of telling Lisa what had transpired tonight. She couldn't blame her. Given how protective Billy was of Sydney, she was sure Holly didn't want to give him any more reason to keep her daughter from her.

Mel watched Holly's face and noticed that she paled and put her hand over her chest as if to try and calm her heartbeat.

"How high is her temperature?" Holly asked. "Did you give her any medicine?"

Mel watched as Holly started pacing. It was clear that Sydney was sick. Mel felt a pang in her chest for Holly. How hard it must be for a mom to be separated from her child when she was sick.

"What did Billy say?" Holly asked. There was a pause. "What do you mean he's not there? Where is he?"

Her pacing picked up speed and she placed a hand on her forehead as if warding off a headache. Mel could hear the voice on the other end of the phone but couldn't make out what she said. Judging by the high pitch and rapid-fire pace of the words, Lisa sounded as if she was having a meltdown.

"How many times has she thrown up?" Holly asked. "Four? Has she been able to keep anything down?"

There was more frantic chatter. Then Holly glanced at Mel and her expression was determined.

"I'll be there in fifteen minutes," Holly said.

Mel bounced up from the couch. "What? You can't!"

Holly turned her back on her.

"See you soon," Holly said and then she lowered her phone from her ear and ended the call.

"Holly, I know you're worried about Sydney, but—" Mel began but Holly interrupted her.

"No, you don't know," Holly said. "What do you have at home? A cat? It's not the same and don't tell me that it is."

"My cat has nothing to do with this," Mel said. She knew Holly was freaking out and lashing out, but she needed not to go near her baby Captain Jack. "You are clearly upset and I get that Sydney has a fever—"

"One hundred and four," Holly said. She began to stride to the back bedroom.

Mel followed hot on her heels. It would be insane for Holly to leave the protection of the suite. They had no idea which crazy Elvis had been the one to shut her in the air vent. They didn't even know why Holly and her bakeries were the target. For a brief second, Mel wondered if Angie was correct and their rival, Olivia Puckett, could be behind this, but it just didn't feel right.

Olivia was consumed with her relationship with Marty and she had to know that blowing up the possible locations for their first franchise would pretty much destroy any chance they had as a couple. Otherwise, yeah, Mel could totally see Olivia driving a car through the front of a building to stop her from franchising.

"All right, one hundred and four is worrisome," Mel said.

Holly didn't even break stride as she shrugged off her fluffy bathrobe and reached for her clothes. Mel turned away at the sight of so much skin, but she didn't leave the room.

"So, where is Billy?" Mel asked. "Why is Lisa caring for Sydney on her own?"

"She said he had to go into the office for something," Holly said.

"Does he normally do that?"

"How should I know? I don't live with them. Maybe it's normal, maybe it's just a freak coincidence that Sydney is sick while her dad is running an errand," Holly said.

"Why did Lisa call you instead of Billy?"

"She said he wasn't answering his phone," Holly said. She tugged on her pants and pulled a shirt over her head then she shoved her feet into a pair of flip-flops.

"His wife is pregnant with their first child," Mel said. "Isn't he the sort who would have his phone fully functional at all times in a situation like that?"

"Yes, but maybe he was in a place with no reception," Holly said. She made to walk around Mel, but Mel grabbed her arm, stopping her.

"Holly, listen to me. Doesn't any of this strike you as odd?" Mel asked. "Especially after what happened tonight."

"What are you saying?" Holly asked. She looked

overwrought and ready to cry and Mel felt bad, she really did, but they could not afford to be stupid right now.

"How do you know that was Lisa?" she asked.

"The display listed her as the caller," Holly said.

"But it could have been someone using her phone," Mel argued. "Did you recognize her voice? Was it absolutely her?"

"Yes, no, maybe, I don't know. You're crazy," Holly said. "Who would do that?"

"Wild guess, but I'd say it's the same person who knocked you out and shoved you in an air vent," Mel said.

"But why?" Holly cried. "Why is someone out to get me?"

"I don't know," Mel said. "But your daughter is your weak spot."

"What if she's really sick and she needs me?" Holly asked. "What am I supposed to do?"

"Call Billy," Mel said.

Holly looked like she was going to shake Mel off and charge the door, but Mel tightened her hold on Holly's arm.

"One phone call," she said. "Just to check."

"Fine, but if he doesn't answer, I'm going," Holly said.

They hustled back to the main room and Holly picked up her phone and called her ex-husband. She held it to her ear, chewing the corner of her thumbnail while she waited.

After several rings, she pulled it away from her ear and shook her head at Mel. "He's not—"

"Hello." A male voice came out of her phone, and Mel and Holly exchanged a startled glance.

"Billy?" Holly asked.

Mel could hear him answer but couldn't make out the words.

"I know it's late," Holly said. "I'm checking on Sydney."

Mel waited, unable to make out what Billy said.

"What do you mean she's fine?" Holly asked. "Lisa—"
She began but Mel shook her head furiously from side to side. If something funky was going on, they needed to ask questions first and not offer up any info.

"I thought I got a message from Lisa, saying that Sydney was sick," Holly said. She paused to listen. "She ate four slices of pizza and then went to bed? Huh, maybe it was an old message that just came through. Could you do me a favor and just peek in on her?"

Billy said something and Holly forced a laugh. "Yeah, that's me, the overprotective one."

Holly resumed pacing while Mel stood in the kitchen watching her.

"Oh, okay," Holly said. "Thanks."

Mel frowned. Clearly, Sydney was fine. What the heck was going on?

"Hey, Billy, is Lisa there?" Holly asked. "She did? Oh, okay, sorry to bother you." There was a pause and then Holly said, "Thanks again. Sleep well."

She ended the call and tossed her phone onto the counter. She dug her hands into her hair, dislodging her ponytail.

"Okay, I am now officially freaking out," Holly said.

"Sydney's fine?" Mel guessed.

"Sleeping like a baby, according to her dad," Holly said. "What's more, Lisa went to bed early because of a back-ache due to her pregnancy."

"Someone is using Lisa's phone then," Mel said. "Trying to lure you out of the hotel, I guess. Where did she want you to go?"

"Lisa and Billy's house."

"I don't think she was ever going to let you get there," Mel said. "We need to call Manny right away."

"This is a nightmare," Holly said. Her phone went off again and she looked at the display. She frowned and picked it up. "Hi, Billy, what's up?"

Mel heard his voice, sounding disturbed, and she looked at Holly's face. Holly paled, looking like she might faint.

"Okay, all right, I'll call you if I hear from her," Holly said and she ended the call.

"What's wrong?" Mel asked.

"Billy said that after we hung up, he went to check on Lisa to see how she was feeling," Holly said. "She wasn't there."

Twenty-five

"I know who murdered Scott," Mel said. She felt woozy as if all the blood had drained from her face. It all made sense now. "It was Lisa and I know why."

"What?" Holly asked. "No, that's impossible. She's not a killer, plus she's pregnant."

"Is she really?" Mel asked. "Have you seen her big, bare belly? Has anyone?"

"Billy must have," Holly said. "But—"

"He said she's been avoiding him," Mel interrupted. "Earlier when he brought Sydney here, he said she won't let him go to the doctor with her. Who does that unless they're hiding something?"

Holly gave her a horrified look.

"What?"

"We had a pool party for Sydney's birthday two weeks

ago," Holly said. "It was superhot, like a freaky warm desert day, and we all went in the pool, everyone except Lisa."

"Because she doesn't want anyone to see," Mel said. "And why does Sydney think babies come out of bellies like kangaroo pouches?"

"Lisa said she thought it was a cute way for her to think of it," Holly said.

"Or did Sydney see something she wasn't supposed to and Lisa lied her way out of it by saying babies come out of pouches?"

"That's nuts. There is no way she could fake a pregnancy," Holly argued. "I've been pregnant. I would know."

"How did you describe the Elvis who grabbed you?" Mel persisted. "You said he had a flabby gut that felt like a pouch. Could he have been a she? Could the pouch have been fake? Could Lisa be faking her pregnancy?"

Mel didn't think Holly could be any paler than she already was. She staggered a bit to the side and Mel caught her around the middle.

"Oh my god, this is crazy, right?"

Mel shrugged. She'd been exposed to a lot of crazy folks over the past few years. Honestly, nothing really surprised her anymore.

"I thought the softness up top was just man boobs but I bet it was a woman. All this time, it's been Lisa," Holly said. "But why?"

"Sydney," Mel said. "Lisa has been playing mother to her while you've been showgirl mom. With you changing your career and being around more, Lisa is going to lose her spot as number one, and if her pregnancy is fake, then she really won't have anything."

The suite's buzzer rang and Mel hurried for the door. "That must be Manny."

She moved the latch aside and peered through the peephole. Standing on the other side was a short, stocky Elvis. Mel knew immediately that it wasn't Marty or Oz. She also noted that the security guard Manny had posted by the door was nowhere to be seen.

She quietly closed the latch, hoping that it wasn't audible on the other side of the thick door.

She stepped back, spun on her heel, and grabbed Holly's wrist as they ran toward the back of the suite.

The buzzer sounded again, and Mel yelled, "Coming," even as she ran in the other direction.

"It's her, isn't it?" Holly asked.

"Yes," Mel said. "But I have a plan."

Holly started to cry and Mel shook her lightly. "Don't fall apart now. I'm going to distract her and you're going to take the service elevator down and then send it back for me."

"No, we have to go together," Holly insisted.

"There's not enough room. It's a single-person ride for the staff to get into the suites quickly so they can care for the guests and not be noticed," Mel said. "Plus, I need to keep her occupied while you send help so we can catch her. If she disappears, there's no knowing what she'll do next. She could go after Sydney. Go right to security and get Manny."

Mel opened the door to the utility closet and punched in the code that she'd seen Mario the chef use. It brought the elevator to them in seconds. Mel shoved Holly into it.

"You can fit," Holly insisted. "I'm sure of it."

Mel shook her head. The elevator was built to rocket one person quickly where they were needed so that the rich guests could live their pampered lives without interruption.

"Go," Mel said. "I'll be fine. She's not after me."

Holly leaned forward and hugged Mel hard. "Be careful."

"Always," Mel said. She hugged Holly back and then hit the button that would jet Holly down to the first floor.

As soon as the doors closed, she turned and raced through the apartment to the front door. She had no plan. She had no strategy. She really hoped she could stall on opening the door until security grabbed the lunatic on the other side.

When she stumbled back into the front room, she gasped. The front door was wide open.

For a second Mel thought about running to the other elevators and getting to safety. It would have been the obvious choice, but what if she went out into the hallway and Lisa found her there? Unless the elevator came right away, she'd be trapped with a person who had already killed once. Did she really want to be victim number two?

She moved as quietly as she could, tiptoeing across the room into the darkened corner. She pressed her back up against the wall and scanned the suite. When they had checked into the luxurious digs, she had felt spoiled by the spacious layout. Now she knew there were two thousand square feet that a psychopath could use to hide and it was up to Mel to find her.

The sound system suddenly came on and club music blared out of the speakers situated all over the suite. Mel jumped and let out a little yip that she was relieved could not be heard over the music. Her heart seemed to hammer in sync with the pounding bass beat. She felt queasy and a little faint.

She tried to remember where the control panel for the stereo was. If she remembered right, there was one in every room, which didn't narrow down the locations where Lisa could be as much as she'd like.

Mel lowered her body toward the floor. Crouching below eye level seemed like a good idea, especially if she could use the furniture to hide behind. She crept out of her dark corner and dashed into the living room, where she hid behind an armchair. She waited but there was no shout or any movement in reaction to her mad dash.

Lisa had to be in one of the bedrooms. Mel darted behind the sofa and then behind a chair. The control panel was within reach and she poked it with her index finger until the music stopped and the lights went out.

There was a crash from one of the bedrooms in back and Mel swiftly dashed down the hallway in the dark. If she could figure out which room, she could slam the door and trap Lisa until help arrived.

The lights snapped on when she was halfway down the hall, and she ducked into the bedroom on her right. It was empty. She darted behind the open door for cover.

"I know you're here, Holly," a voice called out. "Come out, I just want to talk to you."

Mel felt her heart hammer in her chest, and she was amazed Lisa couldn't hear it, too.

"I will find you," Lisa said. It sounded more like a threat than a promise.

And now Mel was sure it was Lisa. She was just as soft-spoken as she'd been when Mel first met her, but now there was a lilt of crazy in it.

Mel figured that Holly had made it down to security by now. She needed only a few minutes until Manny arrived, hopefully with backup, to take the crazy woman out. She just had to stall for five more minutes. Surely she could outmaneuver this woman for five minutes.

There was no place to go from the bedroom, except through the French doors out to the balcony. She hoped the others had left their doors unlocked so that she could enter and exit at will as she tried to lead Lisa around in circles.

She could hear footsteps in the hallway. She had only seconds. She hurried across the bedroom and opened the door. She slid through it, leaving it agape so that Lisa would be lured outside.

Mel stayed in the shadows. She could see the lights of the city and hear the steady grind of the traffic below on the Strip. Just yards below her were thousands of people. So close and yet so far, Mel had never felt quite so alone.

She hugged the wall to her back and moved across the terrace to the next set of doors. The curtains were closed so she reached for the knob and tried to turn it as quietly as possible. It was locked. Damn it.

She moved to the next set. The lights from the room she had left snapped on. Mel reached for the door handle and turned it. Lisa might arrive outside at any minute. It was unlocked. She pulled it open and went to step inside.

The hit when it came was completely unexpected. Mel felt something catch her around the knees and drag her to the ground. She hit the stone hard, knocking the wind out of her. Damn it, Lisa must have used the control panel to turn the lights on in the other room.

"You're not Holly!" the stocky Elvis who had been at the door screamed at her. "Where is Holly?"

Mel didn't have enough air in her lungs to answer. She was wheezing and choking, trying to reinflate her lungs. Elvis's wig was askew, revealing a dark ponytail. Mel's crazy theory had been right. The one stalking Holly had been Lisa.

Out of patience, Lisa grabbed the collar of Mel's shirt and shook her as if she could force the information out of her.

"Lisa, stop," Mel ordered. "Stop!"

Lisa gasped. Her grip on Mel weakened and Mel took the opportunity to shove her off. It was a weak effort but Lisa was so rattled she didn't put up much resistance and Mel scuttled across the patio, putting a lounge chair between them. Lisa lumbered toward her, clearly not respecting Mel's boundaries.

"I know you're faking your pregnancy." Mel reached out and poked Lisa's belly with her pointer finger. It was squishy and firm just like her sister-in-law's belly when she'd been pregnant. Mel had a moment of doubt. Was Lisa really pregnant?

"I'm not faking," Lisa yelled. "I'm not!"

"It was you who looked at the bakery that morning before I went there with Holly, wasn't it?" Mel badgered. "Did Scott show you around, and when you discovered he was a smoker, you figured you'd turn on the gas and with any luck we'd all be blown to smithereens. Was that the plan, Lisa?"

"No, no one was supposed to get hurt," Lisa said. She sagged a bit at the knees.

"And what about the car busting through the window?" Mel asked. "Did you hire someone to do that? Were you hoping Holly would get killed in the accident and then you'd have Sydney all to yourself? Except you almost got Sydney killed that day, didn't you? And how about the shots at the house? Was that you? Did you decide it would just be easier to kill Holly?"

"It's not my fault!" Lisa yelled. She was crying now and she wiped her nose on one sparkly sleeve. "If she had just left everything the way it was I wouldn't have had to hire my brother to drive that car through the bakery window or to shoot out her windows and scare her. I thought I could scare her into staying in the show and only having Sydney on Mondays, but she kept pushing me."

Theory confirmed. Now where the hell was everyone? Surely, Holly had gotten downstairs by now. What could be taking them so long? Mel didn't like the cray-cray look in Lisa's eyes. Her instincts were screaming at her to get out of there so she tried to back away from Lisa before she had a total meltdown.

"Listen, it doesn't have to be this way," Mel said. "We can get you some help and everything will be fine."

"Don't patronize me!" Lisa let out a furious roar and jumped over the lounger onto Mel's side, knocking her to the ground. Mel tried to shake her off but Lisa was strong and had the whole psychotically mad thing going.

"Tell me where Holly is," Lisa demanded.

"She's long gone," Mel wheezed. "She's sending help. If I were you, I'd run for it."

"Liar!"

Mel had the urge to argue, but she figured Lisa would probably crack her skull like a walnut if she thought Mel was wising off.

Instead, Mel closed her eyes and put all of her energy into trying to shake Lisa off. She bucked and writhed and arched her back but Lisa clung like a barnacle.

"Get off me," Mel demanded. She had hoped to sound strong and mean but instead it came out winded and wimpy.

Lisa leaned close and growled in Mel's ear, "Tell me where Holly is."

"Why? So you can kill her?"

Lisa punched Mel in the kidney, making her buckle as the pain ricocheted through her body.

"I wouldn't have to if she'd just kept things the way they were," Lisa said. "Sydney is my daughter. Mine. I'm the one who has raised her since she was a baby, not Holly."

"But what about your baby?" Mel said, knowing it was like poking a bear with a stick. "Don't you want more time with your own child?"

A sound came out of Lisa that made the hair on the back of Mel's neck stand on end. It was an anguished cry, one of misery and heartbreak and rage. Mel shivered.

"There is no baby," Lisa said. She was weeping. "I lost it at ten weeks, but I couldn't tell Billy. He was so happy. I just wanted to give him what Holly had given him. He always says he's over her but how could he be? I mean she's Holly Hartzmark and I'm . . . not."

"I'm sorry," Mel said. "So very sorry."

She didn't know what else to say. She was pinned under a woman who was clearly crazed with grief, and she didn't know what to say or do to get Lisa to let her go.

"Like that does me a damn bit of good," Lisa snapped. She grabbed Mel by the hair on the top of her head and yanked Mel to her knees. The pain made tears fill Mel's eyes and she couldn't see. She tried to grab Lisa's wrist and dig her fingernails into the other woman's skin, but Lisa was relentless. She dragged Mel toward the pool and without warning dunked Mel's head under the water.

Mel didn't have time to suck in a breath or close her mouth. Her head was submerged, and she immediately began flailing and fighting. She tried to punch the arms that held her under but she was losing strength and couldn't connect.

Her lungs began to burn and her eyes felt as if they would pop out of her head. With sudden clarity, she knew she was about to drown. Her life didn't pass before her eyes. There was only one thing that filled her mind. Joe.

His image came to her in a fuzzy, dreamlike visage. He told her he loved her and he leaned in close to kiss her. When his lips met hers, Mel thought that if this was death, it wasn't such a bad way to go.

Twenty-six

It was then that she threw up a gallon of water all over him. The water came out of her lungs as if it was being suctioned out of her nose and mouth. Mel felt as if every part of her head and lungs had been flushed out. She choked and sputtered and began to suck in air in great gulping gasps.

"Cupcake, you just scared me to death," Joe said. Then he hugged her. Hard.

Mel whipped her head around, looking for Lisa. She spotted her unconscious on the ground beside them.

"You're here?" Mel asked Joe. "You're real?"

"Very much so," Joe said. His tight grip on her made it hard for Mel to breathe but she didn't care. In fact, when she began to sob all over him and his grip got even tighter, she welcomed it.

"That was specfreakingtacular!" Oz shouted. "Joe took that crazy woman out in a diving tackle at the same time he grabbed you . . . wow, just wow!"

"Totally, wow," Marty added. His Elvis wig was hanging off the back of his bald head and his eyes were a little bugged as if he couldn't quite believe what had just happened.

"Mel! Mel!" Angie raced out onto the patio. She slipped in the water but Tate caught her before she fell. They both dropped to their knees beside Mel.

"Are you all right?" Angie demanded. She went to elbow Joe out of the way to hug her friend but he wasn't having any of it and Angie was forced to hug them both.

"I'm fine," Mel said. Her voice was raspy. She glanced at the faces around her so full of concern and love. She felt her throat close up. Had she really come as close as she feared to never seeing these people, whom she loved so very much, ever again?

A sob wracked her body and Joe scooped her up into his arms and she buried her face in his neck.

"Let's get you dried off," he said. His voice sounded rough as well, and Mel wrapped her arms around his neck and hugged him close.

Before he stepped into the house, he turned back and nodded at Lisa's unconscious body. "Call Manny. Have him get her out of here."

"So, it's all true what Holly told us when she came screaming through the casino?" Angie asked.

Mel nodded. Angie glanced at Lisa like she was going to do her some harm, but Tate put his arm around her and held her back. Mel gave them a weak smile before Joe carried her into her room.

"We need to get you to the hospital," he said as he set her on the bed. "Let's get you in something dry and catch a cab."

"I don't need to go to the hospital," Mel said. When he looked like he was going to argue, she grabbed him by his tie and pulled him close. "What are you doing here? Did you win the case?"

His hand was shaking as he brushed her sodden bangs off her forehead. "No idea."

Mel frowned. "What do you mean?"

"After we talked on the phone, I couldn't stop thinking about what you said," he replied. "You were right. I have always put my career ahead of us. It wasn't fair to you. When it came time for closing arguments, I passed it off to my colleague and caught the first flight to Vegas."

Mel studied his face as if she couldn't comprehend what he had just said. "But you worked on this case for months, we were almost killed . . . how could you just walk?"

"You are more important to me than any case," Joe said. "As soon as I got that through my thick head, then the only place I wanted to be was by your side. And it's a good thing I got here when I did. You . . . I . . . oh, hell, cupcake, I could have lost you forever."

His voice cracked and Mel cupped his face between her hands and kissed him. She felt as if she couldn't get close enough to him, and she kissed him with all the pent-up longing she had suffered over the past few months.

When they broke apart, they were both breathing hard.

Joe pressed his forehead to hers and said, "I love you, Melanie Cooper."

"I love you, too, Joe DeLaura. I always have." Tears streamed down Mel's cheeks and Joe gently brushed them away with his fingertips.

"Then marry me," he said. "Right here. Right now. Before another day passes. Be my wife."

Mel looked into his dark brown eyes. No one had ever looked at her the way Joe was looking at her now, as if she was his very reason for drawing breath.

"Yes," she said. Then she laughed. "Yes!"

They kissed again and it was quite some time before they left Mel's room.

"I really think I look fine," Mel said. "I almost died last night, so while I might be a little pasty, I'm still alive so that's something."

"This is your wedding," Angie said. "You need to raise the bar a little bit higher than 'alive' looking."

She took Mel's hand in hers as if she expected her to balk and dragged her into the salon at the Blue Hawaiian. Holly was already there talking to two women behind the counter. They were both somewhere in their forties but had enough Botox, hair extensions, and whatnot to appear ageless or at least in their thirties.

"Oh, my," one of the women said and she put her hand to her throat as if Mel had just been fished out of a toilet.

The other one tossed her long blond hair and looked

Mel up and down as if she were a car. Mel wondered if she was going to kick her tires.

"Daisy, Larissa, this is Mel. You have one hour to work your magic," Holly said. "And just so you know, she is marrying her true love so this is important."

"True love?" Larissa perked up.

"I've loved him since I was twelve years old," Mel said with a closed-lip smile.

"Oh my god!" Daisy cried. "True love. This is epic. Let's do this!"

Mel wasn't given a chance to say anything else as she was hustled into a back room, where she was primped, plucked, and polished within an inch of her life.

"No, don't touch," Daisy said when Mel went to rub her right eye. "The glue on your eyelashes hasn't set yet."

"Eyelashes?" Mel asked. That was all she got out as Daisy set to work on her other eye.

"You're going to look amazing," Larissa said, watching Daisy's work from behind her. "Trust us."

Mel would have felt better about the whole thing if her eyelids didn't feel like they were being glued open. She was lying in a reclining chair with Daisy looming over her using a huge magnifying glass and tweezers to place the false eyelashes on Mel's eyelids.

"There," Daisy said finally. "Now don't move."

"I'm going to see if Angie found you a dress yet," Holly said from where she was sitting reading a book with Sydney. "You wait here."

"There was another option?" Mel asked.

She sighed and closed her eyes. This was her wedding

day. She was going to marry Joe DeLaura. It was crazy, rash, and wild, and somehow it felt perfectly right.

She had called her mother earlier, dreading her mother's reaction to missing Mel's wedding. Her mother had shocked her all the way to her core.

"You are marrying dear Joe?" her mother had sputtered as if she couldn't believe it. She always called him "dear Joe," a habit that used to be annoying but now felt quite endearing.

"Yes, Mom, he's here in Vegas, and we're just going to go for it," Mel said. "But if it will hurt you not to be here, we'll wait. We'll do it when we get home in a traditional ceremony that you and I can spend months planning together."

"Are you out of your mind?" Joyce had cried. "Go! Go marry that boy now! He's the love of your life, Mel. You only get so many chances to find true love. Don't blow it."

Mel had been stunned. "You're not mad?"

"Of course not," Joyce said. "We'll plan a huge party for you when you come home."

"Wow," Mel said.

"I love you, baby," Joyce said. "Now go!"

Mel had hung up bemused and bewildered and ready to marry her man. She supposed that being so close to death had kicked her in the caboose. The thought that she wouldn't get to spend her life with Joe—well, it had really clarified what exactly was important to her.

She thought about Lisa and how losing her baby had tipped her over the edge of crazy and she wondered if that's what heartbreak did to some people. It sent them to a dark place that they could never leave. She was scared to think about it. If she lost Joe before she got to pledge her life to his, would she go crazy like Lisa?

The police had grilled Lisa and discovered that her belly was a fake silicone job that she bought online. Apparently, losing her baby had sent her into a tailspin, and she had convinced herself that if she couldn't provide a baby for Billy like Holly had then it was only a matter of time before he left her to return to Holly.

Initially, she had only been trying to stop Holly from opening a bakery so that she wouldn't take Sydney and Billy away from her, but when Scott Jensen had been killed, Lisa had decided she had nothing to lose and that killing Holly by pretending to be a deranged stalker would solve all of her problems, namely, that she would get to raise Sydney as her own and keep her husband.

It was a sad situation and Mel knew that both Billy and Holly felt like they should have seen the crazy in Lisa before she cost Scott his life. Mel knew how they felt. She had been in their shoes before. But out of all this horror, she had found her way back to Joe.

Since Joe had saved her life and asked her to marry him, he was determined to put a ring on her finger as soon as humanly possible. They had been at the courthouse first thing that morning and their wedding was to be held at the famous Viva Las Vegas Wedding Chapel as soon as they could get there. Mel couldn't wait.

"Hey, wake up, princess." Larissa nudged Mel awake. "Let's get you dressed and out of here."

Mel blinked. She hadn't even realized she'd dozed off. She felt her new lashes brush her cheeks when she closed her eyes. Weird.

"I got the dress!" Angie cried. "It's perfect."

"And I have the headpiece," Holly said.

Sydney followed her mother into the room. Angie helped Mel out of her robe while Holly held the dress for Mel to step into. It was a fifties retro tea-length dress with a crinoline under the skirt and V neckline in a soft white silk that felt as comfy as pajamas.

Angie closed the hidden zipper on the side while Daisy and Larissa fussed with Mel's veil, which consisted of a pearl-encrusted headband with a pouf of delicate white chiffon hanging off the back. Angie dropped a pair of demure white open-toe pumps on the ground to complete the look.

Finally satisfied, they all stepped back and studied Mel. Angie sobbed and put her hands over her cheeks to catch her tears as if she was afraid she might leak all over Mel's gown.

"You look like a princess," Sydney said. Her eyes were wide with wonder, and Mel thought she was very kind, just like her mother.

"Come look," Daisy said and she led Mel over to a tall three-way mirror.

Mel stood in front of the three images and blinked. She touched the side of her face and her reflection did, too. The woman in the mirror was a vision. Mel looked at the others and they were all smiling at her.

"That's me?" she asked.

They all nodded at her, and Mel felt like she was going to cry. She had never felt more beautiful in her life.

"No crying!" Daisy said. "You have a wedding to get to—now go before I cry myself."

Mel glanced at Holly and Angie and realized for the first time that they were wearing matching pink chemise dresses and that Sydney was in an adorable white dress with pink trim.

"The colors reminded me of the bakery," Angie explained. "Is it okay?"

"Are you kidding?" Mel asked. "It's perfect. You all look lovely."

"I don't have to be in it," Holly said. "I know that we haven't known each other very long and you probably have other girlfriends . . ."

"Stop," Mel said. "After what we've been through and now that we're business partners with you owning our very first bakery franchise, I really don't see how our bond could be any stronger. I know you have my back just like I have yours. Besides, since you and Sydney are a package deal, I get an adorable flower girl, too. How perfect is that?"

Sydney grinned and put her hand in Mel's as they left the salon with a wave and walked to the white stretch limo waiting for them outside the hotel.

The driver opened the door for them and tipped his hat as they climbed into the back.

"The gentlemen are waiting for you at the chapel," he said.

"Oh, wow," Mel said. She reached across the seat and squeezed Angie's hand in hers. "This is really happening. I'm really going to become Mrs. Joe DeLaura."

"Yup," said Angie. Then she burst into more happy tears.

Twenty-seven

"You're going to ruin your mascara," Holly said.

"I know but I can't help it," Angie wailed. "I'm just so ha-ha-hap-py."

"She doesn't sound happy," Sydney said.

"Here," Holly said. "Pull gently on your lower eyelids. It'll make your tears recede back into your eyeballs."

Angie sniffed but did as she was told. "Oh, hey, that totally worked."

"I've been to a lot of weddings," Holly said. "And I cry every time."

Mel was surprised to find that at that particular moment she didn't feel like crying. Instead, she was ecstatic, giddy even, that her life was rocketing forward with Joe at her side as her husband. She had never felt luckier in her entire life.

The limo stopped in front of the small white chapel. It was adorable with a petite bell tower and circled by a tall white wrought iron fence, covered in yellow climbing roses. The place looked as if it had soaked in all the crazy, giddy, silly happiness from all the couples who had crossed its threshold over the years. Mel stared out the window as the others climbed out, pausing to take it all in.

Tate was standing out front, looking spectacular in a dove gray tux with tails, a snappy patterned waistcoat, and a black bow tie.

"Hey there, handsome," Angie called out to him. When he looked at her in her spiffy pink dress, he grinned.

"Hey there to you, beautiful," he said. Then he kissed her—per usual it did not remain chaste for long. "Dang! We need to get hitched quick. I've got wedding fever."

Tate helped everyone out of the limo and then reached in for Mel. She took his hand and he gently pulled her out.

"Hey, buddy, are you nervous?" he asked.

"No," she said.

"Good, that's good," he said. He didn't release her hands but instead took her other hand in his so that they stood facing each other.

"Are you okay?" she asked.

"Yeah," he said. When she met his gaze, he looked a little watery.

"Uh-oh," Angie said. She stood on her tiptoes and kissed Tate's cheek then she took Holly's arm and Sydney's hand and led them to the front door. "Have your moment, you two; we'll wait by the door."

"You're my best friend," Tate said. His voice sounded

gruff. He squeezed her hands and Mel squeezed his back and said, "And you're mine."

"Everything's going to change now, isn't it?" he asked.

"In the best possible way," she said.

He nodded, sniffed, and then nodded again. "And you're sure?"

"With all of my heart," she said.

"Good." He blew out a breath. "I'd have helped you escape if you got cold feet and changed your mind; even though I'm pretty sure Angie would hunt me down and skin me."

"I appreciate the offer but it's not necessary," she said. "I just hope . . ."

"What?" Tate asked. He frowned, clearly picking up on her anxiety.

"It's stupid . . . it's just . . . I want to be the perfect wife for Joe," she said.

Tate smiled and then he leaned forward and kissed her forehead. "Do not worry. 'It doesn't matter if the guy is perfect or the girl is perfect, as long as they are perfect for each other.'"

"Oh, *Good Will Hunting*," Mel identified the movie quote. "You know that's in my top ten."

"I've been saving it for your special day," he admitted.

"It was perfect." She laughed and hugged him close.

Twenty-eight

"Tate, the groom is getting antsy," Oz called from the door.

"On my way," he said.

When Mel joined the others in the vestibule, she could hear music playing in the chapel. Holly handed Sydney a basket of pink rose petals and showed her where to walk. Sydney gave Mel a thumbs-up and disappeared into the chapel, looking very serious as she meticulously scattered the petals while she walked. Oz, looking dapper in his tux, held his arm out to Holly and she took it with a smile. Oz winked at Mel and they, too, disappeared into the church. Mel tried to get a peek at her groom, but Angie blocked her.

"No! He can't see you yet," she said. "Now wait until I am all the way down the aisle before you follow, clear? Marty, you're on point."

"Gee, I can't wait to be in your wedding," Mel said. Angie looked at her and she saw Angie's eyes water up again. "Oh, I'm sorry. I was just teasing."

Angie waved a handkerchief at her. "It's not that. I'm just so ha-hap-p-py. We're going to be sisters for real now."

Mel stepped forward and hugged her friend. "You've always been the sister of my heart."

At this, Angie let loose a sob that shook her tiny frame from top to bottom. Tate ran his hand down her back, trying to soothe her while she mopped up her tears.

"I love you," Angie said and she hugged Mel hard before she placed her hand on Tate's elbow and turned to walk down the aisle.

"I love you, too," Mel called after her.

Marty watched them before turning back to face Mel. He looked her over and said, "You look beautiful, Mel."

"Thanks, Marty." Mel beamed. She felt beautiful. It was a pretty cool feeling.

"Listen." Marty paused to clear his throat and he hooked a finger into his tuxedo shirt as if trying to loosen his tie or at least widen it for greater air intake. "I know this is a special moment reserved for dads and daughters, and I know your dad can't be here, and I just want you to know, and it is totally okay if you say no, but I, well, I love you like a daughter, and I would be, er, honored to escort you down the aisle."

His bald head was a deep shade of red and his faded eyes looked watery. Mel didn't hesitate. She threw herself against Marty's bony chest and said, "Yes, please. It would make a perfect day even more so if you would give me away."

At that, Marty howled great big, messy sobs, and Eleanor, the little lady in the cute yellow suit, who organized the weddings at the church, came running with a box of tissue.

Oz appeared in the vestibule, looking alarmed. "Is everything all right? I thought someone was strangling a duck."

"Do you mind?" Marty snapped. "Me and the bride, here, we're having a moment."

Oz glanced between them and a slow smile spread across his face. "Sure," he said. Then he pushed aside the fringe that always hung over his eyes, and he let out a wolf whistle. "I meant to tell you, you're hot stuff, boss."

"Thank you." Mel laughed and shooed him back into the chapel. "We'll be right there."

After Marty had blown his nose several times, and dabbed the tears off his cheeks, he straightened his lapels and crooked his elbow for Mel to take.

Eleanor handed Mel a ribbon-wrapped bouquet of pink roses and lilies of the valley. It was simple and lovely, and breathing in the sweet scent of the flowers helped to ground Mel. In three short steps, she and Marty entered the chapel and Mel glanced up to see Joe standing at the altar.

Her breath caught at the sight of him not just because he looked so very dashing in his tuxedo but because the look in his eyes was one of such total love, she was overcome by it, by him, by the two of them pledging their lives together. She felt her own eyes well with tears of joy, but she blinked them back.

"Ready?" Marty asked. She nodded and together they began their walk down the aisle, matching their steps as Mel took in the faces of the people in attendance who were all so dear to her—Holly and Sydney at the altar beside Angie, looking as pretty as the bouquet in her hands, Tate and Oz standing beside Joe, with Manny standing as witness in the first pew of the tiny chapel.

When Mel and Marty were halfway down the aisle, the music swelled, and Elvis, the young hot version with the bangs falling over his forehead and in a sharp black suit, stepped out from the curtain behind the altar and he began to croon "Love Me Tender." Marty lost his footing for a second and he leaned into Mel and said, "This guy is even better than the brochure promised! He's a ringer for the King and that voice!"

Mel met Joe's gaze and he looked as amused as she felt. She glanced down at her flowers to keep from laughing. They had agreed at city hall to let Marty handle the details of the ceremony, including hiring the minister. She might have known it was going to be Elvis. Somehow it seemed pretty perfect.

Marty solemnly kissed Mel's cheek as he handed her off to Joe and he took his spot as witness in the first pew on the bride's side, mirroring Manny.

While Elvis sang, Joe leaned forward and whispered in Mel's ear, "You are the most beautiful woman I have ever seen. I can't wait to call you my wife."

Mel trembled at the words *my wife* just as the thought

of calling Joe *my husband* filled her with a giddy sense of rightness that she had never known existed before.

"My husband," she whispered back. "I love that, and I love you."

Joe squeezed her hand as Elvis ended his song and the music faded. Mel turned and handed her bouquet to Angie, who looked like she might weep, but was stoically holding it together while surreptitiously tugging on her lower eyelids. Holly looked weepy, too, but she gave Mel a watery smile before ducking her head.

Mel and Joe joined hands and faced each other. Elvis the minister, who really was a ringer for the deceased famous singer, glanced between them with a warm benevolent smile that lifted up a little higher on one side. Mel wondered if he practiced that in the mirror.

"Dearly beloved," he began, "we are gathered here today to witness the union of Joseph DeLaura and Melanie Cooper in holy matrimony."

Eleanor, the petite woman who had been coordinating their event, let out an "Amen!" and Mel felt a giggle start in her middle. She glanced at Joe and noticed he was pressing his lips together as if to keep from laughing.

Elvis continued the traditional ceremony. Mel and Joe exchanged vows, smiling and looking deeply into each other's eyes as they promised to love each other all the days of their life together.

They exchanged the rings that they had bought in a sketchy jewelry store on the Strip. Mel's fingers were shaking as she pushed the white gold band up past Joe's knuckle. When he put the matching diamond band on her finger, he raised her hand to his lips and kissed the knuckle that would keep the symbol of their promises to each other from slipping off her finger.

It was so romantic, Mel thought she might faint, but she didn't because she didn't want to miss a second of this magical moment in her life.

"And now by the power vested in me by the state of Nevada and the soul of the King, I pronounce you—"

Then all hell broke loose. Three different doors that led into the chapel slammed open and men in flak jackets and face shields and carrying big, lethal-looking guns erupted into the room, surrounding them.

"Everyone freeze!" one of the men shouted.

Mel couldn't have moved if she'd tried.

"Hands in the air!"

As one, they all lifted their hands above their heads.

One of the men put a gun to the back of Elvis's head and shouted, "You, down on the ground."

"Wait!" Joe cried. As Elvis was crouching, he said, "'Say man and wife. Say man and wife.'"

"Yeah, I'm kind of busy now," Elvis snapped.

"*The Princess Bride*," Oz said.

"Not playing the movie quote game right now," Tate said out of the corner of his mouth.

Manny stepped forward while reaching into his jacket. One of the officers turned and aimed his gun right at Manny's head.

Holly shrieked and the tension in the room ratcheted even higher.

"Easy," Manny said. He slowly took his hand from

his coat. "I'm a police detective from Arizona. I'm on your side."

"Keep them up," the officer said. He then reached into Manny's jacket and grabbed his ID. He flipped it open and studied it then used his shoulder radio to talk to someone. "We have an out-of-state officer in the chapel. I'll bring him out."

He pushed Manny toward the door. Manny looked over his shoulder at them and said, "I'll see what I can find out."

"Todd Sedowski," the officer with the gun on Elvis said, "you have the right to remain silent . . ."

Another officer cuffed Elvis's hands behind him while he lay on the altar floor on his belly. Mel looked at Joe, who stared back at her in a look that mirrored her complete and total shock.

"Hey, watch the suit, man, these things don't come cheap," Elvis griped.

"I'm pretty sure you can afford it, given that you've scammed a small fortune off of unsuspecting couples," the officer said.

"Oh, Todd, what did you do?" Eleanor cried.

"What did *I* do?" he protested as the officer hauled him to his feet. "This was your idea."

"My idea! Todd, how could you turn on your own mother?" Eleanor squeaked. She looked at the officer beside her. "I swear I had no idea what he was up to."

"Right," the officer said and he clamped a hand on her arm and led her out of the chapel. "Let's go have a chat, shall we?"

As Eleanor was led down the aisle, her head spun around not unlike a demon in a horror film and she screamed, "You're a bad, bad boy, Todd!"

Mel felt the hair on the back of her neck rise.

"See? It's her," Todd said. "She made me do all of this. She's crazy! I didn't do anything wrong, I swear."

"Yeah," the arresting officer scoffed. "We have warrants on you for burglary, assault, and my personal favorite, fraud."

"Fraud?" Joe asked.

"Sorry, sir," the officer said. "But this"—he paused and waved his hand to encompass the church—"is all bogus. This guy isn't ordained to be a dog walker, never mind a minister."

"So, we're not married?" Mel asked.

"Nope," the officer said.

She and Joe exchanged stricken looks.

"I can't believe this! I can't even elope right. Oh, my god, my mother is going to kill me," Mel said.

Recipes

Vanilla Beaned

A Vanilla Cupcake with Vanilla Bean
Buttercream Frosting

Cupcakes

2½ teaspoons baking powder
¼ teaspoon salt
2½ cups flour
¾ cup butter, softened
1½ cups sugar
2 eggs
1½ teaspoons vanilla extract
1¼ cups milk

Frosting

½ cup (1 stick) salted butter, softened
½ cup (1 stick) unsalted butter, softened
1 teaspoon clear vanilla extract
1 vanilla bean with the seeds scraped out, use the seeds
*   discard the bean pod*
4 cups sifted confectioner's sugar
2 tablespoons milk

To make cupcakes: Preheat oven to 350°. Line muffin tins with 24 paper liners, and set aside. In medium bowl, sift together baking powder, salt, and flour, and set aside. In another bowl, cream butter and sugar at medium speed, add eggs, and beat until smooth. Beat in vanilla extract. Alternately add dry ingredients and milk, beating until smooth. Fill cupcake liners ⅔ full. Bake until golden brown, about 20 minutes. Makes 24.

To make frosting: In large bowl, cream butter. Add vanilla extract and vanilla bean seeds. Gradually add sugar, one cup at a time, beating well on medium speed, adding milk as needed. Scrape sides of bowl often. Beat at medium speed until light and fluffy. Keep bowl covered with damp cloth until ready to use. Makes 3 cups.

Frost cooled cupcakes with vanilla buttercream.

Snickerdoodle Cupcakes

A Vanilla Cinnamon Cupcake with
Cinnamon Buttercream Frosting

Cupcakes

3 cups flour
1 tablespoon baking powder
½ teaspoon salt
2 teaspoons cinnamon
1 cup (2 sticks) unsalted butter, softened
1¾ cups sugar
4 large eggs, room temperature
2 teaspoons vanilla
1¼ cups milk

Frosting

½ cup (1 stick) salted butter, softened
½ cup (1 stick) unsalted butter, softened
1 teaspoon clear vanilla extract
1 teaspoon cinnamon
4 cups sifted confectioner's sugar
2 tablespoons milk
2 tablespoons granulated sugar, for dusting
½ teaspoon cinnamon, for dusting

To make cupcakes: Preheat oven to 350°. Line muffin tins with 24 paper liners, and set aside. In medium mixing bowl, sift together flour, baking powder, salt, and cinnamon, and set aside. In large mixing bowl, cream together butter, sugar, eggs, and vanilla. Alternate adding dry ingredients from medium bowl and milk into large mixing bowl until batter is smooth. Fill cupcake liners to ¾ full. Bake for 18 to 20 minutes until golden brown. Makes 24.

To make frosting: In large bowl, cream butter. Add vanilla and cinnamon. Gradually add sugar, one cup at a time, beating well on medium speed. Scrape sides of bowl often. Add milk, and beat at medium speed until light and fluffy. Keep bowl covered with damp cloth until ready to use. Makes 3 cups.

Frost cupcakes. In small mixing bowl, stir together granulated sugar and cinnamon and sprinkle over freshly frosted cupcakes so that sugar and cinnamon will set.

۱٬٬٬۱

The Elvis

A Banana Cupcake with Peanut Butter Frosting

Cupcakes

1½ cups flour
1½ teaspoons baking powder

¼ teaspoon baking soda
¼ teaspoon cinnamon
⅛ teaspoon salt
1 egg
1 cup mashed bananas (3 medium)
¾ cup sugar
¼ cup cooking oil
1 teaspoon vanilla

Frosting

1 cup butter, softened
1 cup creamy peanut butter
4 cups powdered sugar
¼ cup milk
2 teaspoons vanilla

To make cupcakes: Preheat oven to 350°. Line muffin tin with 12 paper liners, and set aside. In medium mixing bowl, combine flour, baking powder, baking soda, cinnamon, and salt, and set aside. In another bowl, combine egg, bananas, sugar, oil, and vanilla. Add wet mixture into dry mixture all at once and stir until just moistened. Do not overmix. Spoon batter evenly into prepared liners and bake for 20 to 22 minutes. Makes 12.

To make frosting: In medium mixing bowl, cream together butter and peanut butter. Add powdered sugar, one cup at a time, and alternate with milk and vanilla. Stir until smooth.

Frost cupcakes.

Cherry Cola Cupcakes

A Chocolate Cola Cupcake with Cherry Cola
Buttercream Frosting

Cupcakes

1½ cups all-purpose flour

¼ teaspoon baking soda

2 teaspoons baking powder

¾ cup unsweetened cocoa powder

⅛ teaspoon salt

½ cup (1 stick) butter, softened

1 cup sugar

2 eggs

⅓ cup Maraschino cherry juice

1 cup cola

Frosting

½ cup (1 stick) salted butter, softened

½ cup (1 stick) unsalted butter, softened

1 tablespoon Maraschino cherry liquid

4 cups sifted confectioner's sugar

2 tablespoons cola

red food coloring (optional)

12 Maraschino cherries

To make cupcakes: Preheat oven to 350°. Line muffin tin with 12 paper liners, and set aside. Sift together flour, baking powder, baking soda, cocoa, and salt, and set aside. In large bowl, cream together butter and sugar until well blended. Add eggs one at a time, beating well with each addition, then stir in cherry juice. Add flour mixture alternately with cola; beat well. Fill cupcake liners evenly and bake for 18 to 20 minutes. Makes 12.

To make frosting: In large bowl, cream butter. Add cherry juice. Gradually add sugar, one cup at a time, beating well on medium speed. Scrape sides of bowl often. Add cola and red food coloring (optional) and beat at medium speed until light and fluffy. Makes 3 cups.

Frost cooled cupcakes and garnish with Maraschino cherry on top.

Turn the page for a special preview of
Jenn McKinlay's next Library Lover's Mystery . . .

BETTER LATE THAN NEVER

Coming soon in hardcover from
Berkley Prime Crime!

"Let the wild rumpus start!" Beth Stanley cried as the cart of books she had stacked to bursting abruptly regurgitated its contents all over the Briar Creek Public Library's main floor with a loud rushing noise followed by slaps and thumps as the books landed on the ground.

"Shhh!" Ms. Cole hissed. She was an old school librarian, nicknamed the lemon because of her frequently puckered disposition, who was in charge of the circulation of materials for the small library located in a small town in coastal Connecticut.

"Sorry, I tried to stop it but I couldn't hold it in," Beth said. She was wearing a crown and carrying a sparkling scepter, which was really a bejeweled cardboard tube from a roll of wrapping paper with a tissue paper flower sticking out of the end.

Lindsey Norris noted the tail pinned to the back of her yoga pants and the pointy ears poking out beneath her crown. With her short, dark hair styled in wild disarray, Beth bore a remarkable resemblance to Max the character she was representing.

"*Where the Wild Things Are* for story time?" Lindsey guessed.

"Best story time book ever," Beth said.

"Brilliant! I love Maurice Sendak," Paula Turner said.

"No one asked you," Ms. Cole said. Her glance was frosty as she took in her part-time clerk with undisguised suspicion.

Paula was the library's newly hired clerk, and with her sleeve of colorful arm tattoos and long hair dyed a deep purple, she had been a challenge for the conservative Ms. Cole to supervise from day one.

"That'll do, people," Lindsey said. She was the director of the small library and tried to maintain some semblance of order. "We have three more loaded book trucks coming in. We need to make room behind the desk."

"There is no more room," Ms. Cole said. Her tone was as dry as butterless toast, and if she were anyone else, Lindsey might have thought she was teasing. Ms. Cole was not.

A monochromatic dresser, Ms. Cole was all in black today as if she were in mourning. Lindsey figured she probably was, given that they were holding their first annual fine amnesty day, which went against everything in which Ms. Cole believed.

She was a punitive sort, who enjoyed using fines and

shushing to curb their patrons' naughty behavior. Lindsey had been trying to get her to roll with the times for a couple of years now. It was a battle.

"Why don't we get the crafternoon ladies to help?" Beth suggested. She was picking up the books that had fallen off her cart. Lindsey and Paula helped her. Ms. Cole did not.

"In what way?" Lindsey asked. She stacked the books back on the cart.

"They can fine sort the book trucks that are already checked in, which will make room for the new ones," Beth said. "In fact, if we wheel the trucks to the meeting room, we can do that while we discuss our book of the week."

"They are not cleared to work in the library," Ms. Cole protested.

"Drastic times," Lindsey said. She looked at Paula and Beth. "Let's wheel the checked-in carts to the crafternoon room to make room for the incoming."

"I really must protest," Ms. Cole said.

"Of course you do," Lindsey said. She met Ms. Cole's upset gaze with her own and tried to channel her inner calm. "Answer me this, do you have a better idea?"

"You mean aside from never having another fine amnesty day ever again?" the lemon asked. "No."

"Then to the crafternoon room it is," Lindsey said.

She, Beth, and Paula each took a cart and pushed it to the back room, where the crafternoon ladies met every Thursday afternoon to eat, discuss a book, and work on a craft.

As they entered, they found Nancy Peyton and Violet

La Rue already in place on the comfy couches placed in the center of the room. Violet had been in charge of the food today, so it was ham and cheese sliders, potato soup, and a veggie platter.

Lindsey felt her stomach rumble. She tried to remember the last time she'd eaten. It must have been last night because when she'd arrived at the library this morning, the book drop had been full to bursting. She'd skipped breakfast to help unload it and hadn't had a chance to think about eating since.

"What's this?" Nancy asked as the parade of carts appeared.

Nancy was Lindsey's landlord as well as one of her crafternoon buddies. A widow, Nancy had inherited her old captain's house when her husband, Jake, went down with his ship many years ago. Nancy then made it into a three-family house and rented out the top two floors. Lindsey lived on the third while Nancy's nephew, Charlie Peyton, lived on the second.

"How married are you to the idea of doing a craft today?" Lindsey asked.

"Not very, why?" Violet asked.

She was dressed in her usual jewel-toned caftan, which made her dark complexion glow. A retired Broadway actress, Violet had an innate grace and flair that, despite her gray hair, which she wore scraped into a tight bun at the back of her head, made her seem eternally youthful. Truly, she could command a room like nobody's business. Right now, her tone was cautious. Smart lady.

"I'm throwing myself on your mercy," Lindsey said.

She bowed with her arms out in obeisance just so they would know she was sincere. "We are so far behind on sorting the books that have been returned, we may never catch up. Would you ladies be willing to help us get these trucks in order?"

Nancy and Violet exchanged a glance. The two ladies were longtime best friends and Lindsey knew they communicated without words. It was no surprise to her when they both faced her and answered at the same time.

"Yes, of course," they said together.

"Is Ms. Cole going to come in here and yell at us for eating near the books?" Violet asked. "Because that would be a problem for me."

"So long as we don't eat over the books, I think we'll be okay," Lindsey said.

"Food, I need food!" Mary Murphy hustled into the room with Charlene La Rue right behind her.

"Girl, every time I see you, you are either eating or napping," Nancy said. "Are you feeling all right?"

She moved to stand beside the food table and loaded a plate for Mary before the woman even had her jacket off.

"Oh, yeah, I'm fine," Mary said. "Just storing up for winter, you know, like a squirrel."

"It's May," Violet said. "You keep packing it in like this and you'll be able to hibernate for two winters."

"Heh-heh." Mary laughed uneasily and her gaze darted to Lindsey.

Lindsey smiled at her to let her know her secret was still safe. The truth was Mary was pregnant with her first child. Lindsey had figured it out, but the others were still clueless. Lindsey had promised Mary she wouldn't say a word to anyone, including Mary's brother, Sully, who Lindsey had an on and off again sort of relationship with, so Mary's news and the fact that Lindsey knew about it made things a teensy bit complicated.

Charlene La Rue paused beside her mother, Violet, to kiss her cheek. Charlene had inherited her mother's slender grace and beauty, but instead of going into theater, Charlene was a television reporter in New Haven. With the career and the husband and kids, her schedule was packed to bursting but she kept her crafternoon Thursday commitment because it was one of the few times she got to spend with her mother and talk about something besides the children.

Thankfully, everyone was on board with fine sorting the books while they discussed their book of the week, Nathanial Hawthorne's *The Scarlet Letter*.

It took three trips to bring all the extra carts into the crafternoon room, but once they were in, they all took a cart and began arranging the books for shelving.

"Question," Charlene asked. "How far do I go following the Dewey number?"

"Meaning?" Beth asked.

"Can I just lump all the 398.2 books together, or do I go all the way to the letter that follows?" Charlene asked.

Lindsey glanced at Beth and said, "I still believe in 398.2—how about you?"

Beth laughed. Mary and the others frowned.

"I don't get it," Nancy said.

"I do." Charlene glanced up from her cart. "Judging by

these books, 398.2 is the base number for fairy tales. Won't Sully and Robbie be happy to know that she still believes in happy ever after."

"Ah, yes, but who will be her Prince Charming?" Violet asked.

"Oh, no," Lindsey said. "There is no charming anyone for me. Thank you very much."

She shook her head back and forth to emphasize her point. She'd been keeping her personal life on the down low and had no intention of sharing any information until she knew where it was going. "We are not discussing my love life or lack thereof, not when we have Beth's new relationship to dissect and discuss."

"Way to throw me under the gossip train," Beth said. Then she grinned. "But since you asked, Aidan is wonderful. He's funny and smart, handsome and kind." She sighed. "I've never been happier."

The woman positively glowed and Lindsey was pretty sure her crown sparkled for real. The other ladies all sighed with her, and Lindsey was relieved to have successfully distracted them.

"Has the *L* word been used yet?" Mary asked through a mouthful of ham and cheese.

"Not yet," Beth said. She fretted her lower lip between her teeth. "Should it have been? We've been dating for three months. Who says it first? Should I say it first? I don't know if I'm ready for that."

"It should just come naturally," Nancy said.

"She's right, but I'd wait and let him say it first," Charlene said. "I knew I was in love with Martin after the first two months, but I let him take the lead on the *L* word. Men can be pretty skittish about declarations of love."

"Ian said it first," Mary said. "Of course, I didn't really have a chance since he said 'I love you' the very first moment he saw me. I think our meeting went something like me saying, 'Hi, I'm Mary,' to which he replied, 'Yes, I'll marry you. I've been madly in love with you since you walked through the door five seconds ago.'"

Lindsey laughed. She could see Ian doing just that. Mary was a lovely woman with thick curls of red-brown hair and sparkling blue eyes and Ian was, well, not so much of a looker. But he had personality by the bucketful and he adored his wife, which Mary never took for granted.

"Speaking of the *L* word and relationships, here's my question about the book," Nancy said. "What does a strong female like Hester see in a spineless sniveler like Dimwit?"

"Dimmesdale," Violet said.

"Whatever," Nancy said. "I hated him."

"I think that was the point. Hawthorne portrays him as weak and Hester as strong even though she's treated very badly for adultery while he hides behind his position and does nothing to protect her," Charlene said. "What did you think of him, Mary?"

"Huh?" Mary asked through a mouthful of soup.

"What did you think about Dimmesdale?"

Mary looked chagrined. "No idea. I didn't finish the book. Frankly, when I got to Hawthorne's eighth use of the word *ignominy*, I quit."

Beth started to laugh and the others joined in.

"I'm serious. That word does not roll through my head," Mary said. "Every time it cropped up, I had to stop and sound it out and it never felt right and then I was just irritated, so I quit."

"Hawthorne loved that word," Lindsey said. "I read a critique where it said he uses *ignominy* sixteen times in the book, *ignominious* seven times, and *ignominiously* once."

"Ugh." Mary looked pained as she spooned more soup into her mouth.

The rest of the crafternooners shared amused looks but no one chastised Mary for quitting on the book. They weren't very strict about that part of being a crafternooner, or any part of being a crafternooner for that matter.

"Lindsey, can I talk to you for a second?"

Lindsey turned to see Paula standing in the doorway. She was holding a book in her hands and looking excited.

"Sure, what is it?" Lindsey asked as she crossed the room.

"This book," Paula said. "It's my sure thing. It has to be the winner for the category of most overdue item."

To keep the staff entertained during the flood of incoming materials, Lindsey had offered up prizes for the staff member who found the most overdue item or the most abused material. The prize was a free pizza because Lindsey had discovered during the past couple of years as director that food was always a motivator for her staff.

"Really?" Lindsey took the book and glanced at the cover. It was *The Catcher in the Rye* and it looked to be in good shape. "How overdue is it?"

"Judging by the slip that was left inside, the book was due on October twenty-third, 1996." Paula pointed to a yellowed piece of paper. "Twenty years."

"No way," Lindsey said.

"Way," Paula said. "So, I'm down for the free pizza from Marco's, right?"

Lindsey pointed to the clock. "The contest goes until closing time today, but so far it looks like you're in the lead."

Paula pumped her fist.

"Did someone say pizza?" Mary asked. She had moved from the soup to the veggie platter but her eyes lit up at the word *pizza*.

"Not for you," Lindsey said. "Go put your name and the book's name on the leader board, Paula. I'd like to keep the book, though."

"Will do," Paula said. She left the room with one more pump of her fist.

"Wow, twenty years overdue. What ILS were they using back then?" Beth asked.

"Dynix," Lindsey said. She glanced at the book, which looked to have been well taken care of over the years. "Remember when we thought that integrated library system was the cutting edge of technology? Let's see, if we calculate the fine at today's going rate of twenty cents per day for twenty years, we're looking at . . . help me out, somebody."

"About seventy-three dollars per year, which would be fourteen hundred sixty dollars," Mary said.

They all looked at her.

"What?" she asked. "I'm good with numbers."

"Impressive," Nancy said.

"Ignominious," Violet joked.

"Good thing you're having an amnesty," Charlene said. "Can you imagine paying that fine?"

"We'd never charge more than the cost of the book, but you're right that it's steep, although not as bad as Keith Richards's library fines I'll bet," Lindsey said.

"Keith Richards the rock star?" Violet asked.

"That's the one," Lindsey said. "Apparently, he was quite the library lover in his youth. In his autobiography, he said the library was the only place he would willingly obey the laws, like silence. And he admitted he was a bookworm who checked out books but never returned them. He has something like fifty years in fines racked up in Dartford, Kent."

"Ha! Can you imagine Ms. Cole taking on Keith Richards?" Nancy asked. "I'd pay to see that."

"Me, too," Violet snorted.

"Who do you suppose had this book checked out for twenty years?" Charlene asked. "And why return it now?"

"I'll bet the lemon knows," Beth said. "She never forgets an overdue book."

"She can't have kept the records that far back, can she?" Lindsey asked.

Beth pointed her scepter at her. "Only one way to find out."

Lindsey shrugged. Holding the book close, she went to find Ms. Cole.

FROM *NEW YORK TIMES* BESTSELLING AUTHOR

JENN MCKINLAY

~~~~~~

THE CUPCAKE BAKERY MYSTERIES

Sprinkle with Murder

Buttercream Bump Off

Death by the Dozen

Red Velvet Revenge

Going, Going, Ganache

Sugar and Iced

Dark Chocolate Demise

Vanilla Beaned

INCLUDES SCRUMPTIOUS RECIPES!

~~~~~~

Praise for the Cupcake Bakery Mysteries

"Delectable...[A] real treat."
—Julie Hyzy, *New York Times* bestselling author
of the White House Chef Mysteries

"A tender cozy full of warm and likable characters and...
tasty concoctions."
—*Publishers Weekly* (starred review)

jennmckinlay.com
facebook.com/JennMcKinlayAuthor
penguin.com

M1212AS0915

FROM *NEW YORK TIMES* BESTSELLING AUTHOR

JENN MCKINLAY

-The Library Lover's Mysteries-

BOOKS CAN BE DECEIVING
DUE OR DIE
BOOK, LINE, AND SINKER
READ IT AND WEEP
ON BORROWED TIME
A LIKELY STORY

Praise for the Library Lover's Mysteries

"Fast-paced and fun…Charming."

—Kate Carlisle, *New York Times* bestselling author

"A sparkling setting, lovely characters, books, knitting, and chowder! What more could any reader ask?"

—Lorna Barrett, *New York Times* bestselling author

"Sure to charm cozy readers everywhere."

—Ellery Adams, *New York Times* bestselling author of the Books by the Bay Mysteries

jennmckinlay.com
facebook.com/JennMcKinlayAuthor
penguin.com